Ciara's Diary

CIARA'S DIARY

1999–2002:
SENSE AND SHIFTABILITY

CIARA KING

Gill Books

Gill Books
Hume Avenue
Park West
Dublin 12
www.gillbooks.ie

Gill Books is an imprint of M.H. Gill & Co.

978 07171 7889 6

Print origination by www.grahamthew.com
Copy-edited by Matthew Parkinson-Bennett
Proofread by Jane Rogers
Printed by CPI Group (UK) Ltd,
Croydon, CRO 4YY

This book is typeset in 12 on 15.5pt Garamond.

This is a work of fiction. Names, characters, businesses,
places, events and incidents are either the products of
the author's imagination or used in a fictitious manner.
Any resemblance to actual persons, living or dead, or
actual events is purely coincidental.

The paper used in this book comes from the wood pulp
of managed forests. For every tree felled, at least one tree
is planted, thereby renewing natural resources.

5 4 3 2 1

For those of you who never got
the shift at a youth club disco, but instead
spent your time dancing to "Thong Song"
by Sisqó.

Acknowledgements

It is so very hard to try and convey just how grateful I am for all the love and support that I have received throughout the journey that has been *Ciara's Diary* and beyond.

To all the team at Gill Books, thank you for taking this project on. A special thanks to Conor Nagle and Catherine Gough for fully understanding what *Ciara's Diary* is and for their hard work, guidance and humour. I've genuinely enjoyed every minute that I've spent with you both.

A special shout out to the incredible radio station that is iRadio, where it all began. It not only gave me my start in radio and a platform to read *Ciara's Diary* in the first place, but also introduced me to some of the greatest friends of my life.

As for the OG that is Chris Greene, thank you for being the main sounding board for *Ciara's Diary* since its conception all those years ago. I'm really proud of how far we've come and what we've created. I love doing radio with you.

Ciara's Diary might never have continued as a regular feature were it not for the very important feedback from listeners of the radio show, who texted and tweeted and messaged every week. It's the listeners that make what we do worthwhile, so thanks for getting it and laughing along with me and Chris.

To Dan Healy, Paul Russell and ALL of my colleagues and friends in RTÉ 2FM, both 'on-air' and off. Thanks for being just a great bunch of people to work alongside, and thanks for all the help with *Ciara's Diary* and the continued support for it. I won't forget it. It's an honour to share the airwaves with you.

To the gang at TV3's *Six O' Clock Show*, thanks for all that you have done for me.

To the incredibly sound Liz Nugent, who has always been on hand to take a call and offer me encouragement and advice from the very beginning.

To my sports guru Phil Egan, who patiently and diligently answered my obscure sports questions at all hours of the day and night.

To Ciara Knight, the queen of comedy on Twitter and the champion of naming chapters of books. You make me laugh so much.

To all my friends who have taken the time to send a text, help me with a contract query, answer an email, take a phone call, encourage me, act as a sounding board, give me a quote or just told me to cop on and enjoy the journey. Thank you.

Lux, Pax, Felicitas to all my former teachers and classmates at Clifden Community School, especially Brendan Flynn, an amazing man who always encouraged my writing and who is an incredible advocate for the Arts in Connemara.

To the girls of Synge Street, I think I was meant to live with you three. Thanks for continually telling me that I was 'nearly there' for the past year!

To all my friends in the village of Roundstone in Connemara, who have always supported me. What beautiful people you are and what an idyllic place it was to grow up and, now, come home to.

To the Roundstone Girls – the custodians of the secrets of the real-life *Ciara's Diary* and the best sisters that a girl could ever ask for.

To my family, on both sides. I'm really proud to be related to all of you.

To my godson Johnny O'Donoghue. I became your godmother on the day that Roger Federer won his 18th Grand Slam title, and this book will be published on 8 September 2017, your first birthday, so I think you might be my lucky charm baby boy. (Don't read this book until you are much older. I'll explain all then.)

To my favourite people, my parents Paddy and Denise, and my brother Patrick. I'm so glad that you are mine.

And, finally, to my brother Darragh, who never got the chance to be a teenager. You are in our hearts always and forever.

Ciara X

About the Author

Ciara King is one half of the presenting duo
behind 2FM's *Chris and Ciara*. In addition to
regularly appearing elsewhere on RTÉ radio, she's a
contributor of roving reports to TV3's *Six O'Clock
Show* and entertainment.ie. She is a native of
Roundstone in Connemara. *Ciara's Diary* is inspired
by her teenage misadventures.

'Girl Power' by Ciara King

I'll tell you what I want, what I really, really want ...
So tell me what you want, what you really, really want.
I'll tell you what I want, what I really, really want ...
– Equal rights for women.

Frigid Jones' Diary

Dear Diary,

Are you there? It's me, Ciara. I would like to write that I received this diary in a profound way like Anne Frank did on her 13th birthday, but I didn't. I bought it ages ago in Mary's of Galway and it cost me, like, £2 or something, and I found it while I was rooting in the attic for my old Dean Cain poster. Then again, Anne Frank wrote a bestseller and lived in an *actual* attic so maybe there's hope for me, too.

I should probably tell you a few things about myself since I'm going to be confiding in you a lot.

I live in the back-arse end of Connemara. I really don't know how this happened, but it's definitely my parents' fault. I feel like I should be living a different life somewhere exotic like Summer Bay, where I would have been adopted by Irene and lived in her beach house, or maybe even somewhere more exotic like Limerick. Anywhere in the world would be more sophisticated than here.

Most days I just spend my time daydreaming, looking out at the sea and dodging seagull shit. And as much as my parents tell me to, like, 'appreciate' growing up somewhere SO beautiful, I'm, like, 'whatever' about the whole place. I mean, ya, it's beautiful and the landscape is inspirational to, like, poets and artists, but I'm not planning on becoming the next Don Conroy or Mary Kingston any time soon, so they need to relax.

Nothing ever exciting happens here. I can literally count on one hand the most exciting things that have happened and they include the time Mr O'Flaherty's goat got into the grounds of our primary school and we stayed in our classroom looking out at that goat for a good hour – petrified, of course.

The only other thing I can think of is the time last July that I met a person from Northern Ireland, having only ever seen them on TV before. He was dark and brooding like a young Heathcliff (as in *Wuthering Heights* Heathcliff, not Heathcliff Huxtable from *The Cosby Show*), and of course I wanted to shift him. I had just seen *Some Mother's Son* and was obsessed with Bobby Sands and the goings on 'up North', and I don't want to be that girl who just shifts people from the Republic either. I should probably try and shift a French exchange student at some stage, that's if they can drag themselves away from the one pint-bottle of Bulmers that five of them are sharing. I could also do with extra help with my French homework.

My family aren't the worst, but I do think of divorcing them a LOT now that we actually have divorce in Ireland. My granny voted against divorce, which is really weird as she doesn't even have a husband. Mum says that if Dad doesn't paint the back kitchen like she asked him to that she'll divorce him, which I think is a really sly thing to say, but it *would* make my life more dramatic. Dad says he'll paint her back kitchen if she's not careful, which doesn't make sense because that's actually what she wants him to do.

I hope that when I'm writing this diary I can channel Carrie Bradshaw from *Sex and The City* because I think I'm the Connemara version of her in a lot of ways, which is again frustrating because she gets to live in exciting New York City and I'm here looking out my window at bog. When I'm sitting in my bedroom writing about my life, I'll have the voice of Sarah Jessica Parker in my head and I'll probably end up writing some really deep stuff like, 'I couldn't help but wonder, are *all* the lads in my school complete losers?', like she does for her relationship column in *Vogue*.

Maybe this diary could be like my own relationship column? There won't be as much talk about sex though. As embarrassing as this is to admit, I'm a total virgin. But I am hoping to change that – I didn't read all those Judy Blume books for nothing. Most of my life is spent thinking about if and when and how I'll lose my virginity. My granny says that good things come to those who wait, but I've been waiting longer than Mayo has to win an All Ireland title. Half of me is afraid to think about sex because I was the first altar girl in the parish, and I've also read enough Maeve Binchy novels in my time to know what happens when you get tempted by the 'you know what'.

My love life is as dry as a river bed in a Trocaire ad. I've shifted a couple of lads, nothing serious. There has barely even been any tongue action. I practise kissing on my arm sometimes so I don't get rusty during my many dry spells, but that's as much craic as Mother Theresa playing 'Never Have I Ever'. I don't tell ANYONE about the arm-kissing because it's really pathetic. Even for me.

Rebecca said that she shifted someone once and it was like shifting a washing machine, and I honestly haven't been able to look at the Hotpoint in the kitchen properly since.

I know that if I am ever going to lose my virginity, my boobs are going to have to help me out in some regard. I'm old enough to know the power of good cleavage – just look at Jordan. She managed to score Dane Bowers from Another Level! Maybe if my boobs actually catch up to my shoulders I'll eventually have more of a chance. I'm not, like, obsessed with them or anything, but I am ready to move on down the alphabet of cup sizes. Usually getting an A in anything would please me, but not in this case.

It's really cool to have somewhere to write down all my deepest darkest thoughts though. It's hard being me at times and I have a lot of feelings about stuff. I can talk to Rebecca, but she says that I'm overly dramatic about things, which is, like, a really sly thing to say because I think I'm just a really deep person like Enya or something. Like, I feel things so emotionally that I couldn't handle the 'will they, won't they' romantic situation between

Dr Quinn Medicine Woman and Sully so I literally had to stop watching it for my own sake.

Being a deep person isn't all that it's cracked up to be. I mean, it's grand if you're as cool as Seamus Heaney, but in the teenage world that I inhabit, it can be tough. Like, there's this girl called Lucy and she doesn't like me, which really gets to me. I don't know why Lucy doesn't like me, maybe it's because she can smell the bang of virgin off me, but she spends most of her time ignoring me. Not that I care, but there's NOTHING worse than being ignored. Unless, of course, you're Anne Frank.

I long to talk about important things, you know, instead of whether or not Man United are going to win the treble or what the lads in my year think of Stifler's mom. I think I'm an old soul in a young person's body, like from Ancient Greece or something. I'm going to Ask Jeeves who I was in a past life then maybe it will all finally make sense.

I think I really want a boyfriend. I daydream all the time about finding 'The One'. You know, like Joey and Pacey in *Dawson's Creek*, even though I can't imagine ANY of the lads that I know having the vocabulary that Joshua Jackson does – they all have the conversational skills of Lorcan in *Fair City*, and that's being nice. Still, I haven't given up hope. There's still time to tackle some of the lads from the school rugby team (see what I did there?). One of them even has a car, which would be handy for shifting in if it was, like, raining outside or something. There isn't really any shelter outside the town hall.

I think I might have wanker's cramp from all the writing so I'm going to go to bed.

Good Night Dear Diary,
Love,
Ciara X

Cousin FIT

Dear Diary,

I know I've said this before, but I think I've met The One. But alas, true love never seems to run smoothly, does it? Well, especially not for me. It seems we have a modern day *Romeo and Juliet* situation on our hands. On one side there is me, Juliet, beloved daughter of the Capulets, and on the other side, Romeo (AKA John), son of the Montagues and a cousin of my nemesis and main arch-rival Lucy.

Of all the men in the whole wide world, why did I have to fall in love with Lucy's cousin?!

If this was episode of *The Simpsons*, I would be Maggie Simpson and Lucy would be the monobrow baby, and my new love would probably live in Shelbyville.

But John is different. Let me tell you about John.

A big gang of us decided to hang out in the local shopping centre as we are teenagers, and obviously grown-ups or the government don't know how to cater for the needs of young adults. On a side note, we really are treated like second-class citizens. Do the people in power not realise that we are the next generation, with feelings and emotions and, like, really deep thoughts about things and stuff. We should really be able to vote for our rights as well. We should be able to shake off these shackles of oppression that have haunted generations of teenagers since the Famine!

Anyway, we were bored and went to the shopping centre. I had heard from one of the girls in my year that there was a leopard print bra in Penneys and I wanted it – no, NEEDED it – in my life. How sexy is that, like? Kat Slater is always wearing leopard print bras in *EastEnders*, and she gets loads of men.

So we're on our way into Penneys and who do we bump into only Lucy, who is standing with this seriously handsome guy. In my head I was like, 'Please God, don't let this be her boyfriend because are you actually serious, that's so unfair, she doesn't deserve him, she is going to ruin my life some day,' but she introduces Rebecca to him as her cousin John while totally ignoring me at the same time. Not that I cared or anything.

From watching Dr Phil on *Oprah* once, I was able to suss out this John guy fairly quickly. His bottom lip was pierced, indicating a bad boy element, he was wearing just enough Dax Wax to give off an air of not actually caring that much and he was wearing a Barcelona football shirt with 'Rivaldo' on the back, which obviously pointed to a deep love of Spanish football.

His eyes were deep and brown and I'm sure passionate, and I'm nearly certain he had a quick glance down at my boobular area. It was like somebody had sent an electric shock through my body. Our eyes met and there was this, like, instant connection. Rebecca said afterwards that it was like I was just standing there staring him out of it. But what does she know? She wasn't in the moment like I was. She didn't know that right then and there I was falling in love at first sight. I knew though that I had to have him, whether he was Lucy's cousin or not.

We had to go then as Rebecca wanted to buy a new CD in Zhivago's called 'Genie in a Bottle' by Christina Aguilera. I have a good sense for these things and reckon she'll just be a flash in the pan. I mean, where is all the real music gone? While I was in Zhivago's I went mooching around and I found this guy called Ricky Martin and his song 'Livin' La Vida Loca'. Now, THAT'S proper music. When I grow up, I'm going to marry him. That's if things don't work out with John obviously.

By the time we met up with the rest of the lads they were being really annoying, quoting some lines from a movie called *Fight Club* that they had snuck into the cinema to see. Everything we did for the rest of the day was like, 'Welcome to Supermac's, the first rule of Supermac's is you DO NOT TALK about Supermac's,' then they would fall around the place bursting their shit laughing and trying to give each other dead legs. Lads are so immature. I don't get it.

All the time though, I was glancing over at John wondering was he glancing over at me. It was in this fair establishment of fast food where me and John finally bonded over our love for animals. (I really like animals.) It turns out that John is a vegetarian as he disagrees with the cruelty that is subjected on animals every day across the world. He has been to protests against animal testing and everything. I'm SO surprised that someone so, like, cultured is cousins with Lucy!

A security guard kicked us out as the lads were sticking chips up their noses and blowing them out and laughing, and then it started raining so we all had to shelter in a bus shelter, which worked out brilliantly as I could stand really close to John then. At one stage our hands brushed off each other and I thought I was going to faint. This is what real love must feel like, Dear Diary.

Lucy of course had to go and ruin it and started shouting, 'Don't stand too close to her John; I heard you might catch frigidness.' The actual irony here is that there is more chance of catching something off Lucy then there is off me. I threw her daggers but then she and John had to go as Lucy's mother came to collect them. Man, Lucy's mother looks rough.

As they drove away and I watched my new Romeo depart from my life, Rebecca told me once again to stop staring, that it was really weird and that I looked like a sad case.

She was shifting the face of Johnny Limp so I don't even know why she cared really. They have been shifting since the youth club disco where I nearly sprained my ankle doing the moonwalk. They are 'going steady', as the Yanks say. They make a weird couple, what with Johnny Limp's limp and Rebecca's arse, but at the same time they work.

Oh God, I just had a thought. What if they fall in love and Rebecca loses her virginity to him? What if she loses her virginity before me? No, she's my best friend in the whole world; she wouldn't do that, would she?!

Goodnight Dear Diary,
Love,
Ciara X

The Immaculate Connection

Dear Diary,

I've got to be honest: being a teenager is really tough. I haven't been able to stop thinking about John since I waved goodbye to him at the bus stop last weekend. I still can't believe he is Lucy's cousin. It's just my luck to be honest. Nothing seems to be straightforward for me in life.

I've spent the past week in class just daydreaming about him. I dug out my Celine Dion *Falling Into You* album, which is basically the best album of all time. I remember hearing this one particular song on my favourite radio station, Atlantic 252. There is this female DJ and it's hilarious because her name is Beverly Hills, like the place, and she played 'It's All Coming Back to Me Now'. There's this particular verse and I think it sums up how I felt when John drove off in the car with Lucy and Lucy's mother:

> *I finished crying in the instant that you left*
> *And I can't remember where or when or how*
> *And I banished every memory*
> *You and I had ever made.*

Seemingly this song is written about the book *Wuthering Heights* and in fairness you could potentially compare me and John to Cathy and Heathcliff. Star-crossed lovers whose families keep them apart? Rebecca told me in History class the last day that I'm being very dramatic about the whole thing. That was, like, so mean of her to say. I think she's just getting uppity in herself because Johnny Limp is her boyfriend now. It's like suddenly she has this new-found confidence. I prefer the old Rebecca.

The two of them are completely wrecking my head anyway. They're constantly lobbing the gob on each other and now sit together in the back of Religion class, like, holding hands underneath the table. What nerds. It's not fair as me and Rebecca always sat beside each other in Religion and used to play fun games like time how long it took the Religion teacher to have a breakdown. (Usually ten minutes tops.) We would talk about the concept of God, and is there actually a God. (We are too scared to say there is not.) We did come to the conclusion that there is no way that Mary was a virgin though. That would mean that there would have to have been an Immaculate Conception, which is something that I just can't get my head around. Also, I'm on the fence about G.O.D. I've been praying to him for at least three years now for bigger boobs and they really haven't grown all that much.

In other important things that I need to share, I have decided to write down important news stories so that when I'm famous in the future, people can write a book about my experiences. Like that Bosnian girl who wrote about all those ceasefires and stuff in this place called Sarajevo, which Bono wrote a song about of course, I don't know much about Bosnia and Herzegovina but I do know that it doesn't do very well in the Eurovision. They probably couldn't afford to do it because they are all war-torn and shit. Ireland must have loads of money as we host it nearly every year!

In terms of important news there is nothing much to report. Oh, bar the fact that President Bill Clinton did something with a cigar to some American chick called Monica Lewinsky. He's been peached. Looks like this other dude called George Bush will become president now. I don't think my dad likes him. He calls him a 'fucking cowboy-hat-wearing horse-riding Republican', but I'm confident he will do a good job. Sucks to be Bill Clinton, but it sucks even more to be Bill Clinton's wife Hillary. She'll leave him now too. Serves him right. But I do seem to have a soft spot for him. He's kinda good-looking in an older man American type of way. Maybe it was because he was president? Does this mean I like people in power? I don't think so, because I don't have any sexual feelings about the Taoiseach OR our President Mary McAleese, so maybe Bill Clinton is just a charming man.

I'm dying to know what he did with that cigar though. I asked my mum, but she smirked and told me to ask my father, who very quickly pulled the paper up in front of his face, and I'm nearly sure the two of them were laughing at me. Way to go Mum and Dad, I'm glad that it's me that is the laughing stock of the family.

Anyway, I'm exhausted from all this news reporting. I feel like a modern day Anne Frank except without the added problem of having to hide from Hitler. Although sometimes my parents completely remind me of him what with their strict regimes, so there are comparisons.

I'm off to dream about John and practise shifting my arm.

Goodnight Dear Diary,
Love,
Ciara X

Lovers' Spliff

Dear Diary,

I feel really weird. The room is spinning every time I try to lie back. My tongue is stuck to the roof of my mouth and my eyes are like, as my dad would say, 'two piss-holes in the snow'. I'm trying to write this, but it's difficult, the words are swirling all over the place and it's like they're jumping off the page if you get me?

I'd imagine this is what it was like for Anne Frank (I'm actually obsessed with her) hiding in that annex awaiting arrest and being found by Hitler's forces. Hitler was just not a good guy. Me and Anne have something in common though. I too think I might be arrested as I've done something, like, SO illegal. I think my parents are onto me too. I made excuses too eagerly to go to bed and muttered something like I was really tired and wanted to go read my entire collection of *The Baby-Sitters Club*. But then I remembered that I haven't read those books since I was 13, and I'm pretty sure my mum gave all those books away to some charity – AGAINST MY WISHES MAY I ADD – and I, like, cried for five days after. No wonder they gave me such weird looks.

But I could just be paranoid too, because Rebecca says that it can happen when you do what I just did.

Oh my God. I better write down a recap of what went on tonight, just in case I die after what I've done. Half of me by the way is delirious with joy because I spent time with John and I think there were some serious intense feelings between us. The other half feels I'll be going to jail in no time. I'm also pretty sure that God is judging me too. That's all I need.

It all started out when Rebecca and I had been over at her older sister's, watching *Sex and the City*. (They show sex scenes and everything, so no wonder my mum won't let me watch it.) It's amazing. It's about these four single women in New York who get up to lots of sex, shopping and writing. They even have sex with guys that they have just met in bars! They are, like, so liberated, it's amazing.

Rebecca says that I am mostly Charlotte but that with the drama I bring on myself I can be like Carrie too. We both agreed that Lucy was definitely a Samantha.

So the next day we decided to go to the local shopping centre because Rebecca wanted to go to Glitzi Bitz. She heard that they were selling necklaces with your name on them like Carrie's necklace in *Sex and the City*. So obviously we needed to get them. We figured that the girls in school would think we were pretty trendy rocking in with those around our necks.

We're in the shopping centre, and get this, who's the first person that I lay my eyes on? John – yes, John! AKA the love of my life and future husband. There's a couple of the lads from school there as well, including Johnny Limp, who's Rebecca's boyfriend.

The only way I can describe the moment I saw John is that it was as if I was there when Moses parted the Red Sea for his people to pass through safely away from the Egyptian pharaoh trying to kill them. We smiled at each other and then the lads said that they were going down by the river to hang out so me and Rebecca went with them. Obviously.

We were down by the benches and John sat down beside me and was asking me did I know anything about joints. I sighed a major sigh of relief for having done Woodwork up until my Junior Cert. Did I know anything about joints?! I mean HELLO. I was the queen of dovetail joints in Woodwork class. I started listing out how I could do a groove joint, a dovetail joint and a mortise and tenon joint. John started laughing and told me I was really funny. I was like okay, sure, but at the same time, I worked really hard in Woodwork class for three years to know all about those joints, and he had just laughed – a woman can be good with wood, you know.

Then him and the lads started rolling some weird tobacco with some papers and then started asking me and Rebecca could we make a roach for them. Finally the penny dropped and I copped what was going on. I was about to partake in something completely illegal, which generations of teenagers had gone through before ... PEER PRESSURE.

Before I really knew what was happening, the joint was passed my way. I looked at John, then I looked at Rebecca, then back at John, and I thought to myself, if dragging on this joint gets me the shift and if John will think I'm cool, then so be it. I inhaled, started coughing straight away, my eyes started stinging, but then John put his arm around me and I knew in my heart that I had done the right thing.

It was passed around a couple of times more. At this stage, John had gone in for the kill and had kissed me. His arm was resting over my shoulder, and his hand was hovering very closely to my left boob, so much so that I thought he was going to go for some outside boobage in front of everyone.

Something strange had come over me by then. I felt like I was sinking through the bench and into the earth below me. I couldn't feel my arse any more. Then I went deathly pale. I was beginning to sweat more than Derek Davis on a bouncy castle. I suddenly became really self-conscious and felt that everyone was laughing at me, but it turns out they were laughing at a rock that looked like Marge Simpson.

It all became too much for me. Of course it did, as I'm such a loser. The next thing I remember is that I'm getting sick into the river and John is holding my hair back asking me over and over again am I okay. I wasn't. Rebecca told me later that I had pulled what our teenage circles call a 'whitey'. John told me I had inhaled too much too soon.

I had to go then. Rebecca walked me home and was giving out about John the whole way there. She said he was a total crusty. I think that might mean he's a bit of a hippie, but I don't think so. He smokes one joint and suddenly Rebecca has him living in a wagon with no running water. I mean, he supports Barcelona football club for God's sake. Just because he's a vegetarian, it doesn't mean he's a crusty. I'm surprised at how narrow minded she's being. I'm not narrow minded about the fact that her boyfriend has one leg shorter than the other.

So now here I am, up in my room, my tongue isn't coming down off the roof of my mouth, I'm SO hungry but can't go down to the kitchen because my parents will know what I did.

I feel like the Gardaí are going to knock on my door any minute now and arrest me, and then I won't be able to do my Leaving Cert, go to college and move to America like everyone else. I'm pretty sure I'm going to appear on the next episode of *Crimewatch*.

I blame Carrie Bradshaw and her stupid necklace for all of this.

Still, I managed to lob the gob.

I think it may FINALLY be true love.

Man, I'm sleepy.

Goodnight Dear Diary,
Love,
Ciara X

A Letter from John to the Ciarainthians

Dear Diary,

I've been suffering serious guilt because of what I did the last evening. I keep on expecting to hear the guards coming and knocking on the front door of the house and arresting me, like in that movie *In the Name of the Father*. Oh God, my mother will probably have to accompany me just like Giuseppe Conlon did for his son. The neighbours will all gather in each other's houses and say, 'Where did it all go wrong, she was such a nice girl, and her, the first female altar girl in the parish.'

Rebecca thinks I'm totally overreacting and that I should just chill. She's all like, 'Relax Ciara, you're not exactly Bob Marley.' Like, does Rebecca not realise that we became pretty close to being like those two girls in *Brokedown Palace* with Claire Danes and Kate Beckinsale? They end up in this Thai prison for the REST of their days because of getting mixed up in drugs.

Rebecca says she thinks that hash should be legalised anyway. But I don't think that's her talking, I'd say it's what Johnny Limp thinks. He is having a major effect on her. Even the last day when we were in the pharmacy buying the latest glittery nail varnish, I'm nearly sure I saw her gazing at the shelf behind the till where the condoms are.

We used to play the game where we would dare each other to ask the pharmacist how much they were and then run out of the shop pissing our holes laughing because then she would think we were having sex, and like, we totally are not, and also how weird would that be, for a total stranger to know you were having sex with someone?

Once, Rebecca dared me to buy them, and I even got as far as asking for them, but then as soon as the lady in the shop turned her back to get them, I legged it out of there because I got nervous. But her gaze definitely lingered on the boxes of Durex too long for my liking. Oh my God, how embarrassing would it be to actually, like, buy real-life condoms one day?!

In all seriousness though, Rebecca and I made a pact not to lose our virginity unless we had someone hot to go to the debs with OR until we get married to our own Aidan or Mr Big. (We are totally obsessed with *Sex and the City*. She likes Aidan, and I like Mr Big.)

My day wasn't uneventful by the way Dear Diary. It was a strange one, as in, Lucy talked to me today. She came up to me at lunch and was like, 'John told me you pulled a whitey and puked everywhere.' I went completely red but held my head up high trying to ignore the heat of my cheeks and went, 'Ya, so?' And then she goes, 'You are such a loser.' It took every fibre of my being not to say anything to her. After all, this is the sort of shit the Montagues and the Capulets had to put up with in *Romeo and Juliet*.

The course of true love does not run smooth.

I took a deep breath and began to walk away, but then the strangest thing happened Dear Diary. Lucy throws this envelope at me and mutters something about John wanting me to have this. As she walked off she said, 'It won't last you know, I told John you were the most frigid girl in school.' And then she disappeared into the school bathrooms. Okay, so that technically might be true, but screw her! Obviously I didn't say this to her because I was too stunned (and scared of her) to react. I seriously hope she gets caught smoking in the school bathrooms and gets detention for life.

I opened up the envelope, and although John has the WORST handwriting that I have ever seen, I managed to decipher it and nearly fainted when I did.

Hey Ciara,

Sorry I couldn't walk you home the last night, I was totally baked. Hope you made it home okay. I reckon the reason you got sick was because you smoked too fast. I can teach you how to do it properly if you want. I've been practising these different songs on my guitar and I've written a song for you, if you would like to hear it, that would be cool. I watched this really cool programme on National Geographic about pandas in their native China, so I think I might start sponsoring one.

I was wondering would you like to meet up this weekend? My aunt keeps wondering why I'm coming up every weekend to stay. Don't worry, I haven't said anything about having a girlfriend, unless you want to be my girlfriend, which would be cool.

There is a peaceful protest for some woman called Aung San Suu Kyi in Burma happening and I was wondering would you go with me? The protests are kinda cool, you just sit around, light candles and sing songs. You can write me a letter and give it to Lucy.

Peace Out,

John

PS I've enclosed two teabags of herbal tea. One is lemon and ginger and the other is green tea. You should try it out.

There it was. My very first love letter. It's, like, SO deep and profound and shit.

If he thinks for a SECOND I'm going to give Lucy a letter to give him, then he has another thing coming. Also, am I his girlfriend now? Because he said in the note that I could be if I wanted to, and I mean, I want to times a million!

I showed Rebecca the note in Religion (she only sat beside me because Johnny Limp wasn't in) and she rolled her eyes and was like, 'What a complete crusty.' I was in two minds to tell her that Johnny Limp isn't much to be writing home about, and that he was nothing but a Massey-Ferguson-driving sheep-shearer who thinks he's Tupac Shakur driving around in that Subaru of his, but I didn't because then she turned around and was all like, 'I'm genuinely happy for you,' which was really sweet because she's my best friend after all.

What am I going to wear when I go meet John? He's into animals it seems, so maybe I could wear my leopard print bra from Penneys?!

I am so high on life right now Dear Diary! I have a boyfriend! Little old me has an actual boyfriend! Now I can potentially get the shift every weekend for the rest of my life!

This is AMAZING.

Goodnight Dear Diary,
Love,
Ciara X

Focail Interest

Dear Diary,

My life is totally OVER. I'm being serious this time. I know in the past that I've had a tendency to be a little dramatic, but this latest situation merits one serious FREAKOUT. I'm currently up in my room with tears streaming down my face.

My parents are MAKING me go to the Gaeltacht. They are making me go to the Gaeltacht for two whole weeks. Two FUCKING weeks. I'm sorry for writing curses Dear Diary but such is my ultimate misery right now. Are they genuinely trying to, like, ruin my whole life?! I mean, why else would they send me to some Irish-speaking concentration camp in Connemara?! They must be trying to ruin my love life at the same time.

Why do they have to ruin my one chance of true love?! John is The One! We are so in love. They are literally breaking my heart by ripping me away from him for TWO WHOLE WEEKS.

Just off the phone to Rebecca who I rang to see if her parents were making her go, but they aren't because they must actually LOVE her. Her and Johnny Limp both got jobs in the local hotel. They are going to have a summer just like Pacey and Joey did in *Dawson's Creek* that time they were MIL (Madly In Love). She did say that she heard that Lucy was going, but I doubt that because there's no way that she'd care enough about her education.

I WISH I WAS ADOPTED like Tom Cruise and Nicole Kidman's children. They wouldn't have sent their daughter to the Gaeltacht.

It's so typical. Just when John is finished his Leaving Cert and everything. SO UNFAIR. This might be my last chance to lose my virginity as John is talking about taking a gap year before he goes to college. He wants to become a yoga teacher and learn how to clear people's chakras. It's far from 'chakras' I was reared Dear Diary, but it sounds AMAZING.

My parents are all like, relax, it's only across the bay and it's only two weeks and I'll come back more cultured with a better understanding of the Irish language, blah, blah, fucking blah. Two weeks is like two years in the life of a teenager. Everything will change. It's bollix, that's what it is.

My life is over, let's just put it out there, I'm finished just as my life was actually about to start getting exciting. The most ironic thing about this whole situation is the fact that my boobs have gone up a cup size. An actual cup size. I didn't want to write about it just in case I was imagining things, but it's true. I'm now a B Cup, but what good does it matter now?

Goodnight Dear Diary,
Love,
Ciara X

PS Sorry for cursing so much, just really at my wit's end.

Lucy, Me and the Bean an Tí

Dear Diary,

So, I'm here. In the back arse end of Connemara. Not even my dramatic breaking down in tears could stop my parents and their pilgrimage to be rid of me. As they drove away, I wondered to myself if I would ever see them again.

I'm in the SMALLEST room of all time with just a bunk bed. I always fantasised about actually having a bunk bed when I was younger, but now I have one, and it can basically fuck off. It doesn't matter anyway, because Lucy got the top bunk. Yes, you heard me. Lucy is here and I'm sharing a room with her.

Sometimes I wonder what I've actually done to God and the Virgin Mary to make them so angry with me that they would subject me to this hell again and again.

I guess you're wondering why I'm being so calm about this whole situation, what with Lucy and me hating each other so much and ending up in the same room at the Gaeltacht at the EXACT same time.

I think it's because I have become immune to the melancholia that life seems to throw at me. I'm a former shell of who I used to be. I mean, I'm a teenage girl whose parents basically abandoned her in a foreign country with my most feared enemy, and to top it all off, my John didn't even get time to say goodbye to me before I left.

He was busy with some 'save the seals sanctuary'.

The other two girls in the room are from Dublin and have already commented on being 'stuck with the two culchies'. They have the coolest clothes though that they bought in the Blanchardstown Shopping Centre, which sounds like an amazing place. All their clothes are Umbro and Nike, and they are so posh. One of them even has a Nokia. She said she'd let me play Snake on it if I wanted.

I was like, 'Ya, cool,' even though, if I was being completely honest, I have no idea what she was talking about.

It's weird because it means in a strange way that me and Lucy are kind of on the same side or something. Our Bean an Tí seems sound, her name is Maureen, but her son is a total weirdo. He just keeps staring at my boobs, I'm sure of it. Lucy was quiet, unusually quiet. I know why too, it's because she's shit at Irish. I'm not going to lie, I do have a superior knowledge of Irish compared to her. She would want to be careful, I heard that if you speak just one word of English, you get expelled and sent home straight away and your school hears about it too. And then you go on record and you're not allowed into any other Irish college in Ireland EVER again.

The Irish language, I mean, do we even need it?! I don't think we'll be even using it in two years' time.

We found our schedule for tomorrow. It just seems to be full of playing basketball from what I can see. Basketball through Irish. Have you ever heard of something so zero craic in your life?

I'm going to grab that cispheil tomorrow and shove it where the sun don't shine, which apparently is everywhere because it's so dull and misty.

I hate being here.

Dinner was interesting, and I'm not being a snob but there was home brand ketchup, and I only ever eat Chef. There wasn't even any Heinz. I'm not being whatever, but tá díomá orm.

Anyway, me and the girls were up in the room there and the Dublin girls were saying that there is a group from Clane coming tomorrow and that the girls are seriously nasty, but that the lads are good craic. We'll probably meet them at the céilí or something. Oh God, I have to go to a céilí. I feel like a character in a Maeve Binchy novel. My life seriously sucks. I'm homesick and I miss John. I also miss my mum, my dad and my brother, which I shouldn't because they LEFT ME HERE TO DIE. The worst thing is I have no one to talk to. I hate Lucy, she hates me and the Dublin girls scare me on some level, so I'm trying to make sure that I'm coming across all cool, so that they will think I'm cool. What sort of teenager misses their parents anyway? A sad sap of a one, that's who.

I'm going to wrap myself around my pillow and pretend that it's John but obviously not try to hump it or anything just in case any of the girls hear me.

I'm going to listen to love songs on my Discman too. I think my dad must have felt bad for leaving me here because he packed some extra batteries in my bag for all those 'God-awful songs by wailing women giving out about men' that I listen to.

Oíche mhaith a dhialann,
Grá mór,
Ciara X

Mo Mi Wadi

Dear Diary,
I swear to God, if I have to drink another glass of MiWadi orange for breakfast, lunch and dinner, I'm actually going to kill someone.

That's the one thing about the past week living in the Gaeltacht, they really love their MiWadi orange. Not even Kia-Ora, but MiWadi. Another thing that seems to be very popular down here is bread and jam suppers with massive pots of tea.

Suipéar is quite a daunting experience. The Bean an Tí, Maureen, speaks Irish at lightning speed and it scares me and the rest of the gang, especially Lucy, because she's a thick. I've been trying to help her with her Irish, but she's dire with, like, a capital D. The next thing I'm going to say is going to sound weird, but: we're really getting on.

We take a daily trip down to the tuck shop where we stock up on Pringles and Minstrels and stuff. We stop along the way for Lucy to smoke her brains out and I have to keep watch. Then she sprays herself in Impulse body spray and we're off again. We eat our stash of goodies with the Dublin girls when the lights go out.

I was joking that we were like the girls from Enid Blyton's *Mallory Towers* having midnight feasts and Lucy gave me a dig and told me to stop being so gay. We're obviously not that close yet.

I always thought that Lucy was the most promiscuous girl that I know, but listening to these Dublin girls talk, she's an angel in comparison.

The Clane girls put out easily it seems and one of them has already been sent home because she was caught sneaking out her bedroom window with a naggin of vodka to meet the rest of the Kildare boys.

The Kildare boys are interesting, they don't seem to have any real names and simply go by nicknames: Johnno, Stevo, Symthy, Henno, Kenno, Podge, Fitzy and Ryano. They go behind the back of the Halla Mór and smoke John Player Blue and talk about fingering young ones. All of them dress in shell suits, I don't think I've seen one of them in a pair of jeans, and at least two of them have bleached blond hair.

Johnno seems really cute. But maybe that's because he has the same name as my John (I'm presuming). I haven't heard from my John. I was expecting a letter or something, but I haven't heard anything. Lucy doesn't know how he is either and she's his cousin. She was like, 'Don't mind him.' She's preoccupied anyway because she fancies the arse off Kenno, but thinks one of the girls from Clane is going steady with him. She likes that as in her own words she sees it as 'more of a challenge'. She figures that if she puts out more then he's more likely to stay with her. What this girl won't do for the shift, I tell you. She was totally smirking when she said all this too which means she really is going to do it. Sometimes I worry for the fact that she might someday have children. Anyway, there's a big céilí tomorrow night in the Halla Mór. Maybe there will be some hot guys to look at, not for me obviously because I'm in a committed relationship, but I can always look, right?

Oíche mhaith a dhialann,
Le grá,
Ciara X

The Siege of Penis

Dear Diary

Ó mo dhia! The Gaeltacht rocks! Why haven't my parents sent me here before? Shame on them! There was me thinking that my parents had basically stuck me in the wilds of another part of Connemara, with the whipping wind and the bare desolate landscape that only Peig Sayers would appreciate, but this place is deadly (I've been saying 'deadly' a lot now because the Dublin girls say it a lot too).

We spent the day kayaking and swimming even though it was freezing. I managed a quick phone call to my parents which has to be strictly between cúig agus a sé a chlog, and get this, it was SO nice to hear their voices. They even sounded like they missed me! Then, after more toast at suipéar, it was time to get ready for the céilí in the Halla Mór!

The Bean an Tí was giving out as Gaeilge go leor. She was rippin (I'm also using this word a lot more because the Dublin girls use it a lot). We think it had something to do with us leaving the immersion on or something but we can't be sure. One of the Dublin girls snuck the Bean an Tí's iron into our room and straightened my hair. I'm not going to lie, I had a big ridey head on me. I looked like one of the girls in *Sex and the City*. I have to get one of these, I'm going to make it my life's mission when I get back home.

The céilí was packed and buzzing. It was full of teenage girls and lads. I wasn't even in there two minutes I'd say when Johnno from Kildare asked me to dance and before I knew it, I was doing the Walls of Limerick, the Siege of Ennis and Stack the Barley. Johnno was woeful in fairness to him and it was more jumping and leppin around than actually dancing, but it was fun. My one, two, threes were fantastic from having Irish dancing lessons as a kid. Lucy spent most of the night outside smoking and chatting to Kenno who she told me afterwards was all about her boobs. The Clane girls spent most of the night behind the hall too. It was weird though, as all the lads they had been with just stood around smelling each other's fingers. It must have been drugs.

The céilí ended and we all had to go back to our teachs. When we got back to the room, Lucy and the Dublin girls told me to stay dressed, that the night wasn't over yet. We all got in under the covers, and waited until the lights went out. Twenty minutes later there were stones being thrown at our window. The Kildare boys were outside with flagons of cider. The Dublin girls were out the window in a shot, followed by Lucy.

I was petrified. I promised myself that I would try to be really good because I had such guilts about taking three drags out of that joint a few weeks back, but here it was again, right under my nose: Teenage Temptation.

Lucy was like, 'Are you coming or not?' I thought to myself, if Anne Frank had been given the opportunity to do this as a teenager, she would have jumped at it, right? So the next thing I know, I'm in a field and one of the Kildare lads is passing me cider. It was warm and tasted like feet, but I didn't care. Lucy and Kenno went behind a shed shifting and then slowly but surely the two Dublin girls disappeared with Symthy and Stevo, and then suddenly it was just me and Johnno sitting there chatting.

It was so silent out in that field. The stars were out, and even Van Gogh couldn't have done it justice. Adults say a lot of the time that teenagers these days are vacant, but even I could see how amazing the sky was. Then again, I'm not like other teenagers. As my parents do say, I guess I am special.

It would have been romantic bar the fact that I do have a boyfriend who is probably really missing me right now.

The next thing I know Johnno has suddenly gotten really close, so close that I can smell his Lynx body spray. I'm thinking this is weird, and suddenly he has lobbed the gob on me and for some reason (maybe it was the cider and the boldness of the whole thing) I'm shifting him right back. Real passionate and all. He tasted of cider and cigarettes and Wrigley's spearmint chewing-gum. We heard voices making their way back to the group so we pulled apart. It was Lucy and Kenno and they said we had to leg it out of there straight away.

So myself, Lucy and the two Dublin girls are jumping walls and trying to make it back to the house across the fields and back roads without being caught. We manage to climb back in the window without making too much noise but Lucy and me can't stop giggling. (I think it was more out of nervousness on my part.) We hopped into bed and it felt like five minutes later we were being woken by the Bean an Tí shouting like a FOG HORN, 'Dúisígí! Dúisígí!' We dragged our tired asses out of bed but we couldn't stop smiling at each other over breakfast. What an amazing high! I don't think I've really been living this teenage life to its full potential.

I am having serious guilts about John though. I shifted Johnno, I mean, it was only for not even two minutes in a field in the back arse end of nowhere, so it's not as if it even meant anything. For the first time in my life, I know how Judas Iscariot felt when he betrayed Jesus. What if Lucy finds out and tells John? BUT what if it turns out that I'm destined to be with this guy from Kildare who I shifted in a field for under two minutes?

God, I love the Gaeltacht. How 'coming of age' is that, Judy Blume!

Oíche mhaith,
Le grá,
Ciara X

Bruce Pillis

Dear Diary,

Well, I'm back from the Gaeltacht and – I miss it! Can you believe that? I had the most fun I think I've ever had in my life. Get this: me and Lucy are, like, best friends now. Once my most feared enemy, she's now like an old friend. I never saw that coming, that's how life can surprise you I guess.

We promised the Dublin girls that we would head to Dublin on the bus someday for a 'Gaeltacht reunion' (knowing full well my parents will NOT let me).

I didn't tell anyone about what happened with me and Johnno from Kildare. He did give me his email address though, so that's cool maybe. I spent ages feeling like a female version of Dick Moran from *Glenroe*, but there was no need because I rang John as soon as I got back as I hadn't heard from him. He went Interrailing in Europe without telling me, and is no doubt boring the hairy nipples off some French girl about the plight of humpback whales.

In other news, and I mean other BIG news, I rang Rebecca and straight away I knew she sounded different. It's only been two weeks, but I had that intuition that only best friends have. I slowly figured out why and my heart sank as the penny began to drop. Rebecca had only gone and lost her virginity to Johnny Limp while I was busy learning Irish at the Gaeltacht.

She said it was really romantic and that they had done it in the back of his Subaru. Not the most romantic place I would have imagined, but each to their own I guess. I asked her the obvious questions, like had she seen fireworks (because that's how they describe it in the movies). She said she hadn't seen any. I asked her did it hurt but she said it didn't really as she's been horse riding since she was a young girl. Johnny Limp also told her that he loved her, which is, like, really sweet, and she said it back, and she said everything has changed so much between them, that they're, like, really close now or something, she can't really describe it.

I can't really describe how I'm feeling either. All I know is I'm jealous. Like, really jealous. How could she have done this behind my back?! We made a pact to save both our flowers until our debs, and now not only has she beaten me too it, she also forgot to tell me how she went on the pill, like, six months ago! She went behind my back and went on the pill! I don't know can we come back from this. The first thing I am doing tomorrow morning is, I'm going to the doctor and I'm going on the pill too. She's not the only person in the whole world that's ever been on the pill, like. That will show her, then I'll have sex with John at his grad and we will be even.

I think I was so shocked that Rebecca had sex that I didn't even tell her that Lucy is, like, one of my really good friends now. Which might cause problems because Rebecca is petrified of her and we have spent most of our years in secondary school bitching solidly about Lucy. At lunch break, free classes, in choir practice, at PE, on the phone, in notes passed back and forth in class, you name it.

Do you think that my hymen is going to stay intact for ever? Life is so unfair. How is this happening to me?

When I heard about Rebecca losing her virginity and the added fact that John has not been in contact with me, I took myself off to the cinema. I made Dad drop me the whole way into town to watch *The Sixth Sense*. I'm probably not supposed to write this, but I'm so pissed off – there's a massive twist at the end and BRUCE WILLIS IS ACTUALLY THE GHOST. What a head-fuck, because all along you think the little boy is the ghost. It's crazy.

I'm here listening to songs that remind me of the Gaeltacht. I have Lou Bega's 'Mambo No. 5' playing on repeat on my CD player.

Goodnight Dear Diary,
Love,
Ciara X

PS Lucy just rang my house looking for me! She must miss me! How cool is that!

In For the Pill

Dear Diary,

I woke up this morning determined to go on the pill. I told my mum I was going for a walk, but I was actually going to the local health centre.

As I was sitting in the waiting room, I was thinking to myself that I don't even know what to ask for, but then I thought that Dr Smith had been my doctor since I was a child, so she'll be able to advise me. Except, when I walk in, it's not Dr Smith, but literally a hot young MALE doctor.

This is almost as bad as going to buy tampons and being served by a male shopkeeper.

I go really red and try to think of another reason to be in there, except I can't as I'm thrown off by the maleness and the hotness.

So he's like, 'How can I help you today?' and I'm staring at the ground whispering, 'I want to go on the pill,' and he's like, 'Sorry, I can't hear you,' and I'm nearly crying of embarrassment at this stage, and I say stronger this time, 'I want to go on the pill.' Then he goes really red, and he's mortified, and I want the ground to open up and swallow me whole.

He asked me how long I had been sexually active for. I told him that I'm not sexually active. He said that usually when teenage girls want to go on the pill, it means that they are sexually active. I don't know why I did this, maybe it was because I was nervous and beginning to sweat or maybe it was because I was embarrassed about the fact that he knew I was a virgin, but I just opened my mouth and started talking and I didn't stop.

I told him about always shifting John and how I let him get outside boobage, but no under-bra boobage, and how I let him put his hand on my ass and how my best friend lost her virginity when I was away at the Gaeltacht and how we had both planned to lose it at the debs. It just all came tumbling out of my mouth.

He just sat there staring at me, his mouth agape. Eventually he regained enough composure and after taking my blood pressure (which must have been sky-high) he gave me a three-month prescription of the pill which had a nice name and a nice box and then he sent me packing. I don't know who was more eager to get out of there, me or him. He did tell me however not to feel pressured into doing anything that I'm not ready to do and I told him that I knew that and that I had made a conscious decision never to give a blow job EVER once I had found out what they were.

It might have been my imagination, but he looked like he was going to fall off his seat.

What a bizarre afternoon I had. I kinda feel like more of a woman now if that makes sense. I mean, they do say going on the pill makes your boobs way bigger. Score. I'm looking forward to these babies becoming more bountiful. And I guess maybe I'm looking forward to actually putting the pill into action!

Who knows!

Goodnight Dear Diary,
Love,
Ciara X

Notting Pill

Dear Diary,

So I've been on the pill now for at least a few weeks. My boobs have been bigger of late, but I genuinely feel that they have become SO much bigger since going on the pill. So that's good. On the down side, I would say that they have become more sensitive too. Like, my nipples are really tender, it's not even funny. (I wonder do your nipples get longer if you're on the pill too?) Also something I noticed is that my cramps at my TOM (Time of the Month) haven't been as bad. Usually I get them SO bad where I need, like, a million hot-water bottles. I think my hormones have been affected too.

Like, I went to see this move called *Notting Hill*. Oh my God, Julia Roberts is my idol. I LOVE her. I started bawling at this one particular scene because I guess, Dear Diary, that we are ALL just girls standing in front of hot guys asking them to love us. (And give us the shift.) Hugh Grant, I totally would by the way. His hair is so floppy and cute. I would shift the face off him you know.

I was talking to Rebecca and I told her about going on the pill and she was like, 'Cool.' She told me that her older sister had all these stories about the girls in sixth year who are on the pill. Seemingly you can get really hairy and grow, like, facial hair! Rebecca's sister said that this girl practically grew a beard! I totally don't want to be a hairy bitch when I'm on the pill. Rebecca said that you could put on a pile of weight on the pill too. That's what she's blaming her weight gain of late on, but honestly I think it's the amount of Freddos and Mega Meanies she's been munching into.

Then Rebecca said something to me that really stung. She said, 'Ciara, why are you even on the pill, you don't even have a boyfriend, and you're still a virgin.' I think she thought she was being funny. I now know how Cher felt in that movie *Clueless* when Tai calls her a virgin who can't drive.

Why am I even friends with her? She's just a selfish person. Just because she's not a virgin she's all uppity now, is it? I wouldn't be getting too uppity over the fact I'm going out with Johnny Limp. (HE HAS A LIMP!)

I'll show her when I start having sex. I'm going to have sex with WAY more people than her. Just you wait. I'm going to have sex left, right AND centre.

Goodnight Dear Diary,
Love,
Ciara X

I'm Loving Frigids Instead

Dear Diary,

Rock on Dear Diary, rock the fuck on. I have been through one of the most AMAZING days of my life. AMAZING. I went to Slane Castle and had the best day of my teenage life. I don't know how I managed it, but I did. I'm so tired and my voice is gone and my ears are ringing but it was completely worth it!

I AM SO IN LOVE WITH ROBBIE WILLIAMS.

Tickets were expensive, like nearly 40 pounds, but I had money saved up from babysitting, so Johnny Limp's older brother, Kieran, got us the tickets. He queued all night beforehand and tickets sold out in record time seemingly. The only obstacle was my parents, but then me and Lucy came up with a fool-proof plan. I told my parents that me, Lucy and Rebecca were going to Galway early Saturday morning and we were staying in Rebecca's on a sleepover after. Amazingly enough my parents didn't bat an eyelid.

So early Saturday morning, we all hopped in a minibus to head to Slane, which is like a million miles up the country somewhere. Everyone mostly slept the whole way. The hot barman that is working in the local hotel for the summer was on the bus too. He is a ride. He looks like someone who should be in *Neighbours* or *Home and Away* or something. He has the most perfect teeth I've ever seen in my life, like one of those guys you see modelling in *Heat* magazine. Is it wrong that I could imagine my tongue running across his perfect set of white teeth? That might be the pill talking. I definitely have some unresolved Judy Blume sexual awakening shit going on. Or maybe it was because I was on my way to my first real concert in a field by a castle that I was so sexually aroused.

We eventually arrived in Slane, it took AGES to park, and then when we did our bus was parked I'd say 20 miles from Slane Castle, so we had to walk. Then we had to queue for what seemed like a year to get in. We were all getting nervous that our bags would be checked though. I only had a couple of cans of cider in mine, so nothing major. One of our group did get pulled aside though as it turned out he had the makings of a joint on him. We all nearly totally freaked the fuck out, as I have this insane fear of being arrested, but they let him in eventually. We all got our wristbands and headed in.

The only way I can describe what I saw in front of me was like a scene out of Enid Blyton's *The Folk of the Faraway Tree*. You know when you went up to the top of the tree and ended up in another world? It was like that, only better. There were millions of people there. Millions! Something like 80,000, someone said after. I've never been in the same place as 80,000 people before, especially when you grow up in a village where the population is, like, twenty on a good day. But people kept on pouring into that field.

There was the main stage and two massive TV screens on either side, then another one on top of the hill in front of the castle. We positioned ourselves midway down the hill. There were hot dog stands and burger and chip vans everywhere, plus the longest bar I have ever seen in my life. The queues for everything were massive too.

David Gray started playing on the main stage and everyone was chilling out, sitting on the grass, sipping cider in the sun, listening to him. He sang 'This Year's Love' and all these, like, really overly amorous couples were practically riding each other. Gomez came on then but I didn't have a clue who they were so

I decided to take a toilet break. If there is one thing I know for sure Dear Diary, I was not made for Portaloos. They were so manky that I can't even begin to tell you. I retched several times while trying to hover and pee into the hole simultaneously. Worse still, before I even got in to do my business, I opened a Portaloo door and there was this guy and a girl in it. The girl's knickers were down around her ankles, and I saw yer man's bare arse. I pretended that it didn't shock me that much, but it did. Were they having, like, real-life sex in a Portaloo? I'd happily stay a virgin for the rest of my life than have actual sex in a Portaloo. How can people genuinely get sexually aroused when they are surrounded by the smell of shite? Fucking farm animals the lot of them.

I got lost for a while but managed to find my way back to the gang eventually. I bumped into a couple of people I knew from school as well. Some of the older lads, who usually wouldn't even look at me, today were all like, 'Hey Ciara'. It's weird because I didn't even know that they knew my name, and now they must think I'm cool because I was at Slane just like them. By the time I did make it back to the group, they were all jumping around to the Happy Mondays' 'Step On', and suddenly it looked like everyone was on drugs. I turned my back for twenty minutes and I came back and everyone was off their faces. People were going crazy! People were shifting the faces off each other, people were pissing in the field quite openly, people were building human pyramids and the ones at the top were flashing their arses! You could see their arses on the massive TV screens across Slane. Imagine if their mothers saw them.

The Stereophonics then came on and the crowd made a surge for the stage. Kelly Jones is such a ride. It was really cool to hear 'Pick a Part That's New' live. Actually it was really cool hearing all their songs live.

But then it was Robbie time. The stage went dark and then suddenly 25,000 lights went flickering across Slane Castle and the intro to 'Let Me Entertain You' started, everyone was screaming and jumping up and down and there was still no sign of Robbie on stage. Suddenly, there he was! He walked out all cocky and started singing:

> *Hell is gone and heaven's here*
> *There's nothing left for you to fear*
> *Shake your ass come over here*
> *Now scream!*

It was incredible. The crowd basically sang the whole song for him. The atmosphere was unlike anything I had ever experienced in my life. The songs kept coming, 'Jesus in a Camper Van', 'Phoenix to the Flames'. 'Strong' was like an out-of-body experience for me. He even gave a shout out to the people in the chip vans, the people down the back and even the posh people who didn't pay!

The best ever though was when he walked out on stage wearing an Irish flag and just went 'Olé, Olé, Olé!' into the mic, which was enough for the 80,000-strong Irish crowd to completely lose their minds! Then Robbie lights a cigarette (true story), stands on stage and starts singing 'Angels', and the whole place is lit up with lighters. It felt like every single person in that field in Slane had a lighter. We sang the majority of the song and then Robbie joined in. I'd never seen or felt anything like it in my life. I was getting really emotional because it was literally the best experience I've ever had in my whole entire life, because East 17 is the only other concert I've ever been to but this, this was truly spectacular.

Just seeing Robbie Williams walking around the stage with the Irish flag draped across his shoulders, and maybe because deep down I'm wildly patriotic or maybe it was all those cans of cider in the sun, but I felt like crying, like really crying. I think it was my 'coming of age moment' that people write about in books. Who would have thought I would have mine in a field in Meath surrounded by 80,000 others.

The only dampener was when I turned around to see where Lucy and Rebecca were during 'Angels' so I could tell them that I loved them, all I could see was Johnny Limp and Rebecca shifting the faces off each other, which nearly ruined the moment, but it didn't at the same time. Nothing could ruin that day for me.

Robbie Williams had 80,000 people basically eating out of the palm of his hand. He will never get back with Take That ever again. He doesn't need to. He's amazing all by himself. It was the most unbelievable experience of my life. I think I will genuinely love Robbie Williams for the rest of my life.

The walk to the bus was annoying though as it was parked basically in Cork. Luckily for me though, the only seat left was beside the hot barman, so we chatted for a good bit about how out of this world the gig was, but I eventually ended up falling asleep, as did he. (So technically you could say that I slept with someone.)

Stayed in Rebecca's then and made my way home after. Came into the house and my parents were acting super weird. Both of them were like, 'So, how was the sleepover?' I was like, 'Ya, it was cool.' Then Dad was like, 'Did ye do anything interesting?' I was like, 'No, just pillow fights and girl talk, the usual,' but then my mother erupts and goes mental and says, 'Don't you pillow fight me! You were at Slane! With Robbie what's his face! Shure didn't we see you on the *Six One News*!' My first reaction was like, 'Wow, I was on TV,' and then my next reaction was like, 'Oh shit, I'm literally dead.'

Which I am. They're pretty mad at me. I'm probably grounded for the rest of my life so the hopes of losing my virginity before

I go back to school in September are probably slim. But do you know what Dear Diary? I wouldn't change a thing about yesterday. Not a thing.

Goodnight Dear Diary,
Love,
Robbie Williams's future wife,
Ciara X

Yes / No Virgin Game

Dear Diary,

Oh man, rough day at school. Joanne from sixth year was going around at lunchtime today trying to trick the younger girls into admitting that they were virgins. I mean, what a really bitchy thing to do! She was calling it the 'Yes/No' game, and basically trying to catch people out, which is so sly on SO many levels.

Unfortunately she cornered me, Lucy and Rebecca when we were sitting at the benches looking at print-outs of Leonardo DiCaprio. We would have been killed if the computer teacher knew what we were at and that the reason the ink cartridges were always so low and running out so quickly was because of our obsession with Leo. It was even mentioned at assembly the last day about wasting school resources and if I'm being totally honest, printing off black and white pictures of celebrities that we plan on sleeping with and/or marrying when we're older isn't exactly planning for our future education, but it will help us with revision notes in the future, as we've got a binder with poly pockets and everything, so it's really professional.

The only person we opposed putting in the scrap book was Brian McFadden from Westlife as Lucy says he reminds her of Nick Carter from the Backstreet Boys and we don't like him, seemingly. I think it's because Lucy was with this guy once that looks like Nick Carter, and when Lucy ignored him at a youth club disco he told everyone she was frigid, which, like, massively insulted Lucy because as she said herself, she's built a reputation on NOT being frigid. So ever since we haven't been allowed play Backstreet Boys in the vicinity of her, and now it looks like poor Westlife are feeling her wrath too. Which is a pity because all those afternoons we spent practising the dance moves to 'Everybody' are worthless now.

Anyway, back to the 'Yes/No' game. I love games so of course, like a total sap, I was like, 'Ask me first.' Joanne was all like, 'Have you ever been to West Cork?' I was like, 'Yes, and I've seen Fungi too,' just to add to the question because it was so easy. Then she goes, 'Have you ever cheated on a test?' I honestly had to think about that, but then realised it was me I was talking about, and knowing how afraid I am to get into trouble with any sort of figure of authority and how I, like, freak out when the guards walk by because I'm afraid I'll be arrested over absolutely nothing, I very confidently said, 'NO'.

It was then that I let my guard down. I was too confident. Joanne played the accordion and won medals at fleadhs, so she didn't initially pose any threat. But then came her next question: 'Are you a virgin?' It caught me completely off guard. Lucy and Rebecca knew the truth, that was between us, the circle of trust. But I didn't need everyone in the school knowing, it's completely my business, and Lucy and Rebecca's too as they know about my reluctance to give my flower to just anyone. The answer was out of my mouth before I knew it. 'YES.' I felt like I had shouted it out, shouted it out so loud that the sound ricocheted off the walls, and the sound vibrations bounced all the way up to the moon, banged off it and came back down to earth echoing all around the school.

Rebecca was so shocked the Curly Wurly she had been eating dropped out of her mouth. Lucy dropped the binder of black and white photos of celebrities we want to sleep with and/or marry on the ground. They knew the repercussions of this, my deepest darkest teenage secret laid bare to Joanne in sixth year. Joanne started laughing and was like, 'Oh my God, that was, like, WAY too easy – you failed!'

Now, Dear Diary, I hate failing anything. I hate failing school tests, I hate failing Credit Union quizzes, and most of all I hate failing the fact that I'm a loser teenager who is still a virgin and probably always will be for the rest of my days. I could feel the tears welling up in my eyes and my face going super red. I cursed Joanne from sixth year in my head, I hoped that she'd fail her Leaving Cert and get a really bad STD all in the one day, I hoped that no one would want to go to the debs with her and that she'd fail her first driving test. I'm not proud of what I felt in my head at that moment, Dear Diary, but I was just so embarrassed and mortified.

Lucy jumped to her feet, squared up to Joanne, told her to fuck off and go stick her accordion up her hole, and that if she didn't do it, Lucy would do it for her. I didn't say it to Lucy at the time, but why would Joanne shove an accordion up her own ass? It didn't make sense. Whatever Lucy said worked anyway, Joanne made a quick getaway. Lucy and Rebecca practically carried me to the school bathroom. I was just so stunned. Lucy paced the bathroom thinking of ways to ruin Joanne's life. The only bright idea she had was that her mother's cousin knew someone who was a judge at some of the school fleadhs and Lucy could get that person to guarantee that Joanne never won ever again. I couldn't see that working but I loved Lucy so much in that moment for being my friend that I didn't try to poke holes in her plan.

Suddenly, in the middle of all the drama, Rebecca pipes up that she's allergic to rubber. Me and Lucy were like, 'What?!' Turns out she's, like, really allergic to rubber as her fanny flared up because herself and Johnny Limp have been at it like rabbits. I knew something was up with Rebecca this weekend! I had, like, tried to call her a million times over the weekend but her mum kept on saying she wasn't there, which I knew was untrue as Rebecca religiously watches reruns of *The Waltons* and *Little*

House on the Prairie on a Saturday as she has a major thing for John Boy Walton and the dad in *Little House on the Prairie*, Charles Ingalls (who I've said before and will say again, is such a total ride).

Anyway, I nearly started crying all over again, firstly I felt sorry for me, secondly I felt sorry for her, picturing her putting condoms on bananas in her bedroom while her parents sat downstairs watching *Nationwide* or some shit. But then suddenly I found everything really hilarious, imagining Rebecca's chubby fingers struggling with a condom wrapper and then fumbling to put it over a lifeless banana, and then, knowing Rebecca, she probably got hungry and ate the banana, and had to go downstairs and get some more for her project. In all seriousness though, Rebecca's throat swelled up and she couldn't breathe, so she had to get her mother and explain to her what had happened, which, like, makes what happened to me SO NOT embarrassing at all!!! She said her mother was sound about it and promised not to tell her dad, but Sunday dinner was pretty awkward.

Lucy couldn't stop laughing, what with me practically telling the whole school I'm a virgin, and Rebecca having an allergic reaction to rubber. She found the whole thing hilarious, and has started calling us 'the Virgin Suicides'. It is kind of funny in fairness.

Dear Diary, I know I might be a virgin for ever more, but at least I have the best two friends that any teenage girl could ask for.

Goodnight Dear Diary,
Love,
Ciara X

Smack My Tits Up

Dear Diary,

Had the most awesome weekend. Me, Lucy and Rebecca snuck out and met some guys!!! Like, real-life guys!

Lucy invited me and Rebecca to stay with her on Friday night because Rebecca and Johnny Limp broke up, which is, like, really devastating, and she found out that he already shifted Saoirse from sixth year and she literally had a teenage meltdown. She bought the school tuck shop out of Mars bars for the week, but then really became psycho when she spotted Johnny Limp walking around the school HOLDING HANDS with Saoirse. Lucy decided to take matters into her own hands and went up to Johnny Limp and slapped him straight across the face, in front of, like, the WHOLE school.

They are holding hands which means they are totally having sex. Lucy may have been justified in her actions, but again, can I just say for the record, that I am totally against violence.

Anyway, Rebecca was a blubbering mess for the week. So Lucy suggested that we stay at hers on Friday night. Her older brother was having friends over and then he was going out, so we could just get into our pyjamas and watch *Clueless* and some horror movie or something. Mum and Dad let me go cause they thought Lucy's mother would be there supervising, but I may have forgotten to mention to them that Lucy's mum was going to be at a 50th, so would be out for most of the night.

So, when me and Rebecca arrived, Lucy's idea of a quiet night had turned into her making dolly mixtures from what ever was in her mother's drinks cabinet. 'Uh-oh' was my first thought, but then Lucy's older brother walked into the room, and I was literally starstruck. He was wearing a rugby shirt with the collar up, a pair of beige cords and Dubarry shoes. He had the cheekiest grin and teeth as white as snow on a mountain. I felt myself blushing, like, going fucking puce. Act cool, Ciara, act cool. He was like, 'Hey Lucy Lou,' and she was like, 'Ugh, whatever.' 'Who are your friends?' She was like, 'This is Ciara and that's Rebecca.' I was like, 'What's up?'

What's up?! I mean, could I have been any uncooler if I tried. Then, in a moment of complete panic, I realised I was still wearing my school jumper. Oh my God, he would think I was a complete teenager. He smiled at me and literally my stomach did a somersault.

He was like, 'Me and the lads are going bushing down by the old mill, sneak out later and join us.' Lucy was like, 'Ya maybe.' I was like, 'OH YA, WE ARE SO GOING.'

After twisting Lucy's arm about how we really should go out if only for Rebecca's sake, she agreed. The three of us got ready and snuck out her bedroom window, which was on the ground floor at the back of the house, and made sure to leave it open so we could sneak back in again. On the way down I was quizzing Lucy on whether her brother had a girlfriend. She was like, 'He's in first year of college, so he's being a bit of a man-whore.' I was like, 'Oh right.' Time to turn on the charm. I opened an extra button on my blouse, just so, you know, he might notice my serious rack.

When we arrived down at the old mill there was a group already gathered drinking cans, and someone had their ghetto-blaster down playing some Prodigy tunes. Lucy's brother rocked over and handed us a couple of cans of cider. Lucy saw a lad that she'd been shifting on and off and made a bee-line for him, and Rebecca saw her cousin and headed over to him.

So then it was just me and Lucy's brother, who was the biggest ride I had ever seen. He was just like, 'So, what do you make of the Prodigy?' And I was like, 'Ya, they're cool.' Then, and I have no idea where this came from, I was like, 'Ya, I saw them at the Trip to Tipp.'

Diary, I never went to the Trip to Tipp. Diary, I never went to the Trip to Tipp because my parents were like, 'You are way too young.' But I had heard about it, and I desperately needed to sound cool.

He was seriously impressed. He was like, 'NO WAY, I was there too. What did you make of Kula Shaker?'

Diary, I haven't a fucking notion who Kula Shaker are, but I was like, 'Um ya, they were okay.' He was like, 'Ya, totally.' I asked him what he was doing in college, he was like, 'Engineering'. I was like, 'That's cool,' even though I also don't have a fucking notion what that even entails.

Lucy then came over and was like, 'Can you make sure Ciara gets back to the house okay?' It turned out Lucy was locking lips with this fella, and then I turned around and Rebecca was sitting down chatting to this kinda chubby fella, and they were laughing, so I was like, here's my chance. Lucy's brother was like, 'Ya, sure.'

We walked back to the house, and we were laughing and getting on great. Then he grabbed my hand and was like, 'I've wanted to kiss you all night,' and then we started shifting, and by shifting, I mean seriously shifting. I have literally never been kissed like this, and his hands, they were literally all over me. It was like he was an octopus. Man, college guys know what they are doing. One minute I was up against a wall in his hallway, the next I was sitting at the edge of his bed in his bedroom. Shit had just got serious. We lay down on the bed and kept on shifting, his hand was up my top and in one movement alone, he had unclipped my bra! What a genius! I can't even open my bra.

Things started getting weird then though cause he was doing a serious amount of grinding, and then I was like, 'Oh my God, he wants to have sex with me!!! I can't have sex for the first time in Lucy's house, with Lucy's older brother!!! He's in college, he's experienced!!! I barely know him!!!'

Luckily, I was saved by the sound of Lucy's mother opening the front door. Both of us jumped up. He was like, 'Shit, go down the back stairs to Lucy's room,' which I did, just in the nick of time. Lucy and Rebecca were scrambling in the window giggling, with Rebecca's fat arse getting stuck, so we literally had to tug her in through the window.

The girls were hammered, so they just fell into bed, and they were seriously hungover when they woke the next day. I didn't tell Lucy what happened with her brother, I don't know how she'd react and I'm scared of her. To think I almost had sex with Lucy's brother!!! Oh Dear Diary, why do I think this will not end well ...

Goodnight Dear Diary,
Love,
Ciara X

Presidential Debrief

Dear Diary,

School was a total bore today. I really could not care less about Sin, Cos, or Tan for that matter. I don't really give a shit about infrastructure or the textile industry of the Mezzogiorno or the fact that global warming may cause all the icebergs to melt and the polar bears will die. I know I should be in a more charitable mood, what with Christmas being just around the corner, but I'm not.

You see, I had the weirdest dream last night. It was one of those dreams that I thought only lads have, like. It was, like, a sexual one!!! The strange thing about this dream was who it featured. Dear Diary, I had a sex dream about President Bill Clinton! I mean, what the fuck?! I've been reading about his trial and what Monica Lewinsky said, and I know there was something about cigars – which I asked my father about, but he just put the paper to his face and refuse to answer.

Anyway, this is what happened in the dream. I'm standing outside this massive office door, I'm wearing a debs dress, the next thing I know, the door opens and President Bill Clinton is all like, 'Come in, Ms King,' with his sexy southern drawl. I enter his office and sit down opposite him. He opens his drawer and takes out two cigars and smirks at me. At this point I happen to look down in the dream and my boobs are humongous. I mean, they are Lolo Ferrari big here, we're talking Jordan times 200. He lights both of the cigars, hands one to me, and we both sit there opposite each smoking the cigars just starring intently at each other. The next thing I know, I'm on his desk and me and President Bill Clinton are shifting the face off each other. I mean, using tongues and everything. Suddenly pictures start falling off the walls in the office and snakes start appearing out of holes in the wall. The president shouts at me to run, that he has to go back to Hillary. I rush out of the office only to see Anne Frank sitting in a waiting area, shaking her head and looking really disappointed in me. There's nothing worse than having a sex dream where Anne Frank is looking at you disappointed. I look down just in time to see my boobs shrinking before my very eyes and I start screaming and screaming, and then Dear Diary, I wake up.

I can't believe that I nearly had sex in a dream with President Bill Clinton. And another weird thing is: Bill Clinton is an AMAZING kisser. I've spent the whole day thinking about him. I can't concentrate. Do I fancy President Clinton? I mean, I've seen him on the TV and in newspapers, he was a proper prick to Hillary, but I mean, let's be honest, he is a bit of a ride.

Is this, like, one of those sexual awakening dreams that Judy Blume was always talking about? Is this what happens when you're ready to have sex? Do you have sex dreams about famous American presidents?? If that's the case, please oh please oh please can my next sex dream be about Nicky Byrne from Westlife. I went onto the internet to ask Jeeves about why I possibly had this type of dream, but all I could really gather is that something called a nocturnal emission happens. Did I have a nocturnal emission last night? Is that what it is?? I mean I've heard the lads in class talking about having 'wet dreams' about various female characters off *Home and Away* and Britney Spears but I don't really understand the concept.

I decided to tell Lucy and Rebecca. Lucy was like, it's totally normal, she has at least four sex dreams a week. I asked her had I had a nocturnal emission and she's like, 'A wet dream?' and I'm like, 'Ya', and she's like, 'Well my older brother used to have wet dreams cause my mother was flat out washing his sheets.' Then she was like, 'Well did you come?' I was like, 'Come where? I didn't leave my room, I was dreaming!' She's like, 'UGH forget it.' Sometimes I wonder about her, I really do. Maybe the pill is messing with my mind? Really thinking of coming off it, I mean what's the point? Also I think my mother is getting suspicious as I'm running out of charities to use when asking her for money to buy it each month.

Life really sucks right now. How annoying that I can't even lose my virginity in a dream.

Goodnight Dear Diary,
Love,
Ciara X

Fall-out Girl

Dear Diary,

Well, it's been a pretty dramatic day in the life of little old me. Just when you think everything in your teenage life is going okay suddenly BANG – it, like, all goes to pieces.

Why are girls such two-faced bitches? Why are women such bitches, how can somebody who is, like, your best friend suddenly become, like, a total back-stabber? I mean Dear Diary, what I have learned from life so far is that this is definitely a man's world, so it's like the suffragettes got trampled by horses for nothing, especially when women turn against each other so readily. Shouldn't we be sticking up for each other and not, like, be so mean to each other?

So me, Lucy and Rebecca had, like, the biggest fall-out of the century, and I mean, like, THE biggest, I actually don't think I'll ever talk to them EVER again, which will make the next year and a bit of school, like, totally awkward. It all started when I confronted Rebecca about what the hell she was up to with the Chemistry teacher. Lucy was, like, smoking her third cigarette in the bathroom at lunch break, and me and Rebecca were just hanging with her. She was like, 'I'm getting extra Chemistry classes so what?' and I was like, 'Why, I thought we had a pact about not doing Chemistry cause it's for nerds and, like, WAY too difficult,' and she was like, 'I need it if I'm going to be doing Medicine when I go to college.' I was like, 'Medicine?!'

This was, like, news to me because me and Rebecca made a pact to do Arts together in the college in Galway, cause that's what teenagers who don't have a notion what they want to do in the future do. We were going to get an apartment together, study a language and go away on Erasmus to another country like Italy. We planned on having romantic moments with Italian stallions called Giovanni and Angelo.

Anyway, after I said all that, Rebecca was like, 'Ciara, I have, like, other dreams, I want to be a doctor, deal with it.' She is such a sly bitch, always wanting to be better than everyone else. I was like, 'Fine. Go study Medicine, I don't give a shit.' Then Lucy, who was smoking her, like, fifth cigarette at this stage, was like, 'Um guys, how come you never asked me to move in with you after we do the Leaving Cert?'

Me and Rebecca just kinda looked at each other. We never mentioned it because we kinda reckoned that Lucy will be pregnant in a couple of years and had no real want or need to go to college. Obviously we never said this to Lucy. She must have read it on our faces though, and was like, 'What the fuck, I wouldn't live with you two boring bitches anyway.'

Rebecca, still thick with me obviously, blurts out, 'Oh, Ciara wasn't so boring when she was shifting the face off your brother in his bedroom.'

I nearly had an actual heart attack but still had the sense to block my face with my hands just in case I got a slap. I managed to blurt out that I didn't sleep with him, which Lucy replied, 'Of course you didn't, everyone knows you're frigid,' and then she walked off.

Rebecca was like, 'Oh my God Ciara, I didn't mean to say that,' and I was just like, 'Whatever, metal motormouth,' which was, like, so totally mean because she is, like, really self conscious about her braces.

The next two classes were seriously shit. In Religion class where we always do our homework, the teacher decided to, like, talk about his personal life, as if we give an actual fuck like! Still, it passed like 40 minutes of the class cause people kept asking him questions so he'd keep talking. We had a computer class next where me, Lucy and Rebecca, like, totally avoided each other, which was shit because we usually spend the time sending each other e-cards about random shit, so I spent the class looking up celebrity autopsy photos on rotten.com.

I couldn't get what Lucy had said about me being 'frigid' out of my head. Does everyone in school think I'm frigid just because I haven't had sex?! What's so great about sex anyway? It doesn't even sound that good. Lucy said that she didn't even feel it go in her first time, but that's not surprising cause when she was in third year a lad, like, put three fingers up there, so at this stage you could probably fit a fist in. Rebecca said it did hurt a bit on her first time, but that it was so romantic because Johnny Limp kept on asking her was she okay. In my mind there is nothing romantic about Johnny Limp being on top of you asking you are you okay. There is nothing okay about that Dear Diary – NOTHING. And she said it didn't last that long, like three thrusts and it was over. Jeez, such a big deal about something that doesn't even last that long.

Doesn't really seem worth the hassle, yet here I am, still none the wiser. I mean, I've asked Jeeves, like, loads of questions cause I've heard all these things, like 'condoms can be washed and reused after sex', but it turns out that's a myth. (I was thinking that's cause you couldn't really dry them on the radiator after.) I also heard that a man's testicles can be damaged if he doesn't have sex when he's turned on, or if he hasn't had sex in a long time. I mean, the last thing I would want to do is damage a man's testicles!!!

Oh I give up. Sex seems like just too much hassle, not to mention all the sexually transmitted diseases you can get these days like gonoreaha and syphillus – and they must be serious because I can't even spell them – and AIDS! Yes, you can get AIDS! But in fairness, I heard that you can get AIDS from sharing a toothbrush too.

I think I just feel that I'm being left behind. I don't want to be one of those characters in a Maeve Binchy novel that stays in the local village and gets impregnated by the parish priest. I want more, I want to see the bright lights of Broadway and little black babies in African orphanages, I want to feel the splash of the surf on my face in Summer Bay and have a coffee with Alf in the surf club. I have a dream, just like Martin Luther King did.

Anyway, am off to bed in, like, totally a really bad mood. Thanks for listening, you're my actual only friend right now Dear Diary.

Goodnight Dear Diary,
Love,
Ciara X

Grá & Order

Dear Diary,

I'm not going to lie, but life has seriously been tough for the past few days. Me, Lucy and Rebecca still aren't talking and to make matters worse, today is Valentine's Day. Yes, Valentine's Day, possibly the worst day in any teenager's life EVER, and the worst thing about today is not only the fact that I'm a virgin who doesn't have a boyfriend, I also don't have my best friends with me.

Me, Lucy and Rebecca have been talking about Valentine's Day for months. We planned on slagging the couples walking around the school at lunchtime holding hands looking like complete saps, and then randomly guess which teachers were secretly riding each other, and then Lucy was going to tell us which lads she had decided to give sexual favours to at the Valentine's disco at the weekend.

Sigh. I really, really miss them. So much so I've even started spending time with my family. I was actually in the middle of watching an episode of *Sabrina the Teenage Witch* and my whole family decided to have a competition on who could make the most noise, so I decided to distract them and started asking my mother and father about how they met and fell in love. I actually wish I had never asked because Mum's answer will literally haunt me for the rest of my days. Mum said she fell for my father after checking out HIS ASS when he was playing pool in the local pub and she knew he was The One. I vomited in my mouth a little bit. They met when they were both in London in the '70s. (God, I hope Dad wasn't in the IRA.) Then she, like, gazed over at him lovingly. When Mum went back to the kitchen I asked Dad what he thought was the most important thing about marriage. He said 'keeping the fire alive', which I guess would explain all the time he spends at the bog cutting turf. He said that there were two words that every man should say to keep a marriage happy and they are the words 'Yes, Dear'. Then he started chuckling to himself. Seriously, my parents are, like, so weird.

Granny, who had silently been sipping hot whiskeys in the corner of the couch, suddenly piped up and turned to my father and said 'I don't know what you're on about, that one came here and trapped you into marriage,' and then she mumbled something about 'taking my eldest boy from me, the Lord save us'. Then she blessed herself. I glanced up to see my mother throwing her daggers from the kitchen, and making like stabbing gestures behind Granny's back.

Then Granny started talking about Granddad. She hiccupped, then told me how he was the most handsome man in the parish, and the best poitín maker for miles and miles, 'But the Lord rest his soul, it was the poitín that took him in the end.' She dabbed at her eyes but then told me to 'Ssshhh' because *Coronation Street* was on.

Old people are weird. You know people in Ireland don't really have the best love stories. A lot of these so-called love stories end in, like, major tragedy. Seriously, even famous Irish love stories were all doomed. I mean, take Michael Collins for example, imagine having sex with Michael Collins. I mean, you would literally just lay back and do it for Ireland and I'd say when they called Michael Collins 'the big fellah', they literally meant 'the big fellah'. God, that Kitty Kiernan was such a lucky bitch. But just like that, it ended in tears when she had forked out shillings or whatever for a wedding dress, and then he went and got assassinated.

Here's another doomed story – Oisín and Niamh. They were, like, happy out in Tír na nÓg, but oh no, Oisín got bored like most men, and wanted to check out what the lads of the Fianna were up to. But then when he got back to Ireland the lads weren't there any more, and Oisín, like, fell off his horse and, like, aged 300 years in a second, and Niamh was probably, like, waiting for him in Tír na nÓg with the dinner going cold, going mad because she probably thought he was having pints with the lads, only to never see him ever again. AND don't get me started on Oisín's father Finn Mac Coul. He stopped his own nephew Diarmuid from, like, marrying Gráinne, the daughter of the king of Ireland, and eventually sabotaged his relationship by, like, killing him. I'd say even the lads in the Fianna were like, 'That's a bit harsh.' Finn Mac Coul – Finn NOT COOL in my opinion!!!!

There's loads more examples too, and they all end in, like, major depression. But there is one Irish love story that has lasted though, and that's Bono and Ali, she must have the patience of a saint.

Anyway, my Valentine's Day at school couldn't have been worse. I was in foul form, and by the time the second class had come around, I felt like burning down the school, so when my French teacher announced to the class that I had done badly in my French adjective test, I actually lost the plot. She was like, 'Can you explain to me, Ms King, why you failed your test?' So in the most stupidest move in my teenage life, I turned around to her and said, 'Well, can you explain to me why you failed to educate me?' There was, like, a sharp intake of breath in the classroom. I thought to myself, 'I'm seriously fucked,' and I was right. Double detention, both breaks, on Valentine's Day. This was not part of the plan Dear Diary.

You see, before school started, I had gone into town and ordered a red rose to be delivered to me at the school, and I'd also sent myself a Valentine's card. Okay, so I know it's really sad, but I did it so that Lucy and Rebecca would come over and ask me who it was from and we would start talking again, AND believe you me, Lucy and Rebecca are, like, the nosiest people in the whole world, so they would have been straight over.

So, at lunchtime, when I was sitting in a classroom on my own, the caretaker dropped in my rose and my Valentine's card, and only Hot Brendan was there to see it. Just when I was feeling like such a stupid loser, the biggest ride in school is on detention with me and asked me who sent me the rose. He's really nice, you know, and handsome in a Ricky Martin type of way. When he was talking, I kept imagining what it would be like to shift him. I'd let him live in my La Vida Loca, Dear Diary. He's like SO good on the school rugby team as well. Imagine if I met The One in detention on Valentine's Day!

Anyway, after that brief moment of happiness in the middle of this torturous day, the agony continued with double Maths – which should be renamed 'Mental Abuse To Humans' in my humble opinion – where Lucy and, like, the new girl looked like they were getting on like a house on fire. I even heard the new girl talking about how her and her parents are going to Sydney for the 2000 Olympics next September, but how she was, like, nervous of missing, like, the start of her Leaving Cert year. I was like, may they shove the Olympic flame up her hole if she doesn't stop boasting, like. Lucy was like, 'Oh my God, I will so go with you!!' In my own mind I was like, how? She'd seriously have to curb buying condoms, the pill and the morning after pill to save the money to go.

Okay, that was mean, and she has a medical card anyway, but that's not the point, I was just jealous, it's really hard seeing, like, one of your ex-best friends becoming best friends with someone who could potentially be your nemesis. Ugh, this has to have been the worst Valentine's Day in the history of all Valentine's Days!

Goodnight Dear Diary,
Love seriously sucks,
Love,
Ciara X

PS Sitting here listening to Guns N' Roses' 'November Rain'. As Chandler in *Friends* would say: 'Could I BE any more depressed?'

Broken Nose and Newfand Foes

Dear Diary,

Well the good news is that me, Lucy and Rebecca are back being best friends again, praise the Lord as Martin Luther King would say, but the bad news is I had to, like, practically break my nose in school to get my best friends back talking to me.

I mean, I didn't set out, like, practically to break my nose, it happened because of my latest nemesis the 'New Girl'. That's right: the 'New Girl'. I decided to try out for the girls basketball team at school, cause I kinda freaked out with the fact that me, Lucy and Rebecca haven't been talking in, like, two weeks. I imagine this is what divorce must feel like, no wonder Ireland were so slow to bring it in.

Anyway, it dawned on me that without Rebecca and Lucy, I really didn't have any friends. My classmates are all right, but at this stage in our school years you hang out with who you hang out with, and it's not like first year, where, like, everyone is, like, best friends 4 eva, and you think that's it, we'll be friends for life, but then you get as far as transition year and you're like, 'Did I really shift him at a youth club disco in like second year?' I mean, you really know who you are and where you're going by fifth year.

So I decided I needed to take up a pastime, and basketball it was. It would also give me the chance to wear the Chicago Bulls T-shirt I bought so that I'd look cool like Michael Jordan. Try-outs were during break and it was freezing. I had also forgotten to shave my legs, so I had to opt for my baggy O'Neill's tracksuit bottoms, which meant I couldn't show off my legs to the lads that happened to be walking around the school.

Everything was fine until I saw that Lucy and Rebecca were also at basketball try-outs. Oh God, I imagined it being, like, really awkward if we were put on opposite teams, and sure enough Lucy, Rebecca and the New Girl were on one team, and I was on the other. I felt like I was on the *Titanic* and I was seriously going down faster than Jack Dawson. The first ten minutes were fine, Lucy took down a couple of the girls on my team without the basketball teacher seeing her, pure sneaky like, the girls were terrified of her. Then suddenly I look up and the New Girl has the ball, and then all I remember is her throwing the ball at me, straight at my face, and that was it, lights out. I literally saw stars, and swirling faces and boom! – the pain hit me, it was a pain even worse than being hit in the boob by a tennis-ball flying at a million miles an hour.

The basketball had hit my nose full on and flattened my top lip, which in turn had whacked my teeth and my braces. Suddenly there was blood everywhere, gushing out of my nose. I managed to uncross my eyes to see Lucy and Rebecca looking down at me all worried like. They managed to get me on my feet and were like, 'Oh my God Ciara are you okay?'

The next thing I know Lucy has launched herself on the New Girl, screaming, 'You did that on purpose you bitch!' and all hell breaks loose. Screams of 'cat fight' rings through the air, and all I can see is a blur of people piling onto the basketball court. The basketball teacher finds me and is like, 'Dear Jesus, your nose looks broken.' I'm hanging on to Rebecca, pumping blood, going 'Broken!!! My nose is broken?!' At the same time, the rugby lads are coming out of the changing room, and I'm not looking attractive, I mean, my face is covered in blood, my lip is swollen and I'm half dead. Then one of them shouts, 'Hey Ciara, it looks like you've got your period on your face,' and Dear Diary, I didn't have the time or energy to disagree with them.

The next thing I knew I was in the back of the basketball instructor's car with Rebecca, heading into town to the doctor's. If I actually had been able to talk, me and Rebecca would have been pissing ourselves laughing that we were in the back of the teacher's car, but as I was half dying, I couldn't. Rebecca was holding my head back and I was like, 'Is it bad?' She couldn't look me in the eye, and I knew it was bad.

I knew at that moment that this incident could change the course of my actual life. The doctor saw me and said, 'Okay Ciara, this might hurt a bit,' and CLICK! He basically clicked my nose back into place. I'm not going to lie Dear Diary, I bawled like a baby, but I tried to be strong, as I thought of all the women before me who have given birth, and through these brave, brave women, I got the strength to continue.

On the upside, I didn't have to go back to school. Dad collected me and said that I looked like I had gone three rounds with Rocky Balboa, but it wasn't until I got home that I realised the extent of the damage. My nose looked like Jim Royle's from *The Royle Family*.

My life is officially over. I am never leaving the house ever again. Now I'll never find a husband, lose my virginity or win an Oscar for best performance by a female actress in a leading role. My face is wonky. Now not only do I have bad eyesight AND braces, I also have a wonky nose.

I feel like taking drugs. That's why teenagers take drugs, right?! To escape from their mundane teenage lives, lives full of broken noses and public humiliation. I could do drugs like those guys in *Trainspotting*, except maybe I wouldn't like to see babies crawling upside-down on ceilings. Maybe I'll take drugs like Leonardo DiCaprio did in the movie *The Beach*, except I wouldn't really want to end up sleeping with Tilda Swinton.

Ya, that's it Dear Diary, I'm going to turn to a life of drugs. I'm sure Lucy can get me some ecstasy or something, ya and, like, I can start going to Creamfields and Godskitchen and start, like, listening to Mark McCabe's 'Maniac 2000' on repeat. Ya, that's what I'll do. Oh no, wait, I can't get into drugs! What was I thinking?! Lent has started!!!

Oh God, why does everything not work out for me. I swear I'm actually cursed!!! I can't even start taking drugs properly. God, I hate this time of year! St Brigid's day and Pancake Tuesday and Ash Wednesday, where the smug girls doing Home Ec swan around with their perfectly made St Brigid's crosses and perfect pancakes and perfect ash on their foreheads. Ugh – those Home Ec girls, they wreck my head. God, I hate everyone right now!!!

The only silver lining is me, Lucy and Rebecca seem to be best friends again, and although my face looks like Worzel Gummidge right now, at least I have my friends back. Lucy just rang me and told me that her and the New Girl got dragged into the headmaster's office and got detention for the week. Lucy said though that she turned around to the New Girl and said, 'If you ever go near Ciara again, I'll start putting my cigarettes out on you.' She reckons the New Girl is freaked, which I don't blame her for, as like, seriously, Lucy can be scarier than the Godfather, but at the same time, it's really sweet of her to say that.

Lucy also said that when I get older I'll really start to enjoy balls flying at my face. Eh, I think it's safe to say that from today, I will not be following in Michael Jordan's footsteps.

Goodnight Dear Diary,
Love,
Ciara X

Lukewarm Brendan

Dear Diary,

Oh my God. I mean, oh my absolute God. I need to confide something, like, really life changing to you. I mean, this is the news of the century, in a 'Bill Clinton did WHAT with that cigar?' kind of way. (I eventually found out. Lucy told me. Gross.)

Okay, so Hot Brendan was acting really, really weird in school. I met him at lunch break and he was like, 'I really, really need to talk to you.' I was like, 'Sure, okay,' thinking I'd have to find more creative ways of telling him that his biceps look, like, HUGE in his rugby kit. He is SO obsessed with his biceps it's not even funny.

Anyway, he asked to meet me down by the park benches in town after school, which immediately put my suspicions on, like, Nancy Drew high awareness. BECAUSE, everybody who has half a brain knows that's where us teenagers go to shift other teenagers!!! I was a bit confused, because I really got the impression that Hot Brendan had no interest in me since our 'interaction' in detention, BUT I thought maybe, just maybe he had changed his mind! I'm not going to deny it Dear Diary, I have imagined having sex with Hot Brendan, I mean he's seriously hot. I've been desperate to talk to him since we hung out during detention on Valentine's Day.

Anyway, I met him at the park benches, he was leaning over the railings of the river smoking a menthol cigarette (he says that they are cigarettes for pregnant woman, so they must be okay, which I think is ridiculous as he shouldn't be smoking when he's on the school rugby team, but he also says they keep the weight off. Again, I'm dubious Dear Diary.) Anyway, he's leaning over the railings looking all, like, art nouveau – I don't even know what that means but Hot Brendan looked it.

Then he just turns to me and stares into my eyes (in my mind I was like, this is seriously romantic) and says, 'Ciara, I brought you here to tell you something.' I was like, 'Go on,' and then he says, 'Ciara, I'm gay.' I was like, 'Okay, weird way to say you're happy, Brendan,' and he was like, 'I like boys,' and I was like, 'Eh, so do I, like.' And then he was like, 'No, Ciara, I'm a homosexual.' I was like, 'OH MY GOD YOU'RE DYING!' and I threw my two arms around him and starting crying.

He was like, 'What? I – I'm not dying.' Through my blubbing I explained to him that Freddie Mercury from Queen was the only homosexual I knew of and he died. Hot Brendan was like, 'Ciara I'm not dying. I like boys, I want to kiss boys.'

I was standing there thinking to myself that this was NOT how I'd seen this conversation going. I think I must have been in shock as I kept asking him was he sure like A MILLION TIMES.

Hot Brendan is gay. I repeat, Hot Brendan is gay. Like as in, gay as Christmas, as gay as a treeful of monkeys, like seriously, as gay as a handbag of rainbows. He's gay.

I asked him had he told his mother. He said she knew before he told her and that the only thing his father said was, 'Well, I knew one of ye would end up like your cousin Declan.' Turns out cousin Declan went on an Erasmus to Spain and never came back, he now lives with an older man named Pedro.

It's really weird when you feel your whole teenage world turned on its axis Dear Diary. An hour before that Hot Brendan was a guy I could potentially lose my virginity to, but now I was beginning to realise that I would NEVER EVER be losing my virginity to Hot Brendan. It's so weird, I mean I, like, fancied the arse off Hot Brendan. I don't understand, how do men even have sex with each other?!

Then a series of thoughts start running through my mind: Oh my God, did I do this to him?! Did I turn him gay?! Oh great, that's all I need. I'm the girl that turns men gay. Oh my God! Does this mean that I could be gay? I mean, out of Rebecca and Lucy, I'd obviously pick Lucy as she does have bigger boobs, although I would, like, never tell her that, but like, Rebecca's got a REALLY nice personality ... Oh my God, I'm even starting to think like a gay person. Luckily Hot Brendan put a stop to it by reassuring me that I'm not gay. He was like, 'Ciara, relax, you like dick just as much as me.' In my mind I was like 'Who is Dick?' and 'Am I now in competition with Hot Brendan?!'

I asked him was he happy and he said extremely. He said he feels free, he feels like he's not lying any more, he's found himself. Fuck me, I wonder what that feels like. To find yourself. My granny says going to Lourdes helps people 'find' themselves, but the idea of praying does not appeal to me right now.

Hot Brendan was worried how the rugby lads would react. I was like, 'Just don't walk around the changing room wearing tank tops.' He rolled his eyes and was like, 'Ciara, seriously, Ireland does not and never will have gay rugby players.' He looked so sad that my heart nearly broke. That's it, I am going to write a strongly worked letter to the Dáil, where I will state with strong urgency the rights for gay Irish rugby players. Hot Brendan is my friend, and if he wants to kiss other hot gay rugby players, then so it should be Dear Diary. He's really happy, and I don't think it's my imagination, but I think he's even more attractive. That must be that whole 'you want what you can't have' thing that Lucy talks about.

Anyway, what an interesting day.
Goodnight Dear Diary,
Love,
Ciara X

Requiem for a Teen

Dear Diary,

Well, I have had the most bizarre experience of my teenage life, and I mean, I've seen and done A LOT in my teenage years, from shifting guys from Dublin in the Gaeltacht and scoring guys with holiday homes at beach parties. I've even participated in St Patrick's Day parades. I mean, I have life experience, but what went down last night really took the biscuit. It was like my very own Irish version of *Sex and the City* but with added drama, no sex and loads of drugs!!!

Yes, Dear Diary – DRUGS!!! I'm talking yokes!!! Tons and tons of yokes!!! To the inexperienced: that means ecstasy! Pills! Five-spots! Hash! Acid! You know, what everyone used to do in, like, the sixties!!!

I went to my very first rave, except it was more of a house party with older people and dance music. Lucy, like, burst into the bathrooms in school on Monday, and was telling me and Rebecca about it. She's mad into dance music and really, really wanted us to go. She said we could stay in her house on the Friday night, get ready in our clubbing gear and go to the party.

Now, I know that sometimes I may come across as naive Dear Diary but I knew, in the pit of my teenage core, that there would be drugs at this party. I once smoked a joint and was so paranoid for like a week after that the Gardaí were going to arrest me. I also pulled a whitey and got sick, so I knew a life of drugs was not for me. Also I'm, like, the prefect on the school bus, and I don't need my reputation ruined by attending a so-called 'rave'.

Then Lucy threw me a bone only the hardiest of teenage girls could resist. She told me her older brother was going to be there. For those not in the know, me and Lucy's brother got down to some serious shifting and heavy petting before Christmas, but bigmouth Rebecca told on me when we were fighting and Lucy hasn't really brought it up since. I mean, it's unwritten teenage code that 'Thou should not covet thy best friend's siblings', but there was such a connection between us. Lucy looked me straight in the face and was like, 'If you go with me to the party, you can shift my brother if you want.' I was like, 'I'm there.'

The week could not go quick enough. It was like that line from the Seamus Heaney poem, 'knelling classes to a close', except instead of going to, like, a funeral, we were going to a rave!!!

Lucy even lent me her 'sacred bible' as she called it, *The Orange Euphoria Album as mixed by Lisa Lashes*, which she had gotten as a Christmas present, and I had listened to 'Bass in the Place London' like a million times by the time Friday had come. Lucy told me not to become one of those girls at school that waits until a track becomes popular and then talks about it, she said the key is to like it before anyone else for added coolness. Now, Dear Diary, coolness is not my strongest point, boobs yes, coolness no, and I realised that attending this party on Friday could do wonders for my reputation. So I was just dying to put my coolness into operation.

Mum dropped me over to Lucy's house on Friday evening and as I was getting out of the car she said 'Be safe.' I was like, 'Ugh, whatever.' I rang the doorbell, and Lucy's brother answered. There he was: Lucy's brother, my heavy petting soulmate. He was like, 'Hey Ciara, good to see you.' I mumbled something, I'm not quite sure what it was cause my heart was pounding and I couldn't think and remember to breathe at the same time, but I made it past him and down to Lucy's room without actually passing out.

Well, what a sight greeted my eyes when I arrived into Lucy's room. Everything was illuminous. I mean everything. It was like a magical unicorn from a faraway land had literally come and puked glitter and feathers and neon all over Lucy and Rebecca. There they were standing before me, dressed in illuminous pink hot pants, illuminous yellow string tops, fluffy boots, and covered in body paint that even the Aboriginals in Australia would cringe at. Lucy had so many glo sticks wrapped around her, I wouldn't have been surprised if she had some coming out of her vagina, and Rebecca, for the love of God, was wearing what turned out to be a bandana on her head.

Oh, we were definitely going clubbing all right. I felt like Posh Spice in, like, her worst nightmare. The girls convinced me to wear a feather boa so I didn't look like a complete square to be fair.

Off we headed, naggins in hand, to the house party. Lucy was babbling on about Lisa Lashes and, like, HOW AMAZING she is, and how she can't wait to go to Godskitchen in the Point and see her and Tiësto playing. I made a note to check out this Tiësto fellow for some more added coolness. On the way Lucy's brother wanted to stop and do a 'transaction', which I thought was weird because we were down by the river and no one was around. Then I noticed a guy sitting on the other side of the river. Lucy's brother put a fiver in a cigarette box and threw it over to him, which I thought was sweet as the guy must be homeless, but two seconds later the guy puts something in the cigarette box and throws it back over to Lucy's brother. He catches it and is like, 'Just had to get a little five spot for the evening that's in it.' I was pretty sure that I had just witnessed some illegal activity, and I'm not going to lie, it made me even hotter for Lucy's brother.

We got to the house party and all I could hear was boom, boom, boom echoing through the walls, the rooms were dimly lit and there was a guy on decks pumping out dance tunes. It was heaving! Everywhere I looked there were girls in fluffy boots and neon boob-tubes and lads dressed in what can only be described as jumpsuits with, like, the Mitsubishi car symbols on them. In fact, there were flags in the house with Mitsubishi symbols on them. I thought to myself that a mechanic who really loves his car lives here.

I lost Lucy and Rebecca straight away cause they had gone to the bathroom to reapply their ridiculous make-up. A guy came over and started chatting to me and was like, 'So you're into dance music,' and I was like, 'Ya totally.' He told me that he had been at Creamfields last year and it was, like, the best night of his life. He was like, 'So what are you into – House, Progressive House, Trance, Techno or Electronic Pop?' I was like, 'Fuck!' in my own head as I didn't have a clue, so I panicked and told him that I liked Scooter, then in my nervous, anxious state I said, 'It's nice to be important, but it's more important to be nice.' He was like, 'Ugh okay, Scooter is, like, cheesy and SO mainstream.' I was like, 'Ya totally, I like totally prefer Fatboy Slim,' which he looked impressed by until I admitted that I knew all the dance moves from the video 'Praise You', and offered to show him, but he declined. He was like, 'You haven't been to many house parties like this, have you?' I was like, 'No.' He was like, 'Listen, I've been to loads of dance festivals and the roughest crowds are hard dance, that's where it's at, you wouldn't find that kind of crowd at a Drum and Bass or House or Techno gig, there's usually a really positive vibe, like here tonight.' Then he popped a pill into his mouth and I was worried that all my Scooter talk had given him a headache.

I wandered around drinking my naggin looking for Rebecca and Lucy who happened to be on the dance floor, which was in the sitting room. Something was weird though, as Lucy was just smiling and dancing while looking at her hand, and Rebecca was sweating buckets, smiling and dancing to herself, drinking pint glasses of water. I went in to the kitchen and Lucy's brother was there. He gave me a massive hug and was like, 'It's SO nice to see you,' but then he started doing like this really weird thing with his lip, as if he was trying to bite it.

It slowly began to dawn on me that I was the only one not on the same buzz as everyone else. I went back out to Lucy and Rebecca who were dancing and laughing and kissing each other. Yokes! They were all fucked on yokes!!! Lucy and Rebecca were kissing each other, it looked like a big neon illuminous lesbian fest, and I was having no part of it. I mean, did the girls not HEAR the Verve saying that 'The Drugs Don't Work'? I knew from, like, Civics class that it would take a while for the girls to 'come down' from whatever they were on, so I slouched in a corner, finished my naggin and fell asleep with the dull, thick sound of Da Hool's 'Meet Her at the Love Parade' ringing in my ears.

When I woke up a couple of hours later, everyone was STILL dancing and I was just like, 'I am going to make like a tree and leave.' I asked Lucy where Rebecca was, and she said 'She's being paranoid in the bathroom,' so I went up to get her, man, she was wasted. We both walked back to Lucy's without Lucy, without me shifting Lucy's brother, and with Rebecca holding on to me for dear life.

What a night Dear Diary.
What a night.
Love,
Ciara X

Procrasterbation Material

Dear Diary,

I really hate my life right now. I'm sitting at the desk in my room cursing the educational system. I've done out a study timetable for my summer exams which are, like, ages away, but I'm trying to get organised. But I've managed to mess it up, I had to redo it three times and I've highlighted the bejaysus out of it too, so now it's a page of neon pink and neon yellow, and I don't even know when the summer exams are on because they're that far away.

Man, I'm bored.

Studying is hard. I never know whether to spend more time on Biology diagrams or Maths formulas or Geography contours or drumlins or glaciated lakes. Earlier I was trying to learn just ten French phrases that I can use in a stupid letter, like, when am I ever going to write a goddamn letter in French anyway? Like, am I suddenly going to start writing to the French president and be all like, 'Bonjour Jacques Chirac, do you have any amenities in your caravan park by the sea?'

I've been listening to my Discman non-stop too. I've also been daydreaming and doodling hearts and crosses all over my refill pads. I've also started doing up lists. So far, I've compiled a pretty comprehensive bunch. I started with a list of why *Home and Away* is better than *Neighbours*, then went on to do a list on all the reasons why Whitney Houston would win in a fight against Mariah Carey and Celine Dion. (Whitney would beat Mariah, but they would both totally trash Celine Dion. I felt bad about that because I, like, love Celine Dion.)

So as you can imagine, studying gives me, like, LOADS of time to think. Like, this time next year, I'll nearly be doing my Leaving Cert! I'm trying to figure out what I'm actually going to do with the rest of my life. I do think I have it narrowed down though. I think, like, I might like to be an artist, like an actress or a musician or a novelist OR the fourth member of Destiny's Child or, like, a peacekeeper and spread peace all over the world like Bono. I'm being serious about this too. All the greats of the world knew their calling in life.

I'm just waiting for that call. Like, Joan of Arc was 13 when she began to hear voices from God and knew then that she had to save France. She also took a vow of chastity, which is basically what I've done too but against my will may I add. It all went a bit pear-shaped for Joan though, what with the whole witch accusations and then being burnt at the stake, but I wouldn't let that happen. No way.

Sometimes I lie in bed and I listen to hear if God is trying to talk to me, but then I get sidetracked thinking about school or about all the mingers I've shifted at youth club discos, or about how the delivery guy Doug Heffernan from *King of Queens* is NOT hot enough to have managed to marry someone as hot as his wife Carrie in the TV programme and I can't concentrate, so I don't know if he has even tried to contact me yet. I wouldn't be opposed to it, I'd probably be scared if he actually started talking to me, but I could handle it, I think.

I would just become this great person and then there would be no more double French, or any need to ever go to Religion class or Maths or Geography or Business Studies, life would be hassle-free. There would be no more exams, no more sitting in my bedroom listening to my parents giving out about *The Late Late Show* downstairs, or hearing my brother kick a football off his bedroom wall even though he has been warned like a million times to stop.

Obviously I'm excited for this period of my life to start, but I would miss secondary school too. I LOVE my friends Lucy and Rebecca and Hot Gay Brendan, like I never want to leave them or see them move on without me, well, let's be honest, maybe not Lucy, as we all know how her future is going to end up. I'm learning to love my time in secondary school. I'm really learning to love myself and I'm getting a better understanding of who I am as a person. I've changed SO much in the last couple of years. I feel like I'm a completely different person than I was when I did my Junior Cert, which feels like years ago. I mean, you can even see that in the poetry that I write.

There is one thing that's missing, and it's not my hymen, Dear Diary.

Sex.

A common problem in many of my diary entries is that fact that, you know, I'm still a virgin. I don't think that you can really experience life and, like, really be yourself if you've 'never thrown the leg over someone' as Lucy puts it.

I've decided that instead of studying, I need to get creative and, like, imagine that I have had sex and that I have life experience, so I've started writing romance stories for girls my age, that maybe haven't had sex, but, like, want to, but don't know how.

Here's one called 'Teenage Dirtbag'.

> *She knew the minute she saw him that she was in trouble. Her heart did a somersault only a gymnast performing for an Olympic gold medal could do. She glanced over her shoulders and his eyes met hers. They were piercing and fiery and held a sense of longing that she was not accustomed to. Her loins moved in mysterious ways. They roared to her like the lion does at the start of an MGM movie. She had to have him. He had to be hers.*
>
> *The bell rang for class, and their gaze parted. He was going to Metalwork, she was going to Home Ec. They were the Romeo and*

Juliet of subjects, she thought to herself as she went on her way. *She knew she would see him again and maybe some day make love to him in the back of a car to the tune of Boyz II Men's 'I'll Make Love to You' that they would have been listening to while sharing earphones on her Discman, and then the batteries would run out and they would just start laughing.*

Home Ec passed in a complete daze as she daydreamed about the two of them. She imagined his smile, his perfectly formed dimples, his rippling muscles and his Calvin Klein underpants slightly showing over his Wrangler jeans. She imagined them kissing with roaming hands and lust-filled hearts. She imagined their first argument and their first make-up where he would tell her that he could never live without her, while he held her and cried.

After Home Ec, it was lunch break. Her heart beat faster as she imagined bumping into him, but alas he had rugby training. She imagined being that rugby ball and him holding her tightly in his big, strong hands. Hands that had been chiselled from the gods above. She imagined those big hands brushing off her JLo ass, but then giggled to herself for having such naughty thoughts. Lunch break passed with the dull chatter of girls in her year talking about what they were going to wear at the disco next weekend.

'How boring,' she thought to herself. She had bigger dreams and thoughts than what she was going to wear to the youth club disco. Girls her age were so immature. She wandered aimlessly towards her school locker. As she searched for her Geography book in the deep dark crevice of the locker, she looked up, and there he was. The scent of Lynx Africa wafted through the air. His Dax Wax glistened in his hair. She felt like the earth had stopped moving. 'Hi,' he said in this thick country accent. 'Hi,' she said and nearly died a little when she smelled the familiar scent of Wrigley's Juicy Fruit off his breath. He looked directly into her

eyes. A bolt of electricity passed between them and she imagined doing really bad things in the back of his car.

He was the only boy in her year that drove a car, the rest of the boys drove tractors. His hand reached up to her face and gently removed an eyelash that had fallen loose from her eyelid. She was never going to wash her face again. 'I'll see you around,' he said as he darted off towards one of the science labs. As he passed, the back of his schoolbag brushed off her chest and she wasn't sure if she had imagined it, but she thought one of her nipples had gone hard. Dazed and confused she ran to the bathroom. Breathing hard, she splashed cold water on her face and tried hard to compose herself. 'Pull yourself together,' she thought to herself, 'he's only a lad.' But as the image of him entered her brain again, she felt her knees go weak and she had to lean against the sink for support.

But she knew it could never be, and although she knew she would yearn for him for the rest of her days, he was, and would always be, the principal's son.

The End.

I'm not going to lie, I'm pretty proud of this one.

Goodnight Dear Diary,
Love,
Ciara X

From Dawson's Creek to Winning Streak

Dear Diary,

Well, the weekend started out like any other in our house. Friday night saw Mum giving out about the fact that she couldn't BELIEVE that Brendan Grace and Phil Coulter were on *The Late Late Show* yet again, which was followed by the usual spiel of why was she bothering to pay for a TV licence, when this was the sort of shit she was paying to see, week in, week out. But Saturday in our house was different.

You see, Granny had gotten three stars on a *Winning Streak* scratch card last week and had popped it in the post convinced that Mike Murphy was going to call her name and that she would be a contestant on the show. So the deal was, after Mass on Saturday night we had to stay glued to the TV to see would her ticket be picked.

Our house on Saturday night looked like a senior citizen Christmas party with every old fogey that Granny had ever played cards or bingo with crammed into the house waiting in anticipation for *Winning Streak* to come on. Granny was certain that the priest had said a quick Mass just so that everyone in the parish could get home fast to watch it.

Neighbours that I didn't even know we had were popping in and out of the house at an awful rate, and of course, I was on tea duty. I swear I made like a million pots of tea, and that's not an exaggeration. Tea is like old people's heroin.

I began to feel worried for Granny because the chances of her scratch card being pulled out were slim to none, and I didn't want her being embarrassed in front of the whole parish when her scratch card wasn't pulled out. But she insisted that she got a 'sign' from above from 'himself', and that her ticket was going to be picked out and that was that.

I worry about these 'signs' that Granny sees. These signs consist of whether or not dolphins are spotted in the bay, or if she hears the cuckoo in March and not April. I can't make head nor tail of them myself, but whatever rocks an old person's boat I guess.

Winning Streak had commenced. There was an obvious air of anticipation and also a bang of TCP (or 'tom cat's piss' as we like to call it) coming from the sitting room of our house. Mike Murphy introduced this week's players, had a quick chat with each contestant, heard random shout-outs to neighbours in Meath and mentions to family in hospitals watching, and then he moved on to play Treasure Island. There were claps when one of the contestants won a car on, like, their first go, with people nudging my granny saying that could be you. Which is hilarious, as she doesn't even drive.

I was totally mortified to be in this situation. How sad. I should have been down at the local benches drinking cans hoping to be shifted by some young lad but instead I was stuck in what seemed like a hospital ward for the living dead. I was also cringing so much for the sad saps in the audience with their banners looking like total eejits every time the camera panned to them.

Winning Streak went to a commercial break and I was sent to make more tea. I felt like one of those girls in the Magdalene Laundries, having to work hard against my own will for old people, but I suffered through it.

The ad break was soon over and things began to get serious. It was the part in *Winning Streak* where they bring on a celebrity to pick out next week's contestants from the big drum. It was actually Phil Coulter, and I thought my mother was going to have a heart attack. My granny, on the other hand, saw this as another sign as she has all of his albums and absolutely loves his version of 'Carrickfergus'. We all waited with bated breath. Again, I was feeling this massive over-protectiveness towards Granny as she was about to be left red-faced in front of everyone like the time she dropped the collection basket in Mass. I think she cried for one week solid after that.

The first ticket is pulled out. It's a man from County Meath. The second ticket is pulled out and it's a man from County Cork. The third ticket is pulled out and it's a woman from County Dublin. (Ever notice how there is always someone from Dublin pulled out of the drum?!) And then, I kid you not, Phil Coulter of 'The Town I Loved So Well' fame as clear as day reads out my granny's name off a scratch card. I don't believe it, I actually don't fucking believe it.

Our house erupts. It's like Italia 90 all over again. But the hero of the day is Phil Coulter and not Packie Bonner. Cups of tea go flying, pieces of barm brack and Mikado biscuits spin through the air, the house phone starts ringing, neighbours start running into the house.

My granny is crying and saying 'Jesus, I'll finally meet him, I'll finally meet Mike Murphy.' (She doesn't know it, but she is getting serious side-eye from the other women at this revelation, the old jealous bitches.) We never get to hear who the last contestant is because there is a full-blown party underway in the house. My father has taken out the whiskey and the sherry and the cans of Guinness that are supposed to be kept for Christmas and it feels like the whole village is in the living room.

Then it dawns on me. Oh fuck. I'm going to be expected to go and sit in the audience of *Winning Streak* with a banner and say some sad shit like, 'Ya, we're really proud of her,' and, like, talk about ourselves and shit. I'm 17. My street cred will be in absolute tatters. I can't so this or I will be a virgin for the rest of my days. God damn Phil Coulter.

School on Monday was just how I anticipated. The news that my granny was going to be on *Winning Streak* was actually announced at school assembly, one of the teachers even had some of the third years making banners for our 'trip'.

Lucy and Rebecca were slagging the absolute shit out of me for most of the day and my English teacher wants me to write an account of my big day in RTÉ for the school newsletter. How has this turned into more work for me? Rebecca and Lucy were all like, 'Think of the money you're going to get from your granny if she wins.' Wait a second. Money. I was so caught up with the fact that I'll be making an ass of myself on national television that I had forgotten about the money. Oh my God. My granny could actually SPIN THE WHEEL and then we'd be rich! Or she would be rich and I would start to be a super awesome granddaughter.

We were due to go up to Dublin the next day to film the episode. Turns out it's a pre-recorded show – NOT LIVE! Who would have thought. The village committee had organised a 35-seater minibus up to Dublin, and I swear, I haven't seen old people this excited since *Michael Collins* was on in the cinema in Galway.

Off we headed with packed sandwiches and flasks of tea, and after a quick toilet stop at Hayden's Hotel in some place called Ballinasloe, we arrived in RTÉ. I don't know what I expected when I arrived there. I guess I thought I'd see Anne Doyle and Brian Dobson just hanging around having the craic, but it wasn't what I expected. It looked like a building from the 1970s. There were no celebrities anywhere, not even Bibi Baskin or Derek Davis. We were all ushered in and brought to Studio One. Granny went off and took her position with the other contestants, and we settled in our seats in the audience. There were literally no hot guys there. I forgot to add that we were all wearing T-shirts with my granny's face on them. It was like the weirdest hen party of all time. I made sure that mine was extra tight because if I was going to lose my cool teenage rep for being a sad sap on *Winning Streak*, then at least I would be the sad teenage sap with great boobs.

All of a sudden, there he was. With teeth as white as when you wash your clothes with Daz – Mike Murphy. It's fair to say, Dear Diary, that Mike Murphy is indeed a RIDE, and the majority of the older ladies, as Lucy would put it, were sliding off their seats with the excitement of seeing him.

Before I knew it we were filming. The audience were cheering and Mike Murphy was starting to talk to contestants one by one. First up was a farmer from County Meath who was doing the show for his sick wife in hospital, blah, blah, blah, a posh woman from Dublin (who straight away I wished wouldn't spin the wheel because that would be so unfair), then some old man from Cork, and then Granny.

My heart was in my mouth, firstly for her and secondly because I knew at any minute that the camera could be on me and I would have to wave my banner like I didn't give a shit, which I totally did because of the mortification of it all. I heard Granny say that she planned on going on a trip to Maggiore if she got to spin the wheel and then Mike Murphy asking her who she had brought with her in the audience, and then the camera is pointed at me, and I don't know what happened but I'm standing up and I'm shouting at the top of my lungs and waving a banner like there is no tomorrow. It was like an out-of-body experience.

Dear Diary, the rest of the show passed in a blur, Granny picked County Galway on the Treasure Island map of course and got through to play the Goldmine game. She got eliminated on the third go but still managed to win 10,000 euro along with the 5,000 she already had. FINALLY, it was time to play Spin the Wheel. Six numbers, three are blank and three reveal the letters WIN. The contestants' numbers are put in the bubble. The posh one from Dublin's number came up twice, first she drew a blank, then got the letter W. The farmer from Cork's number kept on coming up too. Granny's number 4 didn't see the light of day and it was the farmer from Cork who went on to spin the wheel.

I didn't really want to admit it to anyone, but my trip to the *Winning Streak* studio had been the most excitement I had had in a VERY long time. The sheer adrenalin. This must be what sex feels like.

The minibus on the way down from Dublin was great craic and I was happy for my granny. She was like a mini celebrity and even got mentioned at Mass on Sunday AND she got her picture taken with Mike Murphy. It will most likely replace the picture of Padre Pio she has up on her kitchen wall.

She said she plans on donating money to the parish church because of the leaky roof in the sacristy. Screw that. What about her poor granddaughter? I decided against saying anything, even though my street cred will probably be completely gone after this programme airs on Saturday night.

I really don't care though. I supported my granny AND got a whole day off school and avoided double Maths. That's a win bigger than spinning the wheel on *Winning Streak* in my eyes.

Goodnight Dear Diary,
Love,
Ciara X

'I felt a Funeral, in my Brain'

Dear Diary,

I'm so sick of these summer exams. It's not even funny. My parents are being so strict and it's not fair because I am practically an adult at this stage. Didn't Macaulay Culkin, like, divorce his parents or something? Can I do this? Who do I need to talk to?

Like, I know that I have to study to get an education. I'm not some imbecile, and if I was an imbecile, it would SO be their fault because they made me. They should be made feel responsible for what they do in their lives to you know. Ugh. Annoying. Like, if they didn't want to be such nagging dickheads all their lives, maybe they should have worn protection?!

Anyway, school is a big pile of balls. Everyone is getting ready for the end-of-school concert, which basically means participating in the school choir and singing 'Panis Angelicus'. I heard that all the sixth years are going to Santa Ponsa after they finish their Leaving Cert. I'm SO jealous. Sun, sea, hot English guys. Lucy says you would want to buy condoms in bulk in the duty free before you'd go there. She also reckons that the hospitals would be full because of the amount of sexually transmitted diseases out there. Including herself I'd say, but anyway. It's not as if MY parents would let me go anyway because they are so BENT.

I really just want my life to hurry up and start happening. As Muhammad Ali once said, 'I know where I'm going, and I know the truth, and I don't have to be what you want me to be. I'm free to be what I want.' I'm going to live my life just like that.

Dad took me for a driving lesson earlier. He said it was to give me a break from the studying but I reckon the real reason was because Mum was giving out to him about painting the back kitchen and that's the only reason he wanted to get out of the house. The last time Dad took me driving, instead of going forward, I reversed and smashed a tail light, so the fact that he even offered was a surprise. About 20 minutes into the driving lesson I had a near-death experience though.

There should be a scientific study done on suicidal sheep in the Connemara region. There we are, driving along avoiding pot holes, and suddenly this sheep appears from nowhere and practically jumps on the bonnet of the car. I slam on the brakes because of my amazing reflexes and we stop. Then Dad jumps out of the car to see if the sheep is okay?! I'm like, HELLO! Don't you think you should check if your daughter is okay after OH I DON'T KNOW – A NEAR-DEATH EXPERIENCE. The sheep was fine, it ran back to its other dumbass sheep friends. Sheep are the dumbest animals of all time. Wouldn't you think they might take a leaf out of their famous cousin Dolly's book and stop being such rampant arseheads.

Anyway, after that incident Dad decided to end my driving lesson, muttering something about me being like a mini Michael Schumacher and that he'd have to put a warning to farmers everywhere if I ever did get my licence! Totally not fair. But after having, like, my life flash before my very eyes, it got me thinking. It got me thinking about mortality Dear Diary.

I mean, what is the meaning of all this? You only have one life. God is having a serious laugh by making us go through these hellish teenage years. What's the point? He is one sick dude if you ask me.

If I were to die tomorrow, my one main regret in life would be the fact that I'm a lousy virgin loser and I've never experienced a pair of strong manly hands holding me, or I've never experienced the excitement of buying condoms in the vending machines of nightclubs that you successfully get into using a fake ID. Lucy is always buying condoms. Even when she wasn't having sex, she bought them because she wanted to practise giving BJs. She can be really conscientious sometimes. We ended up down the back of the hall with a bunch of bananas and a packet of condoms and Lucy sitting there practising like there was no tomorrow. I'm not going to lie Dear Diary, it was a weird afternoon, but you have to admire the girl for her innovation and her persistence. Maybe Lucy will grow up to be one of those powerful businesswomen, you know, like Samantha in *Sex and the City*.

I wonder if I did die, would anyone actually care that I was dead? You know like the way they cared when Princess Diana was killed in that car crash? Do you think that anyone would stand up in mass and read the famous poem 'Do Not Stand at My Grave and Weep'? Instead though, the version at my funeral would be: 'Do not stand at my grave and weep, I am not there, I killed a sheep.'

I really don't think anyone would care. I really doubt it. Not even Mum and Dad. They would just be pissed that they would have no one to hoover the house on a Saturday. I wonder who would cry more out of Lucy and Rebecca, because let's face it, they would so miss me because I am the only normal one out of the three of us, what with Rebecca's emotional eating habits and her ability to eat a Mars bar in ten seconds flat. If I died, she'd probably put the company behind Mars bars out of business. And Lucy! Jesus, Lucy would probably go on a pillaging spree through villages across Ireland like the Vikings and the Normans before her and like seriously plunder LOADS of guys. Mothers would literally have to lock up their sons as she would be so upset that I was dead.

I would also insist that all the priests at my funeral would be women, although I don't think my granny would be too pleased as she reckons that there is no place for women in the church, except for those that are on their knees. She doesn't even like nuns, as she says she doesn't trust them. Which is funny, because every time she sees one, she's nearly tripping over herself to kiss their asses. She's all like, 'Hello, sister,' 'How are you sister,' 'God be with you sister.' Sister my hole like.

She thinks that *Father Ted* is an abomination to human kind, but forgives Brendan Grace for playing a priest in it as she always gets a good giggle out of him on *The Late Late Show*. She says she always prays for his soul every Saturday night at Mass so he'll give up those 'God-awful' cigarettes. Like, what women actually pray for the soul of Brendan Grace? I ask you?

I have my songs all chosen for the funeral Mass too: Mariah Carey's 'Hero', Shania Twain's 'You're Still the One', Des'ree's 'I'm Kissing You', Seal's 'Kiss From a Rose' and THE ultimate saddest song of all time, 'Wind Beneath My Wings' by Bette Midler from the movie *Beaches*. If that doesn't have people roaring crying in the pews then I don't know what will. All the while these songs are playing I would like a montage of, like, the saddest Disney movies playing on a projector above my coffin, like the scene where Bambi's mother dies or where in *The Lion King*, Mufasa is lying dead and Simba is trying to wake him up, or where Belle's father is ripped away from her in *Beauty and the Beast*. Just to add to the emotion of the ceremony like.

Everyone in the parish would talk about how it was the saddest funeral the area has ever seen and all the lads I've scored at youth club discos would be all up in the front seats of the church crying and thinking to themselves, 'Why didn't I have sex with her?' Oh, they would regret it all right Dear Diary, oh yes they would. At some stage I'd like a gospel choir to make an appearance like from the movie *Sister Act*, but I haven't really given much more thought to the final details of the actual funeral, or like, what celebrities I'd actually have there. See, even when I'm dead, I'm still trying to bring other people happiness. It's hard being so selfless at the same time.

Oh my God Dear Diary, I'm having SUCH an Emily Dickinson moment right now! I have literally 'felt a funeral in my brain'. Sometimes I really surprise myself at how deep I am.

Goodnight Dear Diary,
Love,
Ciara X

Lucy Loo

Dear Diary,

I know I have said before that dramatic things have happened me in these teenage years that I have had, but nothing, and I mean NOTHING could prepare me, Lucy, Rebecca and Hot Gay Brendan for the day we had today. It was like an episode of *Party of Five* or *7th Heaven* except it was real life and none of us are as hot as Mary from *7th Heaven*, not even Hot Gay Brendan.

Lucy rang and asked us if me, Rebecca and Hot Gay Brendan would go into the city with her for the day. I was like, YES, get me out of here, my parents are wrecking my buzz. I thought she sounded weird on the phone, but I was like, whatever, she can be a moody bitch at times, so I didn't think much about it.

We all met and got the bus into the city, which is an hour-and-a-half drive from home. Straightaway it was obvious that Lucy had been crying and she was as white as a sheet. We all went down the back of the bus, which is, like, an unwritten rule for teenagers travelling by public transport. We were like, 'Lucy, spill, what's up?' She was like, 'I'm late,' and I was like, 'Late for what?!' She was like, 'No, you don't understand – I'm LATE.'

Rebecca straight away reached for another pack of Monster Munch and looked shocked. I was like, 'What on earth is going on here?' and it wasn't until Hot Gay Brendan literally spelled it out to me that I realised she was talking about her period. Then Lucy started crying and said that she had unprotected sex with some lad that's a friend of her cousins, but he swore that he had pulled out in time. Again I was confused, pulled out in time for what?! The *Six One News*?

Then Hot Gay Brendan started talking about how guys can, like, pre-come before they actually, you know, go the whole hog. I'm confused. So guys can, like, do it, but then like, do it straight away again?

Rebecca at this stage had switched to Mega Meanies and looked petrified. This was honestly the most horrific and dramatic thing EVER. The bus journey was the longest bus journey of our young lives, and it was like everything from that moment on was going to change in, like, an Anne Frank kind of way. Lucy could be pregnant. Lucy could literally be pregnant. I mean, I know I've said this would always happen, but I didn't think it would actually happen in real life. (On a side note, does this mean that I am psychic?)

Half of me was really mad at her for being so stupid. I mean, we have read numerous teen magazines about fooling around, heavy petting, and how unprotected sex can lead to pregnancy! Oh God. What if she ended up in one of those laundry places and had to get her hair cut off and then we'd never see her again? I could imagine Lucy telling her mother and it being like a scene from *The Snapper* where Sharon Curley tells her father Dessie Curley that she got pregnant by Georgie Burgess.

Anyway Lucy had a plan, and the plan was that all four of us were to buy pregnancy tests and then meet in the bathroom of Supermac's and Lucy would do all four tests. There is a load of pharmacies in the city, so we decided to split up and meet back in the square in half an hour.

I stopped in at Easons though cause I wanted a clearer idea of what I was dealing with. I found our biology book from school and thought that it was actually really ironic that I was reading it out of school time, but after I read what I read, I couldn't help but think she was screwed.

Did you know, Dear Diary, that when men ejaculate they, like, release over 200 million sperm? Did that mean that Lucy had over 200 million chances of being pregnant? I mean, God knows I'm no mathematician, but that did seem like quite a high chance. Sperm can also live for up to five days after coming out of a man's you-know-what. Women don't stand a chance. I remember seeing a video in Biology class before and thinking to myself that they looked like cute little tadpoles swimming, but no, Dear Diary. Sperm are not cute. Sperm are devious little fuckers swimming faster than Michelle Smith in the 1996 Atlanta Olympics up to our poor fallopian tubes and innocent ovaries. Once again, that Tammy Wynette song where she sings 'sometimes it's hard to be a woman' popped into my head and I, like, totally understood where she was coming from.

I went into the pharmacy but then suddenly, like, had a mini heart attack for what I was about to do. My palms started sweating, I kinda skulked around the shampoo section, waited until there was nobody at the counter and grabbed the nearest pregnancy test that I could see. I got nervous though and ended up buying loads of extra shit like lip balm and breath mints and hangover cures or some shit. I wanted to scream at the person behind the counter that I wasn't pregnant and that I was a big old virgin so that she wouldn't judge me. But then I literally ran out the door and went to meet the rest of the gang in the Square.

They were all waiting for me nervously, Lucy smoking fags, Rebecca eating a Mars bar and Hot Gay Brendan just standing there looking hot. He confided to me on the way over to Supermac's that he had kind of liked buying the pregnancy test because he can't think of any situation in the future where he'll be buying a pregnancy test for a girl again. I told him maybe some day he could have a baby. Arnold Schwarzenegger was able to have one in that movie *Junior*. He was like, 'Maybe, we'll see,' and right then and there I wished with all my heart that Hot Gay Brendan would have a baby someday. But then he said,

'Remember when you promised me that you'd have a baby for me?' I was like, 'What now?!' He said, 'Do you not remember that you said that you would do a Phoebe from *Friends* on it and be a surrogate mother?' I was like, 'Oh shit'. I had been drinking a lot of cider that night. I ain't getting fat for no gay couple, even if Elton John flew into town and impregnated me himself. I decided against saying that to Hot Gay Brendan though. And I also decided to stop promising stupid shit to my friends when I'm drunk.

We went into the bathroom of Supermac's, we made Hot Gay Brendan stay outside to keep watch, for whom we weren't sure, but we felt that this was the sort of situation where we needed someone to keep watch. We crowded into one of the bathroom stalls. Lucy peed on all four pregnancy sticks (she has some bladder in fairness to her) and then we waited and waited. We put Rebecca in charge of reading the instructions which in hindsight probably wasn't such a good idea, what with her being in such close proximity to fast food. Rebecca said that one line on the test meant you're pregnant and two lines meant it's negative. First test comes up and it's one clear blue line. We freak out. Lucy starts crying again, and I'm trying to calm her down, saying 'It's okay,' and she's all like, 'It's not okay. You don't understand, you've never even had sex!'

Like how SLY was that, but I decided to let it go considering the situation that we were in. The second test, the same one blue line, and the third, just one blue line. The fourth one didn't work, and no line came up. At this stage Lucy had practically fallen down the toilet in shock, Rebecca is puffing off her inhaler at an awful rate and I try to make a joke about being able to eat all the Supermac's you want now because it looks like you might be eating for two. She didn't find it funny. There was massive tension in the air. Then Rebecca goes, 'Oh wait you guys, One blue line means NEGATIVE, TWO blue lines means pregnant. You're not pregnant, Lucy!' I'd never seen Lucy so much want to hit and hug Rebecca at the same time. We double-checked Lucy's pissy pregnancy tests and ya, she's not up the duff.

We all started screaming. The relief. I mean, babies are cute for like five minutes but, like, you have to keep them for ever. They are not just for Christmas, like. We went out, told Hot Gay Brendan, then bought the most amount of food we have ever purchased in Supermac's EVER, with Rebecca of course just ordering that bit more than us. It was the strangest of days Dear Diary. It has put me off the thought of ever having sex though, which is a bummer.

Do you know what I actually feel like doing? I feel like going into the Metalwork class in school and asking someone in there to make us all chastity belts, and making them weld them right onto us until we are least finished our Leaving Cert.

Goodnight Dear Diary,
Love,
Ciara X

Moan of Arc

Dear Diary,
Well it's almost that time of year again! I mean, this very day NEXT YEAR is going to be the beginning of the rest of my life. I'll be getting my Leaving Cert results!

It's probably the most momentous occasion of any Irish teenager's life. I mean, what happens on results day literally changes your life. I'm after freaking myself out even thinking about it. Even though it's next year, I can still feel a major panic coming on. I actually meant to start studying this summer to get ahead of all the nerds in my year, but the thought of opening a book and trying to make head or tail of the Modh Coinníollach makes me think I'd rather give Lucy continuous STD tests for the rest of the summer.

Like, what am I going to do with the rest of my life? I don't say this to too many people, but I think I'm, like, destined for big things. When I say big things, I mean I was put on this earth in, like, a Joan of Arc kind of way. There are so many similarities between us. I know I've discussed this before, but I really feel it to be true. The two of us grew up in tiny villages in the back arse end of nowhere. She had a warrior soul like I have. Like, I'm convinced if my family were to look back over our ancestors, we'd find a link between our family and Gráinne Mhaol. She was a passionate pirate queen and somewhat attractive – just like me! But she's linked to the county of Mayo, and I'd rather not be, thanks!

The only thing that hasn't happened me yet is that whole divine guidance thing. Do I think that I would be the sort of girl that God would try to get in contact with at some stage? Yes I do Dear Diary. There have been, like, all these signs. Take into account that I was the first altar girl in the parish – ever. Secondly, I've been to Knock on numerous occasions. Thirdly – I'm still a virgin. It's a well-known fact that God favours us. Once last year when I went to see the school guidance teacher, he figured through various tests that maybe I should go down the religious route. Which makes sense because my granny says she prays every day that my brother will make the right decision and enrol in Maynooth to go into the priesthood. It drives my mother mad. But what if it's not my younger brother, what if it's meant to be me?!

I've never revealed this to anyone, but I've always thought of myself as a very spiritual person. And in all honesty if God was going to come and give anyone in this godforsaken village a message, it would definitely be me. Would I freak out if God or the Virgin Mary appeared to me? TOTALLY. Once I watched a movie called *The Children of Fatima*, and I swear to God, I avoided hanging out with my friends near mountains for, like, ages.

There's no denying it, there is something out there that my tiny teenage mind can't quite comprehend at the moment. On a side note, I've always thought that Jesus was a bit of a ride, even though that whole sandal/robe thing is a complete fashion no-no. Knowing my luck, I'll probably end up a nun or something. Why is it that when I'm learning *Hamlet*, that line he says to Ophelia, 'Get thee to a nunnery,' always send shivers down my spine? I, like, totally identify with Ophelia's character too. But it's mainly Joan of Arc these days. But like, I wouldn't want to end up burning on a stake, that would be shit.

I don't know, maybe my destiny lies elsewhere. Maybe I should apply to do Arts in NUI Galway. Creative people do Arts right? I write poetry, I'm creative. Ya, even if God did get in contact, I'd have a couple of issues that I would like to clear up with him first. I think I have a couple of ideas to make Mass better craic. Here are a few:

1. *Hot priests. Seriously, priests with big ridey heads on them on the altar, now THAT would get me going to Mass.*
2. *Hot female priests! Come on, everyone knows that sex sells Dear Diary, and all the men in the parish would be only dying to go to Mass if the women were hot.*
3. *Happier pictures. No one wants to see Jesus nailed to the cross half dead like that, and even though there's only a tiny piece of cloth covering his manhood, it's just not sexy because he is half dead.*
4. *Musical candles. Like a light-a-candle jukebox. Put in money, say a prayer or whatever, and then it plays your favourite song instead of, like, getting all depressed when the choir starts singing 'Nearer, My God, to Thee'.*
5. *Themed Masses. Like an Adam and Eve theme or, like, a pope theme.*
6. *Find a way of using episodes of* Father Ted *to get valuable lessons across. My mother hasn't stopped saying that* Father Ted *is the BEST thing to ever happen to the Catholic Church.*
7. *Have an 'Invite the Protestants' night. To most Catholics, they seem fairly exotic, it might be good to mix things up, maybe have a Protestant versus Catholic table quiz or something. You never know, we could end up marrying each other too.*

That's all I've gotten to so far Dear Diary. I think I've made some valid points.

Anyway, I better go here. Lucy is mad to go out because it's Leaving Cert results night and she says that the lads will look hotter to us because they've finished secondary school and are all more mature and stuff. I'm going to go out on a limb here and say that lads don't ever really mature. Sometimes I wonder am I an old head on young shoulders? It's the sacrifice of being me I guess.

Anyway, I don't know why Lucy has such a bee in her bonnet to go out and meet the Leaving Cert lads, seeing as she has shifted most of them anyway. It's not like they are a new challenge to her, and Lord knows, she loves the old challenge so she does.

Hot Gay Brendan is excited because he heard that one of the lads who got his results got enough points to do Fashion Design in the Dublin Institute of Technology and he wants to investigate. I was like, 'Investigate what?' And he was like, 'The fact that he might be gay because he's doing Fashion Design.' I then had to give him a lecture on the fact that just because he was doing Fashion Design does not make him gay. He was like, 'Whatever.' He said he had a mad horn on him, and he wants to go out and use his own 'gaydar'. Which is funny because it's like a radar but for gay people. I really hope he doesn't wear his George Michael T-shirt out again tonight. He needs to buy new clothes.

I suppose I better go and get myself ready and make some sort of an effort. I've got really bad period pains though and I just cried watching an ad on TV so it might not be the best idea.

Cheers God for my cervix!

Goodnight Dear Diary,
Love,
Ciara X

9/11

Dear Diary,

Had the strangest day. We've been back in school now for the past week, but today was unlike any day I've ever had in school ever. As I'm writing this, I'm actually scared for humanity, and I'll you something for sure Dear Diary, I am NEVER getting on a plane again for the rest of my life.

Sixth year as been just as I imagined it would be so far – SO stressful. I don't know what I did for the universe to conspire against me but the timetable this semester is a motherfucker. Double Maths on a Monday morning. I literally felt like quitting my Leaving Cert when I saw that. As if this year isn't going to be hard enough, throw double Maths on a Monday into the mix. But the only other doubles I have are double French on a Thursday and double Biology on a Friday, so in the grand scheme of things, it's actually okay!

Rebecca came into school much more relaxed now that Saoirse is doing Fashion Design in Dublin, she doesn't have to worry about seeing Johnny Limp and Saoirse walking around the school together and shifting the faces off each other. I don't care what Rebecca says, once Saoirse from sixth year last year meets hot sophisticated guys from Dublin she'll dump Johnny Limp and he'll come a-hobblin' back to Rebecca.

Hot Gay Brendan reckons that all the lads that Saoirse will meet doing Fashion Design will be gay. How do I explain to him that not all men who work in fashion are gay? He's going through a phase now where he is obsessed with Dolce and Gabbana. He thinks he's in a niche here because he's the only gay rugby player in the school, which makes me laugh because there's nothing more gay than rugby. Men walking around changing rooms showering and covering themselves in shower gel, then whipping each other's arses with towels. And then the actual game of rugby itself. Shoving your head under other men's arses, tackling big mucky men to the ground, balls in your face, and then hugging each other after they score a try?! It's a big gayfest. Hot Gay Brendan says that I have a really weird view of what being gay is, but I think I'm right and he's just pissed off because he's afraid to tell the rest of the lads that he's an arse bandit. Me and Rebecca call him our little arse bandit which I think he secretly loves, but then Lucy nearly ruined it when she revealed that she's a bit of an arse bandit herself. We really didn't need to know that, and I don't even want to hazard a guess at what she's actually talking about.

Lucy came back into sixth year with a bang. She has started seeing the bouncer guy from when we were out on the Leaving Cert results night. It turns out that you can 'put out' behind the back of a nightclub and boom, a man can be hooked, who would have thought it, eh?

Maybe I should put out more? No, I'm just going to concentrate on my Leaving Cert instead. Anyway, this bouncer guy is a little bit older, so Lucy feels like she has to up her game and everyone that's anyone is a getting a Brazilian these days, and I'm not talking about Pele and Ronaldo here Dear Diary, I'm talking about the lady garden. Me, Lucy and Rebecca always head to Supervalu together to stock up on Immac. But all of a sudden, Lucy comes into school walking funny, which in fairness is, like, the norm after the weekend for her, but it turns out that she had Immaced her nether regions, left it on for too long and, in her own words, 'burnt the box off herself'. Her poor, poor box. For so many reasons.

This is exactly the type of stuff that I am trying to avoid even thinking about for the next year. I don't need these mindless distractions of Lucy and her box or Hot Gay Brendan and his insecurity issues with the rugby lads, or Rebecca asking me did I notice that she dyed her moustache over the weekend, or the fact that everyone all of a sudden is talking about paninis. I haven't a fucking clue what they are, but I think they're a sandwich from Italy or something.

I need to focus on my Leaving Cert. I made an appointment to see the career guidance counsellor. The last time I went was in transition year when I was, like, trying to 'find myself', and she told me I should focus on a career with God. I still don't know why she said that. My mother nearly hit the roof. Maybe it's the fact that I have 'virgin' literally written across my forehead at this stage. Anyway, it was another fruitless trip because I came out of the office and she basically tried to convince me to apply for Spanish and Commerce in Cork, and it wasn't until I walked away that I realised that we don't even do Spanish in our school. What planet are these adults on?! How are these people in charge of us? How unfair is that? I know I don't have to fill out a CAO form for another couple of months, but seriously.

I was in such frustrated form heading out to the prefab for English that I nearly didn't notice the teachers running around talking in shocked whispers. Something had happened. At first I thought that the History teacher had finally kicked the bucket because he looks like he should have died in Ancient Rome. We estimate that he's about 107 years old. So initially, I thought that poor old Nero had finally popped his Roman clogs, but no, it wasn't that.

I don't even know how to write this Dear Diary, but the English teacher told us that two planes crashed into the Twin Towers in New York City, and that the Twin Towers have crumbled and are no more. There was a really weird buzz in the classroom. The smarter, more forward-thinking part of my brain immediately thought this could be a potential article on the comprehension part of English Paper 1 next June, but the other half of my brain was just really confused as to why this had happened. How could two planes fly into the Twin Towers? By the end of the English class, the teacher told us that a plane had flown into the Pentagon too. I only really knew the Pentagon from movies like *Independence Day*, but I knew it was serious.

Everyone was kind of quiet on the school bus on the way home. We stopped for a short break on the way back and everyone clambered into the nearest pub, and there it was, on Sky News. People started talking about some guy called Osama bin Laden and the Al-Kaieeda. I can't even spell that, never mind get my head around what they actually are. But they did it on purpose and the news was saying that it was a terrorist attack.

By the time I got off the bus, there was a load of neighbours in my house and everyone was staring at the TV. Already there were stories about a niece from up the country that was supposed to have been working in the Twin Towers that day but called in sick so didn't go to work. Everyone is literally in shock. It's like looking at a movie, but it actually happened in real life. This is like a modern day *Titanic* moment. I think this will be one of those moments in years to come where you'll remember where you were the day the Towers came down.

I hope this is not a bad omen for the year ahead because it feels like it might be. I'm going to bed now, a little bit more afraid of the world than I usually am.

Goodnight Dear Diary,
Love,
Ciara X

Foot-in-Mouth Disease

Dear Diary,

Well, school is in full swing: my back aches from carrying 10 million books and I have to start studying for my Leaving Cert. We should be allowed to sue. I'll end up looking like Quasimodo from *The Hunchback of Notre Dame*. Man, I'll never get a husband at this rate, not that I'm concentrating on that or anything because I have to seriously focus on my Leaving Cert and getting into college. I mean that, too. I'm going to be the first person in the vicinity to go to college in Trinity. Then I'll be invited back to give talks in my local primary school.

I don't know though, I have a feeling that Trinity might be full of knobs. You know the type Dear Diary. They sit around wearing berets that they got in Paris on 'Erasmus'. They smoke and talk about politics and probably debate 'issues'.

I think I need to go somewhere more Arty Farty like NUI Galway – the City of the Tribes and hippies, and home of the Saw Doctors and Michael D. Higgins (who writes poetry and looks like a real-life leprechaun). Plus, it's close enough to home in case I get homesick or need my clothes washed or something.

Dublin is too far away. I think I've been there literally once in my life, when Granny was on Winning Streak and we were in the posh area of Dublin where RTÉ is. Dad says he reckons that everyone in RTÉ is related to each other, but I think that's highly unlikely. Dublin is a scary place, though. I reckon you wouldn't be able to walk down the street without getting mugged or something. It's not like the way it's portrayed in *Fair City*, that's for sure. It does have a Supermac's on O'Connell Street, so I'll give it that. Why is it that people outside of Dublin don't like Dublin and people in Dublin don't like outside of it? It's a weird one. Maybe they're smug because they're the capital, but at least it's not Cork Dear Diary. As my granny would say, there is something for small mercies.

Do you know what though, I do feel lucky to live in Ireland right now, what with what's just happened in New York. It's only been a few days since those planes flew into the Twin Towers and the whole world has gone mad. It's in literally every newspaper and it's on the news constantly, and every country leader says they're going to stand 'shoulder to shoulder' with the USA. All the images on TV are of the American flag and people crying. It's making me a little bit afraid of the world.

My granny says she is never flying again, which is hilarious because she'll be on that plane to Medjugorje as soon as the parish priest gives a hint of a trip! She's been to Lourdes twice, Knock every year for a 100 years and Ballinspittle once, so her lifelong dream is to go to Medjugorje – the only place she hasn't visited that the Virgin Mary seemingly has.

There are a couple of things I'm afraid of, so I'm going to write a list:

- *Failing my Leaving Cert*
- *Lucy getting pregnant before she does her Leaving Cert*
- *The IRA*
- *David Beckham ever wearing a sarong again*
- *Starving children in Africa*
- *Brazilians (the waxing, not the people)*
- *Never losing my virginity*
- *Losing my virginity to a Turkish waiter and ending up in* Woman's Way *magazine*
- *Osama bin Laden*
- *Not getting enough points in my Leaving Cert to go to college*

- *Getting older and ending up like Shirley Valentine*
- *Being a virgin who can't drive*
- *My boobs never reaching their full potential*
- *AIDS*
- *My house computer getting a virus, too*
- *The Chinese*
- *Calculus, Algebra, Sin, Cos and Tan*
- *Leonardo DiCaprio never winning an Oscar*
- *Being attacked by a shark*
- *Being buried in the Dublin Mountains*
- *People from up North*
- *Slobodan Milosevic and Hitler*
- *Anthrax*
- *Jim McDonald from* Coronation Street
- *Ethnic Albanian extremists in Kosovo*
- *Earthquakes*
- *The banshee and actually hearing one*
- *Missing the school bus in the morning*
- *My uterus accidentally falling out*
- *Getting toxic shock syndrome from tampons*
- *Sven-Goran Eriksson*
- *The Leaning Tower of Pisa falling over*
- *Actually being 'Touched by an Angel'*
- *Foot and mouth disease*
- Dawson's Creek *ever ending*

I feel happy to have those fears off my chest now Dear Diary.

Goodnight!
Love,
Ciara X

Johnny Gimp

Dear Diary,

September is literally my favourite time of year. It's just that everything is so pretty. Also the summer is over so I don't have to worry about shaving my legs until the debs or, like, Christmas or something. Once, and don't tell anyone this, I let the hair on my legs grow for, like, four months. It was a particularly cold winter in my defence, and it took about four of my dad's BIC razors to shave all the hair off. It's not like anyone is looking anyway. I wear tracksuit bottoms in PE because my legs are too white for mankind and also I'm afraid that all the lads might get erections. Lucy sometimes doesn't wear a supportive bra in PE because she says she loves distracting the lads when we're playing indoor soccer against them. She says the lads take themselves so seriously thinking that they're the next Roy Keane or Ryan Giggs, but once she starts running they think she's Pamela Anderson running up and down that beach in *Baywatch* and then she easily scores against them.

I'm not going to lie, watching Lucy's boobs bounce is mesmerising, but I don't think that using your bountiful bosoms will get you that far in life. Then again, maybe I'm just jealous, my boobs don't seem to have the same vigour as Lucy's when running around. I often wonder how the model Jordan is actually able to exercise, or like, if she was ever with a man, would they not suffocate underneath the weight of them? Anyway, I should spend more time revising for my Leaving Cert than contemplating whether or not Katie Price can kill a man with her boobs. It just shows you how much I need to practise concentrating.

I'm prone to procrastination, a lot like the character Hamlet in fairness. I'm really trying to identify with him for my revision to help me when it comes to sitting English Paper 2. His family are so messed up! I can imagine them all on an episode of the *Jerry Springer Show*. Hamlet's sitting there, then his mother walks out and the crowd boos because, let's be fair, her husband was barely dead when she married his brother. Then Claudius rocks out and the crowd go mental, and suddenly Hamlet makes a go for him and starts screaming 'You killed my father!' and he has to be dragged off him by a bouncer. Gertrude takes Claudius's side. Next they bring out Ophelia, and she just sits there holding a tissue crying, and Hamlet's shouting, 'Do you see what you've done, you've broken this family, Elsinore is screwed now!' The big twist would be that Jerry Springer would bring out Hamlet's best friend Horatio on stage, and then Horatio admits that he is gay and totally in love with Hamlet, and then Ophelia faints and Hamlet storms off stage saying he literally can't take it any more and everything stinks, and the cameras follow him as he tries to find his way out of the studio only to be greeted by the ghost of his father smoking a cigar outside the back door, and the crowd are like, 'OOOHHHHH-HHHHHH!' This is as far as I've gotten in my Jerry Springer/ Hamlet daydream, but it has helped me to try and get my head around the absolute head-fuck that is Shakespeare. I think he must have been having a serious laugh at everyone, either that or he had serious issues. He's what my dad would call a complete cowboy.

Hot Gay Brendan complained to the English teacher about the fact that Oscar Wilde is not on the curriculum. He's gotten a new obsession with Oscar Wilde. He just read *The Importance of Being Earnest* and won't stop quoting it. I told him it was more in his line to start studying for his Leaving Cert and read the books that we will have to do exams on. He's just cocky because this will be his second time doing the Leaving Cert. He told me that Oscar Wilde is one of the most important gay men to him since Freddie Mercury and that I should support him. Support him?! I was the one who wrote a strongly worded letter to the *Irish Times* about equal rights for gay rugby players, and okay, it wasn't published, but it's not fair for him to say that I should support him! I mean, I'm even going to the debs with him, knowing that I can't lose my virginity to him. What else can I do to support him? I've even promised to dress up as that man from George Michael's 'Outside' video at Halloween so we could go as George Michael and that guy he got caught doing in the bathroom that time. I think we both must be stressed out or something because it's unusual for Hot Gay Brendan to be a dick. I'm not taking on his emotional gay baggage though. I have to concentrate on the Leaving Cert.

I had to do that with Rebecca already today. She was really upset in school because word had gone around that Johnny Limp had an accident in his Subaru, seemingly he nearly died, blah, blah, blah, and suddenly Rebecca gets really emotional and starts imagining her life without Johnny Limp and decides that she's still in love with him and can't live without him. Rebecca and Johnny Limp are certainly not love's young dream. They are no Joey and Dawson, or Miley and Biddy, and they're not even together any more. Anyway, Johnny Limp didn't nearly die, and he only tipped the side of his Subaru, so it's all a bit dramatic. The reason behind it is that one of the lads was hungry after training so they drove all the way into the city, a good hour-and-a-half drive, to go to Supermac's because Dopey Pete has a thing for chicken tenders. Anyway, Johnny Limp ate so many burgers and got the meat sweats, but instead of pulling in and taking his hoody off, he tried to do it while driving. Johnny Limp isn't a fast driver. Maybe it's something to do with his limp, one leg being shorter than the other or something, so he finds it hard to press down on the accelerator. Look, I'm glad they're okay. The lengths that lads will go to for burgers though.

I think that they're spoilt by their mothers too. What is it about Irish mothers and their sons? It's like ever since Brenda Fricker won an Oscar for playing Christy Brown's mother in *My Left Foot* every Irish mother across the country felt like they had to up their game or something. It won't do them any good in the long run. Especially when their sons don't turn out like Daniel Day-Lewis.

In other news, Rebecca would want to get Johnny Limp out of her head, because I heard through my granny that Johnny Limp's aunt was saying that Johnny Limp's mother wants him gone from home when he finishes the Leaving Cert, and wants him to apply for a visa and head to Australia to his older brother Michael Limp. Or join the guards. Ya, that's exactly what the guards need, Johnny bloody Limp.

Australia seems to be mentioned more and more these days Dear Diary. It's like everyone is going. Why, I wonder? Is it because we've watched so many episodes of *Home and Away* and, like, think we are half Australian? I actually don't know much about Australia bar *Home and Away*, *The Flying Doctors*, a hot Australian rugby player called Ben Tune, and once I watched this really weird movie called *Walkabout* where a man leaves his children in the outback and they are befriended by a little Aboriginal boy and everyone is naked and there is a lot of body paint. It was so weird. Isn't that Tasmanian devil cartoon from Australia too?

Anyway Dear Diary, I am exhausted. I've done so much writing about Johnny Limp that I haven't even looked at my irregular verbs for French tomorrow.

Goodnight Dear Diary,
Love,
Ciara X

Finger Blaster 2000

Dear Diary,

I'm in weird form. As autumn creeps in and brings such beauty with it, it also brings many woes. My skin is now totally dry and I'm getting spots. Like, you'd think the fact that I am nearly 18 years of age would mean I wouldn't have to deal with this shite any more. But no, I woke up this morning with a spot the size of Carrantuohill on my face. I nearly emptied half a bottle of Clearasil on it, but that just burnt the shite out of my face and now my skin looks raw and irritated.

If I'm being honest Dear Diary, I have spent much of my teenage years raw and irritated. Like, when does my life actually start? Has it started already? Is this it? When I get to thinking about all these deep and philosophical things I always think of the opening lines of Coolio's 'Gangsta's Paradise':

> *As I walk through the valley of the shadow of death,*
> *I take a look at my life and realise there's nothin' left,*
> *Cause I've been blastin' and laughin' so long,*
> *That even my momma thinks that my mind is gone*

The valley of the shadow of death has been the five-and-a-half years I've spent being a teenager imprisoned on these school grounds, and now there's nothing left for me here. I've been blasting and laughing so long with Lucy, Rebecca and Hot Gay Brendan that my mum does say she thinks they might be a bad influence on me. I personally think that society is a bad influence on me. There's all these bullshit fairytales about being a teenager and growing into your body and about losing your virginity, but I think Judy Blume was talking through her hole. Because here I am, not long before my 18th birthday and I'm covered in spots and I'm just honestly pondering my very existence on this earth.

I feel stressed out, and it's not just because of the Leaving Cert, but I feel I have so much on right now that I can't handle it. Like, literally in the next two months I'll turn 18, there's the school Halloween disco, and then in November there is the debs. So that is what everyone is talking about at breaktime. Most of the time I'm just sitting there trying to think how on earth I'm going to pass Maths Paper 1 next June and most of my peers are like, 'Oh my God, what are you going to wear to the Halloween disco?' In fairness, I have managed to convince Hot Gay Brendan to drop the whole concept of him dressing up as George Michael and me as the guy he got caught doing in the bathroom. Lucy has decided to dig out her old reliable 'sexy kitten outfit' but has also decided to dress up as a Bond girl called 'Pussy Galore'. In her mind combining the sexy kitten and the bond girl Pussy Galore means she can literally offer people 'double the pussy'. She spent most of the study period today roaring laughing at herself for coming up with that one. At this stage Dear Diary, I don't have the heart or the energy to stop her. She is relentless. I'll give her that.

She's still seeing the bouncer guy, or as she calls him Mr Finger Blaster 2000, but I worry that he will distract her from her Leaving Cert. Rebecca made the mistake of asking her why she calls him Mr Finger Blaster 2000 and nearly got sick in her lunch. When I quizzed her about it, she said she didn't even want to talk about it but reckons that one day Lucy's vagina is going to end up on a National Geographic documentary. I don't think I even want to know.

There's rumours going around the school that the Costello twins are dressing as the Twin Towers, and have even started putting their costumes together in Metalwork class during breaktime. That is so awful. The world is still so numb. People, like, died, even Irish people. These lads think they're hilarious. I've always found the Costello twins really weird since first year when they used to just hang around with each other and talk to no one and they even had their own secret sign language, the absolute nerds.

Then Hot Gay Brendan said that some of the rugby lads are going as Osama bin Laden. Like, it's a school disco, everyone needs to relax and have some cop on and respect. Rebecca wants me to practise the dance moves to Michael Jackson's 'Thriller' as she's going as a werewolf, but I just don't know can we top our dance routine to the Backstreet Boys' 'Everybody', so there's really no point. Also, I'm in sixth year, I'm nearly 18, I'm probably getting too old for dance routines. I also don't think that the costume I plan on wearing would be comfortable enough to do a dance routine in.

I'm planning on going as Anne Frank. I'm going to get a cardboard box and put it over my head and body, so that can be the annex she lived in. It's easy to do my hair like hers, and I've got these big sad eyes, so I just need ankle socks and flat shoes and I'm ready to go. I can buy a pretend diary and talk with a German accent for the night. It will be grand. The uneducated at the school Halloween disco probably won't know who I am, but I'm totally okay with that Dear Diary. Seriously don't care what anyone in school thinks of me any more because I don't even want to shift any of them anyway, not even the lads from the rugby team.

Rebecca says that I've, like, really matured so much these past couple of months. She says that I have stopped obsessing over my boobs growing and losing my virginity, so much so that I barely talk about it any more. I still think about both those subjects, like, ALL the time though.

I think I honestly blame Judy Blume, Nancy Drew, the Hardy Boys plus the Spice Girls for making me think that I would have lost my flower at this stage, that by now my cherry would have been popped, or someone would have finally speared my Britney, or even let me join the six-inch-deep club, that someone would have sailed up my delta of love, boldly gone where no man has dared go before, or finally voted my hymen OFF the island. But no, Dear Diary. This has not happened yet. My boobs are grand, no major changes there. There are times of the month when they are bigger than usual. I find that push-up and padded bras help. They are perky so I've at least another 15 good years with them. I just need to get over everything that I have obsessed about over the past five-and-a-half years, and again, just concentrate on my Leaving Cert, getting into college and meeting hot French guys that are over on Erasmus.

Hot Gay Brendan says that the only reason he is half considering doing Italian in first year of college is because he wants to do a year abroad with Italian stallions in Italy. He has this whole vision of his first kiss being with a man on a gondola in Venice. He's worse than I am. What would they be feeding each other? Cornettos?! He should concentrate on the Leaving Cert and leave his Italian daydreams for when he actually gets into college.

I think I've said 'concentrate on the Leaving Cert' an awful lot in these diary entries and it's only October. This is going to be a LONG year.

Goodnight Dear Diary,
Love,
Ciara X

Earth, Wind, Land and Sea me after Class

Dear Diary,

I'm here supposed to be doing a study revision plan for the mid term, but no matter what I do, I can't seem to concentrate. I find myself just staring at walls for long periods of time. Or listening to the radio. Or sitting listening to the dulcet tones of Brian Dobson's voice coming from the TV in the sitting room. Why do I feel that I will spend most of my time thinking about studying for the Leaving Cert instead of actually studying for the Leaving Cert? I'm putting a lot of pressure on myself already and if I'm being honest Dear Diary, I'm easily distracted too.

Like, there's this new song on 2FM at the moment. It's by this seriously hot Spanish guy Enrique Iglesias and it's called 'Hero' and I find myself totally fantasising when I'm listening to it. It's so romantic. Like, Enrique is a total ride, imagine him singing 'I can be your hero baby, I can kiss away the pain,' like, to your face! I've felt a familiar stirring in my teenage loins of late. I'm trying really hard to prevent thoughts of lust so that I can concentrate on my Leaving Cert, but it's really hard and I can't stop fantasising about shifting the face off Enrique Iglesias. I'm only human and that song is on the radio all of the time now. I told Lucy and Rebecca that I can't stop thinking about Enrique and Lucy told me to relax.

She said the next thing I would be doing is wrapping barbed wire around my thighs to keep my passions under control like a member of Opus Dei. I hadn't a notion what she was talking about but then Lucy tells me that her mother's brother is part of this religious cult in London and that she heard that they wrap barbed wire around themselves to stop them from having sex, it's something to do with mortifying the flesh. I was mortified just listening to the story. Seemingly Lucy's uncle moved over to London in the seventies and was taken into a bedsit by members of Opus Dei and has stayed there ever since. Lucy's family don't talk about it. I might as well be a member of Opus Dei, ain't no mortification of the flesh going on here. I may never even be touched by another human being for the rest of my days. But I guess that will give me more of a chance to study for my Leaving Cert.

I've started concentrating on Biology revision. Why did I pick this subject for my Leaving Cert again? Why do I even have to know about the different functions of the skin, or elements found in amino acids? If I was being honest Dear Diary, I don't even know what amino acids are or why we need them. I seem to be eternally confused by translocation and transpiration, and don't even get me started on plasmolysis. Spirogyra haunts my dreams, and the only thing I seem to have a vague inkling about is viruses and bacteria, mainly due to my unhealthy fascination with AIDS – that's why Freddie Mercury died – and the fact that Lucy is walking around with a cold sore the size of Mount Vesuvius on her mouth. Cold sores are caused by herpes, which is a virus, right? But also is it not a sexually transmitted disease and could Lucy have possibly gotten it from, you know, sampling the sausage one too many times? I kept my mouth shut when she said it was just because her immune system was low. Well, if she didn't spend so much time gallivanting with the new bouncer boyfriend during the week (he works weekends) maybe her 'immune system' would be fine. Anyway, she's pissed off with him as he won't go near her with that crater on her lip so she's thinking of breaking it off with him. Which I personally think is a bit dramatic, but at the same time, I could barely eat my lunch and look at her at the same time.

Anyway, we quickly forgot about Lucy and her cold sore when a rumour went around school that we had a new substitute Geography teacher because our usual Geography teacher had broken his leg climbing a mountain over the weekend. Everyone thought this was funny because he had actually been teaching us about mountains last week so everyone was like, 'I wonder did he count the contours on the way down,' and, 'It's all downhill for him now,' and then a couple of the lads starting singing, 'Ain't no mountain high enough, ain't no valley low enough, ain't no river wide enough to keep us from getting to you, Murph.' Which is funny as his name is Mr Murphy, but then we all felt bad when we heard that he had to be airlifted off the side of the mountain and it was on the news and everything.

I know this is probably going to sound selfish but I began to get really worried about my Leaving Cert then, because what if this teacher is really bad and can't teach properly? I was right to be worried, it turned out. It was worse than that. Our new substitute teacher is a complete and utter ride. I walked into class and nearly fainted. He looks like Enrique Iglesias, David Beckham and Leonardo DiCaprio all rolled into one. He has that cheeky smile, like a young Freddie Prinze Jr. I calculated in my head how long it would be for us to be legally allowed to be together as a couple, and I kinda figured that once I made it into second year of college, it should be all right. So that's just seven months until the Leaving Cert, and three months to see if I get the points for Arts in NUI Galway, so that means I'd be starting college in September 2002. Say I pass my first year exams in June, and get into second year of college, that means I'll just have to wait until September 2003, and that's only two years away, which broken down is only, like, 730 days, which I could totally do. That is also the most Maths that I have done in my nearly six years in school. Go figure. It's amazing what you can do if you really put your mind to it.

Here's the thing, though. I couldn't concentrate. My loins were going mad. They were like a bear needing to be fed after a long winter of hibernation. He was wearing a white shirt and you could totally see his nipples. I'm so happy that teenage girls can't get erections because I reckon there would have been an epidemic in class. He sat on the side of the teacher's desk, all cool like. His name is Mr O'Rourke (how hot is that) and he said that he'll be covering the class until Mr Murphy's leg gets better. I could see all the girls in the class silently wishing that Mr Murphy's leg will never get better. He said he hopes to do some school outings with us so we can 'connect' with the geography that we are studying and has planned a trip to a local drumlin for us next week. Glacial erosion has never been as sexy Dear Diary. I made a mental note to study the shit out of drumlins before next week, so I could impress him with my massive brain. He then started the class talking about chemical weathering. Oh, there was some serious chemical weathering going on all right, not in the atmosphere, but in the inner chambers of my heart. He came around the classroom at one stage to check on our diagrams of acid rain and prevailing winds and all that shite and when he checked mine, I could literally smell him as he leaned in so close. I went totally red and told myself to cop on.

This is not good Dear Diary. This is literally the last distraction that I needed while trying to study for my Leaving Cert. I blame Enrique Iglesias and that damn song. I was happy to get out of that class and into Business Studies and immerse myself in the Sale of Goods and Supply of Services Act 1980. The business teacher was telling us about this new product that has been launched in the USA called the 'iPod'. She says that we soon won't have to use our Discmans or MP3 players, and that they will be a thing of the past. I seriously doubt that. I love my Discman, buying batteries for it is a bitch but I'm never getting rid of it.

Anyway, I'm going to try and get some sleep here, my mind is racing thinking about Geography class tomorrow. Time to dig out the old bottle of Tommy Girl that I only use on special occasions!

Goodnight Dear Diary,
Love,
Ciara X

Legally Frigid

Dear Diary,

It's my birthday! I'm officially 18 years of age! 18! I am quite sad that my 18th birthday has fallen in such a time of turmoil for the world. Since September 11th, things have been weird. Today, I was reading the paper to see what was on the front page of this, my 18th birthday, and it was all about a *Washington Post* worker who has been confirmed as the ninth victim of anthrax. Anthrax-infected mail has been showing up in Florida, Washington and New York since the September 11th attacks. I'm not going to lie Dear Diary, it made me REALLY nervous opening my birthday cards this morning. It's a bummer that it's such bad news on this, my glorious 18th birthday. But you know what Dear Diary, Anne Frank had to celebrate her birthday in an annex in Amsterdam when her life, and the lives of her family were at serious risk from Nazis. So in her memory I'll soldier on, anthrax or no anthrax.

The 21st of October, such an amazing date to have a birthday on. It's no coincidence that on this day in 1945 in France, women finally got the vote as part of the suffragette movement, and then a strong feisty female was born nearly 40 years later – as in, ME Dear Diary! Also, did you know that on this date in 1971, Disneyland in Orlando opened for the first time? Again, no coincidence that the happiest place on earth opened on my birthday. I am also honoured to share my birthday with Alfred Nobel, a scientist and an inventor, and of course my beloved Paul Ince (who plays for Middlesbrough now which is so lame but I still love him) and of course the lyrical genius that is Tony

Mortimer from East 17 (whose breakup I am still not over by the way). But it's my 18th birthday, so I'm not going to be sad, I'm going to be happy!

Woke up to a strange package this morning in my room from my parents! Turns out they're actually really sound! It's a mobile phone! I can now communicate with people from the outside world and I don't have to spend my time whispering down the house phone to Lucy, Rebecca and Hot Gay Brendan within earshot of my parents! It's a Nokia 3310 and I don't think I've ever seen anything as beautiful in my life. I have my own number and everything and I straight away looked for Snake on it because I think my parents are sick of me playing it on their phone. I think I love this phone more than my Game Boy and Discman combined. The only way it could have been better is if I could listen to music on it, but you can't have it every way.

Lucy is the only other person with a mobile that I know so my parents also bought me a 'pay as you go' voucher and I texted her straight away! It's SO MUCH FUN. I spent ages just staring at the screen of my new phone waiting for her to text back, as I got a delivery report that the message had been delivered. It felt like 10 hours later when she replied with 'LOL, U R FRID8'. It took me a second for me to cop on to the fact that she was calling me a frigid. I've never been called frigid on an electronic device before, it's usually to my face.

She's changed her tune from last night. So Rebecca, Lucy and Hot Gay Brendan had a surprise party for me last night. It was a surprise in that it was just the four of us down by the park benches. They were really sweet in fairness. They got some buns and put candles in them and sang 'Happy Birthday' and gave me a birthday card, and they had all chipped in and bought me a bottle of DKNY. Hot Gay Brendan says it's the latest perfume from a fashion designer called Donna Karan. My first bottle of designer perfume! I feel like Enya or Mary McAleese if I'm being honest. Lucy had also bought some cider which we drank out of disposable cups until the end of the night when we just started swigging straight from the bottles.

Rebecca has decided that she doesn't want to be a doctor any more, she wants to be a vet because now she hates people all of a sudden (she's still totally heartbroken over Johnny Limp in fairness). I think she was crying at some stage, but we're all so used to her crying that I think we just ignored it. She said, and I quote, that she would 'much rather shove her hand up a cow's arse and have a good old root around than have to give an old man a medical'. Which I thought was a little harsh in fairness. Hot Gay Brendan has decided to come out to the rugby lads. He said he's finally going to pluck up the courage and just do it. He's going to do it the next time there is a schools rugby match, in the dressing room. Lucy, then egging him on, suggested that he should wait until half-time and that he should try and incorporate Al Pacino's inspirational speech in *Any Given Sunday*. Honestly, I think he's making a big deal out of this and making it all too theatrical. I kind of said that to him too and he got offended and was all like, 'It's the rugby guys Ciara – they're like my brothers.' As if that was meant to explain anything.

The drunker Lucy got the more she kept telling us that she just KNOWS this is the year I'm going to lose my virginity. She can feel it in her famous waters seemingly. I'm surprised that she can feel anything down there to be honest.

Maybe it was the cups of cider that I was downing but I couldn't help looking around at Lucy, Rebecca and Hot Gay Brendan and, like, really LOVING the fact that they are my friends. But then I got sad, because some part of me thinks that this is the last year that we'll all hang around with each other before college. Which then made me freak out about a question that the hot substitute teacher gave us for homework over the weekend to help us study for the Leaving Cert about national resources playing a major role in the economic development of Ireland, and maybe it was the cider taking effect, but I got sad thinking about the depletion of Ireland's fish stocks, so I went home.

Lucy gave me Afroman's single 'Because I Got High' as it's the number one song on my 18th birthday, so I listened to it for a while, but then my batteries ran out.

I had a nice day today though, even though my 18th birthday fell on a Sunday. Which is lame. Granny came over and Mum cooked a nice meal but then Granny had too many hot whiskeys and started saying that Sundays hadn't been the same since *Glenroe* finished last May and that RTÉ is an abomination for finishing it up and that the only saving grace at the minute is this storyline on *Fair City* which she is OBSESSED with. There's some bad guy called Billy Meehan abusing Carol and his mistress Tracey and now seemingly Tracey is a prostitute, which Granny finds appalling and has been trying to get onto Joe Duffy all week to complain about it. Dad reckons her bad form is down to the fact that she's not over Tipperary beating Galway in the All-Ireland Hurling Final. She can really hold a grudge.

So that's it Dear Diary. That was my 18th birthday in a nutshell. I can't help but think of the parallels in my life, and my journey to get to this point. I can see elements of this journey in Walt Disney's *The Lion King*. I feel like Simba being held high over the kingdom of lions in Africa. This is where life begins now for little old me. I have learned my wisdom from Mufasa, I have best friends like Timon and Pumbaa and I am ready to face my future in Pride Rock, if that makes sense. Scar represents all the difficult adults that I may encounter on this journey, but nothing can change the fact that I've made it this far. I am 18 years old. And it's been one hell of a long road to get here. There have been some serious trials and tribulations, there have been tears, fears and heartbreak and serious period pains. There have been summer romances and awkward shifting and that one time when Lucy's brother dry humped me. There have been dodgy hairstyles and times that I have cried myself to sleep at night because someone didn't have my back. There have been annoying teachers, and peer pressure and celebrity breakups. Some might say I've had an unhealthy obsession with my boobs, but they are growing Dear Diary, they are growing.

This is my 18th birthday on this earth, and I know that I am still a virgin, but I'm okay with this, because right now, I am living the real circle of life.

Goodnight Dear Diary,
Love,
Ciara X

Brave Hearts

Dear Diary,

Mid term is almost over and I am freaking out because I barely did any study for my Leaving Cert and now I think I'm going to fail my Leaving Cert and not get enough points to do Arts in NUI Galway and I'll end up living in this house with my parents for the rest of my life. That's what's going to happen to me. You might think I'm being a bit dramatic but I'm SO not. I went and did the ONE thing that I said I wouldn't do this year, but I went and did it anyway because when God was dishing out willpower he must have forgotten to give me any. I shifted someone at the school Halloween disco and now I can't stop thinking about him and wondering is he, like, ever going to text me. I gave my number to a boy for the first time, and not, like, my house number that I used to give to lads in first year. Is he going to ring me? Do I have a boyfriend now? Is this a good idea, what with my Leaving Cert and all? Are we going to go to the debs together? Am I going to lose my virginity to him? Is he 'The One' that Carrie always goes on about in *Sex and the City*? I'm literally having a panic attack. Lucy rang me and was like, 'Take a chill pill – you only shifted him.' But what Lucy doesn't realise, because I haven't told ANYONE, and I mean ANYONE, is more happened than just shifting.

I don't know how to feel about it, it was an experience that I've never had before. But my boob was touched. My left one. And not outside bra either. Just under the bra, but no nipple because honestly it probably would have fallen off with the shock of it all. I feel lots of feelings right now. Mainly guilt, but I think that's because I was the first altar girl in the parish, and the other feeling I have is, well, I REALLY want that to happen again. Like, how can I concentrate on the Modh Coinníollach when I have all these, like, sexual feelings running through my teenage loins? My poor loins. They have laid low for many years like a dormant Mount Vesuvius, but they just had to go and erupt in this my very important Leaving Cert year. Hot Gay Brendan says he knows how I feel. He said if he erupted right now, he'd cover the city of Pompeii AND its population twice over.

So, who would have thought the school Halloween disco would have had so much drama, but it did. I went with my Anne Frank costume. I remember from reading her diary her talking about wearing her sister's hand-me-downs, so everything was too big for her. I opted for a white blouse, a dark sweater, mid-calf-length skirt, ankle socks that I haven't worn since my First Communion and plain black shoes. My hair is shoulder-length anyway so I just stuck it behind my ear with a bobby pin. It wasn't the sexiest I've ever looked, but I just wanted to do a good job portraying one of my heroes. I also took one of the glow-in-the-dark stars that I have stuck on my ceiling and stuck it to the side of my jumper. Millions of Jews had to wear them to be identified. It's called the Star of David. He must have been someone important but I really don't know that much about him.

The cardboard box that was to be the actual annex was harder, but I just got one from the local shop and covered it in brown paper and kind of drew a chimney on it and some roof slates. I had to insert myself into it, so it kind of ended up looking like I was a TV, but I also carried an actual copy of Anne Frank's diary in my hand so dumbasses in my school would actually get it and I wouldn't have to spend the night explaining myself. I did think about staying silent for the school Halloween party because in fairness, Anne Frank had to stay quiet for the majority of her time in the annex, but then I figured I would be bored out of my mind.

I arrived at the disco and straight away there were problems, as my box wouldn't fit in through the door as it was too wide, so I had to shimmy in sideways. Then the jokes started. The lads from my year kept coming up to me, poking their heads into the cardboard box and saying stuff like, 'Look, Ciara, I'm in your box.' They thought they were hilarious and it took me ages to figure out that they actually meant my vagina. I tried explaining to them that it was an actual representation of an annex in Amsterdam, but it was just wasted on them.

Lucy rocks in dressed as Britney Spears in the music video 'Baby One More Time'. She had her hair in pigtails and THE shortest skirt of all time, knee-high socks and her Adidas runners. She looked hot in fairness, and was half locked, as was Rebecca, who rocked in wearing just a pair of jeans and a T-shirt that had a piece of paper sellotaped onto it saying 'Lucy's Gowl'. Lucy was cracking herself laughing saying it was her idea because she does have the most famous 'gowl' in all the region. Hot Gay Brendan stole the show though. He walked in, all six foot two inches of him, dressed as Shirley Temple Bar from the telly bingo. The rugby lads were straight over to him, some of them seemed genuinely impressed, others called him a 'gaylord', but in an affectionate way because when he came out to the team they said they didn't care because he's like an Irish Jonah Lomu. As gorgeous as Hot Gay Brendan is as a man, he is an even more beautiful woman. The prick. There is literally no end to his beauty. He seemed happy out, half cut, going around playing telly bingo with his little bingo machine.

The disco was okay. I spent most of it in the bathrooms with a very drunk Lucy and Rebecca. They had snuck me a couple of cans because I couldn't hide anything in my box on the way in, so I pretty much downed them. I couldn't do much dancing as my box made it awkward for me to move, so I went outside at some stage to get some air, as my head was beginning to feel fussy too. And that's when I saw him.

Honestly Dear Diary, he looked like a member of the Fianna, like Cú Chulainn and Finn Mac Coul and Diarmuid all rolled into one. He was dressed like Mel Gibson from *Braveheart* – William Wallace. Turns out that I kind of knew him when I was younger as we used to run in the community games together but he had gone away to a boarding school in first year. His name was Danny and he was SO cute. Like really, really cute. He smiled at me and I think that was the moment I fell head over heels for him. We chatted for ages. He told me that he loved my Anne Frank costume and that it was really cool that I was highlighting the plight of the Jewish people, and how he wanted to do Engineering in NUI Galway but didn't know would he get the points, and that boarding school was okay but sometimes he missed his family. I could have listened to him all night. He shared his cider with me. No one has ever done that with me before. At one stage Rebecca stumbled out, got sick in the bushes and headed back into the disco again.

That's when Danny went in for the shift. He kind of lunged at me, like Mel Gibson running down the battlefield in *Braveheart*. Except he got blocked by my box. Dear Diary, he literally tore the box off me trying to passionately shift the face off me. I didn't care. We were up against the town hall shifting the faces off each other, and maybe it was the cider, but when he started putting his hand up my top, I didn't want to stop him, he was going further and further up, and I was like, 'Oh Jesus Christ,' but then Lucy came out and said that I had to help her because Rebecca had fallen asleep in the toilet and Lucy couldn't wake her. I could have literally killed Rebecca and Lucy right there. I went to help, we managed to get her on the bus, and all three of us were staying in Lucy's house anyway. Danny did walk me to the bus after I had gone back up to get him. He asked did I have a mobile phone, and I said that I did and we exchanged numbers, then he gave me another quick shift and went on his way. Lucy said my face was covered in blue and white paint and that it looked like I had gone three rounds with William Wallace himself, which I kind of did in fairness!

I can barely think straight. He's amazing BUT I have to get him out of my head because it's my Leaving Cert.

I have to go get more phone credit, just in case he texts, because he will text, won't he?

Goodnight Dear Diary,
Love,
Ciara X

Danny the Champion Arsehole of the World

Dear Diary,

I am literally the angriest I've been in my whole entire life. Angry with a capital A. I texted Danny yesterday and he hasn't even had the respect to text me back?! Like, what the actual hell? I got phone credit yesterday and texted him straight away and he definitely got it, because I got a delivered message and I've heard nothing since, and I just checked my email for the third time today which is NOT an easy thing to do, waiting for this heap of shit dial-up connection, and nothing. I don't understand what's happened.

Like, I wasn't even able to concentrate in class all day because I've been so upset. I had to fight back tears in double Maths, but that might have been down to the fact that we were doing statistics and probability and the probability of me failing my Leaving Cert is pretty high. I will literally fail my Leaving Cert if Danny doesn't get in contact.

Lucy and Rebecca are totally pissed off with him too. They are all like, 'Men are such dicks.' Lucy said I should just have some 'me time' to try and relax my mind. She said I should brush that beaver. I was like, 'What?!' She was like, 'You know, audition the finger puppets.' I was like, 'Seriously Lucy, what are you on about?!' She was like, 'You need to enjoy a night in with the girls, beat around the bush, buff the muff, butter the biscuit, club the clam, part the pink sea, play the hairy banjo – you know what I'm saying.' I was totally lost until she said that I should knock one off to a poster of Nicky Byrne from Westlife, and then it dawned on me that she meant, like, masturbation.

But only lads masturbate, right? Lucy says no, that when she's feeling low, she gives her bean an old flick. I nearly got sick. Is there nothing she won't do to herself? Her poor, poor bean.

I decided to just put a million curses onto Danny instead. Granny is, like, always putting curses on people, from the postman to the local butcher to the woman who beats her at bingo the whole time. But I think she just doesn't like that woman because she met Daniel O'Donnell before and Granny can't handle the jealousy.

So in study class, when I should have been studying, I wrote down a list of curses that I was going to mentally put on him. The first one is kind of evil.

1. *'May you die without a priest in the town.' (Which is a bit harsh as I don't actually want him to die.)*
2. *'May your obituary be written in weasel's piss.' (This is my granny's favourite curse, but again, I don't want Danny to die.)*
3. *'May you get the runs on your wedding night.' (NO! I actually don't want him to marry anyone.)*
4. *'May the cat eat you and the devil eat the cat.'*

Here's a good one:

5. *'May the devil make a ladder of your backbones while picking apples in the garden of hell.'*

Ya, I like that one. Lucy says that the next time I see him I should say 'When you were born, you were so ugly, the nurse slapped your mother,' but in fairness that couldn't possibly be true because he is literally the most beautiful man that I have ever seen, and I don't understand why he hasn't texted me back.

Has he gone off me? He couldn't have met someone else because he goes to an all-boys school. Oh God, please don't tell me that I have another Hot Gay Brendan situation on my hands. I literally couldn't deal with it if that was the case. Why is it that it feels like men have all the power, like, why is it that I'm sitting here feeling really shit about myself because he hasn't been in contact with me? Carrie would not put up with this if this was a *Sex and the City*-type scenario. She would call the girls and they would head out to some cool club in New York and of course I can't do that, because I'm 18 and I'm basically trapped in this village and there's, like, one bus a week that passes through.

Oh my God, Danny is such a skank. He's a shithead. He's about as useful in my life as Anne Frank getting a drum set for Christmas. He is the opposite of Superman, he is No-man. I hope he steps on pieces of Lego for the rest of his days.

Not even all of this venting is making me feel better. I feel crap and I feel so stupid because I've been daydreaming about how things are going to unfold between us and I've been daydreaming about the debs, and I had imagined us slow-dancing to Westlife's 'Queen of my Heart' and then Danny whispering in my ear, 'Ciara, you are the queen of my heart,' and then we'd go to a hotel room, and he would smell of Davidoff Cool Water cologne, and I'd be wearing Tommy Girl, and then we would just go and totally have sex and it would be the most perfect night of my life. But that daydream has been totally ruined now, why are lads such total and utter DICKS.

Oh my God Dear Diary, he just texted me! He said he was totally sorry for not being in contact but that his phone was confiscated and the brothers at the school only gave it back to him now. He texted me loads of kisses and said that he totally misses me. Oh my God, he is SO sweet and such a cutie. I totally love him. Do you know what he said? He said he's going to bed now listening to John Lennon's 'Imagine' on his Discman and thinking of me lying next to him. How amazing is that! I actually think he likes me Dear Diary, he really likes ME. Someone finally likes me. I'm, like, SO happy right now.

Goodnight Dear Diary,
Love,
Ciara X

Oceans in Heaven

Dear Diary,

I know that I should be studying for my Christmas exams, but my head is so full of thoughts about Danny, my boyfriend. I actually have a boyfriend. He asked me to be his girlfriend on the phone the last evening. I was like, 'Okay ya, cool,' trying to be really casual, but actually feeling like I wanted to scream 'Marry me!' down the phone. I'm not going to tell my parents as they'll just see this as a massive distraction from studying for my Leaving Cert, and I know, of ALL years to finally meet The One. I think he asked me to be his girlfriend after I was the perfect cinema date. He took me to see *Ocean's Eleven* in the cinema in Galway. We chatted the whole way into Galway and listened to the radio and it turns out he totally loves Kate Winslet's song 'What If' and he knows all the words. I thought that was really sweet until he started talking about her topless scene in *Titanic* and I was jealous. I can't compete with Kate Winslet! She's so hot.

Speaking of hot, so are the majority of the cast in *Ocean's Eleven*. I've never seen so many good-looking people in the one movie. If I hadn't been sitting beside the best-looking guy in Ireland, I would totally have been daydreaming about losing my virginity to Brad Pitt, George Clooney, Matt Damon, Don Cheadle or maybe even Julia Roberts. I was on high alert in fairness, and my palms were really sweaty because I was nervous, and I kept on having to rub them off my jeans to stop them from being so clammy. I was nervous you see because I thought he might go in for the shift because Lucy told me that lads love going in for the shift in the cinema. She said that the key is to go to the cinema during the day, go right to the back row and just spend the movie fiddling with each other.

Like, that is not classy. The cinema is really expensive and if you want to fiddle with each other, then just go down the back of the town hall like everyone else. She told me about the time she went to see *Shrek* with her ex the bouncer, and how they had gone to town on each other on the back row. She has literally ruined that movie for me. I don't think I ever want to see it now, even though everyone keeps on doing impressions of the donkey in it and talking about how onions have layers or some shit. All I'd ever be thinking if I watched that movie is which parts Lucy and her bouncer boyfriend were sucking the faces off each other during.

Anyway, I couldn't really concentrate during *Ocean's Eleven* because I was afraid that I would drop popcorn all over me or get it stuck in my teeth, and my palms were sweaty and I could smell Danny's Lynx shower gel and it was unnerving me as it was just so nice to have someone sitting beside me that, like, wanted to sit beside me and that might actually like me.

After the cinema, we went to the McDonald's drive thru and just sat in the car stuffing our faces. Danny was so funny because he kept on doing the dance moves to Kylie Minogue's 'Can't Get You Out of My Head' when it came on the radio. He was doing all these robot moves, and I just couldn't stop laughing and honestly Dear Diary, it was the happiest I've been since Lucy's older brother dry humped me on his bed that one time.

We drove home with the windows down, which wasn't so great as Danny was afraid that his mother would give out about the smell of fast food in the car, and it's winter so obviously I was freezing, but then Danny put his hand on my leg and I literally didn't care that there were sub-zero temperatures outside as it was hotter than the Sahara desert in my heart. I didn't move my legs for the whole duration of the journey just in case he took his hand off. We pulled up outside my house and it got really awkward and we were just sitting there and in my mind I was like, 'Will you just shift me,' and then he did and it was amazing, tongue and everything. He tried to move closer but the handbrake was between us so it was annoying. At least, I think it was the handbrake. Then the smell of his air freshener was really apparent and all I could smell was pine, so I was concentrating on that, but then Danny reached across and put his hand on the outside of my jumper on one boob and I thanked my lucky stars that I had worn my favourite padded bra from Penneys. I thought he was going to attempt to put it up my top but then the front door of my house opened suddenly and my dad came out. I've never seen Danny move so quick in all my life. I was MORTIFIED. Dad didn't even see us, he was just going out to his car to put something in the boot. The spell had been broken. Nothing like the appearance of a teenage girl's father to stop her getting some.

Fathers are so annoying. As Lucy always says to me, 'At least you have one.' She found out lately that her dad is living in Thailand with some young one. She has now started refusing to talk about Leonardo DiCaprio's movie *The Beach* because seemingly it was filmed over there. It makes me feel bad for her because it was literally her favourite movie of all time.

Anyway, I said a quick goodbye to Danny and jumped out of the car because Dad totally ruined the moment for me. I went up to my room and tried to do some study just so my parents wouldn't give out to me, but I really couldn't have cared less about looking at an aerial photograph of Sligo town and analysing its road infrastructure or how the region has a long history of human settlement. Hot substitute teacher or no hot substitute teacher (who I still totally fancy by the way).

Did I mention that Danny is now my boyfriend? When he rang me and asked me and I said all right he said, 'Sweet.' How cool is that. He said he was going to ask me to my face in the car to make it even more official and be respectful, but then my dad came out and nearly RUINED MY LIFE. He was cut off then because he ran out of phone credit.

Here's the thing Dear Diary. Now I'm freaking out. The debs is next week and I'm sharing a room with Hot Gay Brendan because he's gay. Danny is coming to the afters. Will I still be a virgin by Christmas?! Imagine that. Oh my God, I'm so scared. I'm not on the pill any more or anything. Am I ready for this? I've done so much talking about it. No, I can't, I just can't. It's my Leaving Cert year, and it would be just my luck to get pregnant.

Sorry, just back. I had to go there for a while and sit with my head between my legs to stop myself from freaking out. It's too soon. What if Danny expects me to put out? What if I don't put out and he goes off me? But then, what if we do, like, do it, and it's not good, or I'm not good? What if I get nervous and end up just lying there like a sack of potatoes? Rebecca says her first time with Johnny Limp was only all right. Which is weird because at the time she basically told us that it was really romantic. Suddenly, now that they are over, she's all like, 'I was freezing and it was all over in less than five minutes.' I need to ask Jeeves about how to have sex. What if my parents see me looking that up on the computer though? Maybe I'll get a book on it. Or just keep on buying more magazines and checking out their weekly sex positions.

I know I should be revising for my Christmas exams, but desperate times call for desperate measures.

If I'm finally going to fornicate, I'm going to have to do some research.

Goodnight Dear Diary,
Love,
Ciara X

'Oh Danny boy, your pipe, your pipe is calling'

Dear Diary,

I'm so tired. Like, this is the most tired I've ever been in my life, and I can't concentrate on my Christmas exams because I am still so buzzed from the debs. Yes, it finally happened Dear Diary – the debs. What a night it was too. It was everything and nothing that I had imagined it to be. I'm so relieved that we're actually even having a debs because our school is banned from so many hotels that we had to wait until December and pretend that we were a youth drama group from Mullingar having their Christmas party.

Danny was meeting us at the hotel at the afters. My parents took LOADS of photos of me and my granny came around and so did some of the neighbours, which was nice. Everyone made a big fuss, which was lovely but, like, totally embarrassing at the same time. I had to pose for loads of photos and then Hot Gay Brendan arrived, looking SO gorgeous in his white tux. Granny's eyes nearly fell out of her head when she saw the white tux and she asked Hot Gay Brendan had somebody sent it over from America as she had never seen anything like it in her life. She told him that he looked like a young Rock Hudson and told me that I looked like Doris Day, which is so not true because she is a blonde and I am a total brunette.

When Hot Gay Brendan was out of earshot, she pulled me aside and asked me was Hot Gay Brendan one of those homosexuals that she's read about in the news. I said, 'Yes Granny, Hot

Gay Brendan is gay,' and she smiled knowingly and said, 'I knew a few of them in my day, great dancers they are.' Then she said, 'At least I won't worry about you losing your virtue tonight because that fella in there wouldn't get up on you to get over a wall,' and off she walked to make herself another hot whiskey. Little did she know what I was planning on doing.

You see Dear Diary, Lucy had donated something to me from her stash – just in case. I can barely write the words. I feel SO guilty. But I had, in my possession, at that moment – a condom. It's not the first time in my life that I felt like Claire Danes in that movie *Brokedown Palace* where she has those illegal drugs and ends up in a Thai prison, except I was in my home with this sexual contraband. I had it hidden in my wash bag and packed in my rucksack for the night away. I also had Immaced the bejaysus out of my nether regions – so physically, I was good to go.

I said goodbye to my parents and got really emotional because the next time they saw me I would be different. I wouldn't be their little girl any more, but a woman of the world. A mature adult female who probably would have changed for ever. I think I must have had tears in my eyes as Hot Gay Brendan was like, 'Are you okay?' and I was all like, 'Ya, I think I got some glitter in my eye,' but honestly at that moment I felt like the character Benny in Maeve Binchy's novel *Circle of Friends*.

We arrived at the hotel to get the bus, which would take over an hour and a half, and Lucy and Rebecca were there waiting. They both looked totally gorgeous and Hot Gay Brendan took loads of photos of us on his disposable camera. Lucy had invited some petrified-looking lad from another school and he was nervously hovering around her. He was right to be nervous because the first thing that Lucy said to me was that she was looking forward to banging his brains out later. Poor guy. Rebecca was okay, Johnny Limp was there but there was no sign of the Saoirse one. She did say that her heart skipped a beat when she saw him in his tux and then she said that he's still using the Zippo lighter that she got him for Christmas last year and maybe that's a MAJOR sign that he is still in love with her. My heart literally broke for her. The way Johnny Limp was throwing the Buckfast back into him, he wouldn't be any use to anyone in an hour.

The bus in was fine. The driver had to stop a million times to let the lads off to take a whizz, but we got there eventually! The hotel looked amazing, full of Christmas lights and trees, and the function room looked incredible, like a mini teenage Christmas wedding.

Lucy was throwing the vodka back into her like there was no tomorrow. She was being really touchy feely with her date, Tom, who was looking even more nervous than before. We were all seated for the dinner and that was great craic. We had dropped our things in the hotel rooms beforehand, and I glanced quickly at the bed and then nearly fainted at the thought of what I might do later, so then I had to go into the bathroom and literally sit down and breathe. After dinner, the music started and everyone hit the dancefloor. It was awesome. We had to queue to get our professional photo taken, but it was cool.

People began arriving to the afters. Straight away I saw Saoirse from sixth year last year and Johnny Limp swaying over to her. Rebecca spotted it too and immediately I saw her lip begin to wobble. Not tonight. NOT tonight. Straight into the toilets we went with her. Lucy offered to put out a cigarette on Saoirse's dress but we both advised her not to.

When we came out of the toilets Danny was standing there in a tux, looking like Leonardo DiCaprio, and if I could have had an orgasm, I would have. He was holding a rose in his hand, and I got really nervous, but I was, like, SO happy at the same time.

The tables had been cleared off at this stage and everyone was on the dancefloor. The DJ played 'Rock the Boat' and everyone was down on the dancefloor rocking back and forth. Which was too much of a task for poor Fergal in my year as he ended up puking on the side of the dancefloor, so we all had to clear off while the poor staff cleaned it up. Then everyone went nuts to Mark McCabe's 'Maniac 2000' and were shouting 'Oggie, oggie, oggie. Oi! Oi! Oi!' It was just about time for Christmas songs! The DJ played 'Fairytale of New York', Wham's 'Last Christmas' and Mariah Carey's 'All I Want for Christmas Is You'. And there, on that dancefloor, with Lucy (whose boobs were beginning to fall out of her dress), Rebecca (who was crying), Hot Gay Brendan (who was breaking out his George Michael dance moves) and my Danny, was probably the happiest that I have felt in all my teenage years. But then a fight broke out and we had to get off the dancefloor again.

We all went into the residents bar then. Rebecca was in better form because she had seen Johnny Limp step on Saoirse from sixth year last year's dress, and he tore it and she stormed out. Lucy was propped up at the bar shifting the face off Tom, who was beginning to grope her like a wild animal. Hot Gay Brendan was flirting with the Polish bartender who couldn't understand a word that he said. So then suddenly Danny appears by my side, takes my hand and whispers, 'Let's disappear.' So off we went to the hotel room. My heart was in my mouth and I was so nervous that I didn't stop talking, and then I couldn't find the key to get into the room, but then I did and it was fine. So we went in and took off our shoes and stuff and Danny lay on the bed, and then I went into the bathroom to, like, brush my teeth and spray myself with Impulse body spray and take off my dress and put on these, like, silk pyjamas that I got in Penneys, and then I checked myself in the mirror a million times, silently said goodbye to my hymen, and went back out. And then, Dear Diary, that's when I saw it.

Danny lying there, under the covers, snoring loudly in the bed. He had fallen asleep. ASLEEP. Dead to the world, conked out. Old Danny boy had called it a night and was getting himself some good old shut-eye. I literally could have cried ... in total and utter RELIEF. Dear Diary, I wasn't ready to lose my virginity. Who was I kidding?

The next thing there's a knock on the door and it's Hot Gay Brendan, and he's like, 'Hey, can I stay here?' and I was like, 'Ya.' Two seconds later, there's another knock on the door and it's Rebecca. She's all like, 'Guys, I'm lonely and I miss Johnny Limp, can I stay here?' I was like, 'Come in.' So we all hopped into the bed, me beside Danny who was out of it, Hot Gay Brendan on the other side, and Rebecca in the bed beside him. Hot Gay Brendan was making jokes about swapping places but I was having none of it just in case his hands roamed anywhere near Danny. Then, just when we are all getting settled and Rebecca had finally stopped crying, there's a loud banging on the door, and it's a drunken Lucy giving out about Tom being a total frigid. The poor lad. So Lucy hopped into the single bed, and me, Danny, Rebecca and Hot Gay Brendan AND Lucy all fell asleep wrapped around each other at about five in the morning. So technically Dear Diary, you could say that I slept with not one but four different people last night, and I guess that will have to do for now.

Goodnight Dear Diary,
Love,
Ciara X

Lucy in the Sky with Hymens

Dear Diary,
Well, 2002 has started off with a bang. Literally. I'm here in my room trying to study and I can't because I am freaking out for Lucy. Lucy, Lucy, Lucy.

It all started when we went over to Lucy's on Friday night to try out her new GHD. Rebecca, Lucy, Hot Gay Brendan and me knew we had a free house because Lucy's mum goes to Weight Watchers on a Friday night. Straight away, I knew something was up with her. She was so distracted and not herself. She was in the middle of GHDing Rebecca's hair when all of a sudden all we could smell was burning hair and we realised it was Rebecca's and we just about saved a massive chunk of it being burnt to a crisp. She didn't even join in when we were going through *OK* magazine and commenting on whether we'd do Gareth Gates or not (Hot Gay Brendan totally would by the way, as would Rebecca as she thinks his stutter is cute, I totally wouldn't as he looks like he is 12 years of age, but I do think he has a beautiful voice.) There was just no chat out of her.

I thought that maybe she was upset because her dad's now going to have a baby with the young one he went off to Thailand with and I tried to talk to her about it with tips that I had picked up from watching Dr Phil on *Oprah*, but then she told me to shut the fuck up talking about babies. It was really awkward.

Here's the thing about Lucy. She is always in good form. She's not, like, a massive thinker about life and the only thing deep about her is her vagina. So when she's acting like this you know there is something seriously wrong with her. Rebecca, me and

Hot Gay Brendan left because it was so weird and walked up the road wondering what the hell was wrong with her. Hot Gay Brendan reckoned she was worried about the mocks in February but Lucy couldn't care less about exams and school, so that couldn't be it. Rebecca thought maybe she was on her period and was feeling hormonal, but Lucy is the sort of girl to give you a blow-by-blow account of her menstrual cycle with updates on cramps and bloatedness. If she could get us up her cervix, she would have us as an audience for when the lining of her uterus is shed each month. That's how open she is about things. I couldn't put my finger on it, but something was seriously up.

I went home and spent most of the weekend studying and texting Danny. I texted Lucy a couple of times as well, but she didn't answer. Then my mobile rang and it was Hot Gay Brendan sounding overly excited. He was all like, ' I know what's wrong with Lucy,' and I was like, 'What?' and he was like, 'She thinks she's pregnant for REAL this time.' I nearly dropped my mobile on the floor. Hot Gay Brendan knew something was up so went back down to her house after he had walked me and Rebecca home, and Lucy had burst out crying and told him. It was the bouncer that I thought Lucy had broken up with. So herself and Hot Gay Brendan are going to town to buy a pregnancy test. I'm surprised there is a pharmacy in the vicinity that Lucy hasn't bought a pregnancy test from. Hot Gay Brendan is going to ring me after, so now I'm just left here waiting in my room trying to guess whether or not Lucy is pregnant again.

I mean, this isn't the first scare. I remember the time that me, Rebecca and Lucy crammed into a toilet cubicle in Supermac's when Lucy thought she was pregnant before, and that was a false alarm, then there was the time that Lucy made me, her and Rebecca all do pregnancy tests for the craic, only to find out after that she had thought she was pregnant and didn't want to do a test on her own, and now this! Seriously, in her Leaving Cert year?! After talking to Brendan I tried to put my head back in the books to distract myself, trying to learn about 'risk management' for Business Studies, which is the identification, assessment and prioritisation of risks and monitoring and control of the probability and/or impact of unfortunate events. Being Lucy's friend is like trying to deal with risk management. Why it is that everything to do with Lucy leads to a series of unfortunate events?

That's it. I've had enough. I am going to write her a letter to tell her to keep her legs closed for once and for all. This is the last thing that I need in my Leaving Cert year; it's the last thing that any of us need!

Maybe it's best not to write that sort of letter to Lucy right now. I know, I'll write to someone for help. Someone I haven't written to in a while – Aung San Suu Kyi. She's been under house arrest in Burma since 1989, I'm sure she would only be delighted with some correspondence and news from the outside. It will also totally help distract me until Hot Gay Brendan rings with the news on Lucy.

> *Dear Aung San Suu Kyi,*
> *How are you? Long time no talk. I think the last time I wrote you a letter was to inform you about a demonstration I was involved with for the people of Burma in Ireland. If I'm being honest, I only went because my then boyfriend John was a massive fan of yours and I was only doing it to impress him. At the time I couldn't even pick Burma out on a map, but I have learned since not to do things to try and impress boys because John turned out to be a total dick and headed off Interrailing and I haven't heard from him since.*

How are things going under house arrest? You must be bored out of your mind at this stage. I know the feeling, sometimes I'm in my house for too long and I get serious cabin fever. My parents start wrecking my head, they're always at me to study or clean my room or turn my music down. Total buzzkills. Do you miss your family? Sometimes I wish mine were under house arrest in Burma, but I wouldn't wish that on you Aung San Suu Kyi, as they would drive you demented. My father would probably shush you every time the Six One News was on and good luck to you even opening your mouth when the weather was on. You might get a break when the news for the deaf came on though as he doesn't understand sign language.

You must miss your husband though? I'd say you are literally dying for the shift? Have you had the shift since 1989? I really hope you have. Sometimes I think about you and your husband being so far apart, and I think about me and my boyfriend Danny. He goes to boarding school, like, three hours away and I never get to see him. So I totally get what you and your husband are dealing with.

Here are a couple of things that are going on in the world right now:

1. *Everyone is petrified of Osama bin Laden, but everyone thinks that he is hanging out in caves in Afghanistan so you're safe where you are.*
2. *The new currency in Europe now is called the euro and everyone is trying to get their heads around it.*
3. *The war in Sierra Leone is over (if I'm being really honest, I've no idea where that it is).*
4. *Kylie Minogue just got voted sexiest pop star. It's because of these hot pants that she wore in that 'Spinning Around' video. It's a great track, you should check it out.*

Anyway, the real reason that I am writing is because of my friend Lucy, and I'm asking you to say a prayer for her. I know you probably keep all your prayers for the people of Burma but if you could include Lucy, I'd really appreciate it. She's a really great person and friend, but right now I'm waiting to hear if she's pregnant or not. I'm going to level with you, my friend Lucy is fond of the penis Aung San Suu Kyi, and sometimes this gets her into trouble. Usually I'd pray to dead relatives or neighbours asking for help with this sort of thing but I don't think that anyone is listening to me as my boobs haven't gotten any bigger and I'm still a virgin, but I'm hoping they are going to redeem themselves coming up to my Leaving Cert.

I'm sitting here waiting for Hot Gay Brendan to text me. He's my gorgeous gay friend that I thought I was in love with once. Do you have gay people in Burma? I hope so. We don't have many in Ireland, but I'm hoping that will change. I know this is a big ask okay, but is there any chance that maybe you could write to my friend Lucy and give her some words of wisdom and maybe get her to focus on her Leaving Cert? She might not have a notion of who you are, but I could try and explain to her, and I'm sure she'd appreciate the correspondence. Some day.

I better go now, I'll write again Aung San Suu Kyi, best of luck with house arrest and everything in Burma. I'd say the Burmese people think that you're great altogether.

Lots of love,

Ciara

Just off the phone to Hot Gay Brendan. Lucy is NOT pregnant. Oh for God's sake. This is just ridiculous. My heart can't take this. I'm going to tie Lucy's fallopian tubes together myself if I have to. Enough is enough. I've wasted the day worrying about her when I should have been studying for my Leaving Cert.

Anyway I better go, we're going to go drinking down at the benches to celebrate.

Goodnight Dear Diary,
Love,
Ciara X

Stone the Flamin' Crows, Danny!

Dear Diary,

I'm really angry right now. I'm really angry at myself. I'm angry at the educational system and I'm just angry at being stuck in this teenage body in general. The mocks are coming up soon and, like, everyone knows that they are not a clear indicator of whether or not you'll pass your Leaving Cert and get into college. I have past exam papers coming out my eyeballs. Like, you literally cannot hazard a guess as to what's going to come up! How can a teenager study 20 things fully, knowing that maybe four of the topics might appear on an exam paper? Our brain capacity can't be able for that! It's so unfair. As teenagers we get treated so badly by the educational system in this country. I'm telling you something Dear Diary, once the Leaving Cert is finished, and the World Cup is over, I am going to write a strongly worded letter to our Taoiseach Bertie Ahern, and our President Mary McAleese. Everyone is always talking about 'reform' on the *Six One News*, maybe it's a time for a Leaving Cert reform?! How do you feel about that, Irish government?!

Anyway, I think I'm just in bad form because I stupidly chose not to do Home Economics as a subject in school. Like, what was I thinking? How was I even allowed do Woodwork up until my Junior Cert?! Oh no, I just had to be different, didn't I?! I just had to have morals about girls being able to do Woodwork too, and why should I have to choose Home Economics because women have been chained to the kitchen sink in this country for generations and blah, blah, blah. Lucy and Rebecca were showing me some questions from the Home Ec exam papers in 2000, and

I'm literally beyond jealous. Like, listen to this: 'Using beef or lamb, give instructions for preparing, cooking and serving a main course dish suitable for a celebration dinner for four teenagers.'

That was a legit question?! Firstly, where do they think these teenagers go to school – Mallory Towers?! Secondly, the only place that Irish teenagers go to celebrate anything is to the chipper after a night out, and the only thing they are celebrating is either getting the shift or the fact that they have managed to go a whole night without puking up whatever alcoholic concoction they have swimming in their stomachs from their parents' drinks cabinet. Here's another one: 'State how the frozen dish should be defrosted and prepared for serving.' How you can even go about trying to get four foolscap pages about banging something in the microwave and hitting the defrost button is beyond me! It's actually ludicrous. I swear, if Lucy and Rebecca get more points in the Leaving Cert than me I'll lose the rag altogether. Although Lucy really seems to have put her head down after the whole pregnancy scare. She's even been wearing her school uniform within regulation guidelines and everything. I think it's the first time in six years that I haven't seen Lucy's thighs as she has her skirt down below her actual knees.

She candidly told me and Rebecca in the bathroom that she is going off dick until June, which I honestly think is SO mature of her. Anyway – again – why oh why did I choose to do Business Studies for my Leaving Cert? I read one article about Richard Branson throwing a party for his staff and I was hooked, it was my own fault. My only hope is to read this book called *It's a Long Way from Penny Apples*, it's written by this businessman called Bill Cullen. He's always on *The Late Late Show* with Pat Kenny. He grew up in the inner slums of Dublin city and sold apples but now he's, like, this really rich businessman. Hopefully I can use examples from his book, but it's not on the curriculum so I don't know. All I do know is that I'm sitting here trying to get my head around the Industrial Relations Act 1990. There always seems to be people walking up and down waving signs outside workplaces and factories on the news, so maybe I'll gain some inspiration from that, but mainly I just want them to get back to work. Maybe if they spent more time actually working and not patrolling up and down our TV screens, they wouldn't be in whatever industrial dispute they're in. My dad says that big Jim Larkin would be turning in his grave if he heard me say that but I don't care because I don't even know who that is.

Anyway, I've got other things to worry about. I was talking to Danny on the phone and he was telling me about this major drama that went on in his Technical Drawing class today. Two of the lads are in serious trouble because a massive fight broke out between them and they were literally beating the shit out of each other with T-squares, and the teacher had to intervene and everything, and now all the lads have to be questioned by the headmaster. Something happened at GAA training between the two and Danny said that one of the lads launched himself at the other lad like Eric Cantona kung fu kicking that guy in the crowd in 1995. Danny is so pissed off though as he says he likes both of them. He says everyone is taking sides and it's so head-wrecking he feels like heading off to Australia after the Leaving Cert and when the World Cup is over. I was like, 'Eh, okay, hold up a minute – what?!' Then he said, 'Ya,' and that he's really thinking about going. He's going to see whether or not he gets the points for Civil Engineering in NUI Galway and if he does, he'll wait until after the course to go.

Jesus, Mary and Joseph: if you guys are listening to me right now, could you help a girl out?! Please, please, please! Let Danny get the points for Civil Engineering in NUI Galway because then at least I can stall him until 2005/2006. He just can't go.

I'd go mad. I'm left with two options: either make him think that Australia is the worst, or get pregnant.

I've started compiling a list of reasons why Australia is shit. I know I should be studying for my Leaving Cert but desperate times call for desperate measures.

- *Firstly, it's really, really, really far away. I heard that if you go by plane to Australia you're literally on the plane for three days and your legs swell up and you could get a clot, and then you would have to have your leg amputated.*
- *Kylie Minogue is literally the only person to come out of Australia, and I'm not adding Rolf Harris to this list because he writes depressing songs about little boys and horses, and if I'm being honest, should we really trust a man who writes songs about 'two little boys'? It's just plain weird.*
- *It's too hot over there. It's sunny and warm at Christmastime for God's sake. It's just unnatural.*
- *You can literally be killed by anything that moves in Australia, from spiders and snakes to infested koala bears and kangaroos. Never trust an animal that can jump, as my father says.*
- *Also, I don't buy the term 'Aboriginals', why aren't they called 'originals' as they were the first people originally there?*
- *The country is full of people probably related to a whole load of Irish criminals that we sent over years ago.*
- *Also, a dingo once ran off with someone's baby. Mum said it was all over the news at the time. There was even a movie about it, Meryl Streep was in it and even got nominated for an Oscar because of it. Why would you move to a country where a dingo can run off with your baby?*
- *And finally, they talk funny. They put shrimp on a barbecue without even boiling them first and they drink beer during the day just to cool down.*

That's all I've written so far Dear Diary, but if I think of more, I'll write them down.

Goodnight Dear Diary,
Love,
Ciara X

Are you there, God? It's me, Ciara

Dear Diary,

I'm taking a break from studying for my mocks to chill out about the fact that I'm studying for my mocks. What I've learned so far is that I'm not ready to sit my Leaving Cert, that's for sure. The mock exam papers are like something from outer space. It's like the past five and a half years of my education have been a complete and utter waste. I had my French mock yesterday and I might as well be learning Japanese for all the good it did. I made sure to learn off French words for 'planes', 'Twin Towers', 'New York' and 'America' because I was sure one of the compositions would focus on that, but nothing came up. Maybe they're actually waiting until the Leaving Cert exams themselves but surely 9/11 is going to come up in some capacity. I mean, what's the point of something so catastrophic happening in the world and then it NOT being mentioned in the Leaving Cert examinations in Ireland 2002? Pointless.

Honestly, the mocks have been so bad that I've turned to something that I've doubted for the past while – religion. That's right Dear Diary, I've turned to God. I've started going to Mass again and everything. It's funny though, I was thinking that God kind of owes me one. When I was at Mass, I was thinking about all the times I was an altar girl – sorry, correction, the first altar girl in the parish – and all the times that I read from the book of Ecclesiastes. Does God not know how much time I spent learning how to pronounce that before I said it up on the altar? Or when I did the responsorial psalms and didn't get the response from the congregation that I was hoping for. Don't get me started on the amount of times I went around waiting for people to get the money out for the collection baskets, and then bringing them up to the altar and worrying about the fact that all the old men in the church would be checking out my arse when I did. I've done my time.

I don't know is God listening to me though. Sometimes I think it's because he listens to my thoughts on the whole Virgin Mary situation. As much as I try to see that situation from different sides, I still come back to the fact that there was NO way that she was an actual virgin and I still feel really sorry for Joseph. That poor guy was completely duped by all of them. Or maybe it's because the only thing I've prayed to God about over these past few years has been to ask him for bigger boobs or asking him for a bit of a miracle to help me lose my virginity. In hindsight, maybe that wasn't really the way to go since I'm now looking for God's help with passing my exams. Granny has been on to me telling me that she has been praying to St Joseph of Cupertino, seemingly he's the patron saint of exam takers, but then my aunt told me about this guy called St Thomas of Aquinas, he's the patron saint of students.

I feel really sorry for those guys. When God was doling out which saint was patron saint of whatever, he really gave them the short end of the stick. Like, look at St Brigid, she's the patron saint of Ireland, poets, dairymaids, blacksmiths, healers, cattle, fugitives, Irish nuns, midwives, and newborn babies. It's simply because God can see that women can multitask I guess. It's also a pity that God couldn't have made a patron saint for helping hapless teenage girls lose their virginity. Mass would be full every Saturday night, that's for sure.

Sorry for going so deep and religious. I can be a really deep person at times. Danny is doing his mocks too, so we've barely been texting but that's okay, I want him to concentrate and do really well because if he doesn't get the points for Civil

Engineering in NUI Galway, there's that whole elephant in the room about him getting a visa and going to Australia. God, it's literally ruined Australia for me. I now hate a country that I've never even been to but have grown up watching on the TV. *The Flying Doctors* was on non-stop in my house growing up. It's where I learned the term 'bush fire' that we used to slag Lucy when she thought she had a sexually transmitted disease. And don't get me started on *Home and Away*. The thoughts of Danny going to Australia have literally ruined *Home and Away* for me. Australian girls are seriously hot and they're so cool they can surf. I can't surf to save my life, and I don't have a wet suit to look sexy in, and when salt water gets in my hair I end up looking like Worzel Gummidge. I've started watching more episodes of *Shortland Street* and *The Bill*. The characters are so less hot, so they make me feel better about myself.

Valentine's Day is also coming up and because it's the first Valentine's Day that I actually have a boyfriend, I won't have to ring the local florist to send a rose to the school for me from a 'secret admirer'. I don't know what to get for Danny. I don't want to get him aftershave because that is such a cliché, but I also don't want to give him my virginity on Valentine's Day because that's so lame too. I'd much rather lose it on, like, St Patrick's Day because as I've always said, at least you could lie back and do it for your country at the same time. There's no point losing your virginity on, like, Christmas Day or your birthday because if it goes wrong and you end up hating the person you lose your virginity with, you'll always be reminded of that fact on special occasions. I honestly think it's much better to lose your virginity on a random Friday after the youth club or something, than on an actual occasion, but maybe I'm overthinking it. I do have a tendency to do that. I overthink things to the point that I create scenarios in my head that never actually happen.

I mean, have you ever heard a teenage girl panic that she's pregnant even though she hasn't even had sex yet? Seriously, like, every second week I freak out that I'll get pregnant before my Leaving Cert and then I remember that I haven't even had sex yet. It's SO hard to be a woman. Mr Murphy the hot substitute teacher (who I don't think is hot any more by the way, since he decided to share EVERY detail of his wedding plans) got engaged a couple of weeks ago on top of one of the McGillycuddy Reeks, and now drops the fact in in EVERY Geography class. I wouldn't be surprised to see a question in our Geography mock paper tomorrow about what exact contour on the McGillycuddy Reeks he actually got engaged on. Like, it's great that they are in love and everything but, like, I can't even imagine the teachers having sex outside of school. They are literally not human to us. We have our own shit to worry about.

Speaking about my Geography mock paper though, I really better get back to it and do some study and pray extra hard tonight to St Joseph and St Jude and St Thomas Aquinas and God and Mary and Princess Diana, and Mother Teresa and Michael Collins and Anne Frank, and Bono and Enya and literally anyone that can help me at this stage.

Pray for me Dear Diary.

Goodnight Dear Diary,
Love,
Ciara X

My Fanny Valentine

Dear Diary,

I am SO excited! Tomorrow is Valentine's Day and for literally the first time in my teenage life I have an actual boyfriend for Valentine's Day. And I'm not talking about some sad sap that you play tonsil tennis with at the youth club Valentine's disco, I'm talking, like, a REAL relationship. Like Britney and Justin or Bono and Ali, Brad and Jennifer, Demi and Bruce (well, before they got the divorce), Gay Byrne and Kathleen Watkins, Brian and Glenda, David and Victoria, Elton and David, Dolce and Gabbana, Madonna and Guy – the list is endless. I'm trying to think of famous Irish lovers and love stories that I can compare to myself and Danny, but all the Irish stories I can think of are so sad and always end up with someone dying.

My granny told me this one story about this guy with a ridiculous surname called Joseph Plunkett, and he was this dude that had something to do with something called the 1916 Rising, like, YEARS ago, and he had this bird on the go called Grace Gifford. I think Joseph Plunkett was a bit of a cowboy because he was captured and ordered to be executed, but Granny said it was SO romantic because they got married in this famous jail the night before he was supposed to be killed, and seemingly Grace Gifford wore widow's clothes for the rest of her life because she was, like, totally devastated.

Granny's eyes well up every time she tells that story and she would say that he was one of the greatest figures in the Irish Republican Brotherhood. Seemingly Granddad used to sing the song 'Grace' after he had a couple of whiskeys in him in the local pub in the late eighties when the song became big because one of the lads from the Dubliners sang it, but then Granny would always end the story by saying that Granddad was just like Joseph Plunkett – a feckin eejit. I don't know if that's one of the best Irish love stories. Firstly, they got married in a jail, secondly, there's no way she got the ride because he was brought back to his cell, like, straight away, and the very next day he was shot! Then she wore widow's clothes for the rest of her life?! No man would have gone near her! Her fashion sense went out the window and for what?! We didn't even get all the counties in Ireland after all of that. Why did the women have to suffer for the mistakes of the men, Dear Diary?

Actually, why do women always have to suffer for the mistakes of men? It's ridiculous, but I'm not in the mood to hate on men because my Danny wouldn't be stupid enough to get caught and then executed. My Danny is smarter than that and will probably get over 600 points in the Leaving Cert. He texted me earlier on to say that he had ordered me something special that would be delivered to school tomorrow.

I was talking to Lucy and Rebecca and Hot Gay Brendan and was, like, asking them for advice on what to ask him for. I know they were all kind of rolling their eyes at me because I was talking non-stop about Danny and Valentine's Day, but so what – I've listened to them and advised them all on their love lives and breakups and infatuations and craziness and pregnancy scares and gayness, so if I wanted to talk about Danny and Valentine's, I was well within my rights. Lucy said that she had a suggestion for what I could ask Danny for. I was delighted because I couldn't really think of anything off the top of my head. She goes, 'I think you should ask him for cunnilingus for Valentine's.' Then her, Hot Gay Brendan and Rebecca all started breaking their holes laughing. I was like, 'What's cunnilingus?'

and they all looked at me like I had ten heads. Lucy was like, 'Ciara, are you serious?' and I was like, 'Ya.' Then she gave me this weird look and said that it was a new range that the Body Shop had launched especially for Valentine's Day and that she read recently in *OK* magazine that Catherine Zeta Jones swears by it. It was weird though because as she was going through the different products that are available in cunnilingus, like shower gel, soap, body cream (which is rich in vitamin E) and body spray, Rebecca and Hot Gay Brendan were literally crying with laughter. At least Lucy was being productive in helping me with what to ask Danny for. And the way I look at it is, if this cunnilingus is good enough for Catherine Zeta Jones, then it's good enough for me. So I texted Danny after first break and told him if he wanted to pick me up a cunnilingus set from the Body Shop that I would be happy, but obviously not to spend too much money on it because I'd love him if he gave me the cunnilingus set or not.

I've made him a CD with all his favourite songs, so that when he leaves me and goes back to boarding school he can listen to the CD on his Discman. I put loads of romantic songs on it, like Guns N' Roses' 'November Rain', Tracy Chapman's 'Fast Car', because we listen to that when we are actually in his car and he does drive a little faster, which gives me a little bit of a thrill if I'm being honest, but then I think of the road safety ads on TV that are SO sad and have ruined many great songs for me, and so I tell him to slow down. I remember the first time we drove to the cinema together and he sang Kate Winslet's 'What If' at the top of his lungs and it was amazing and literally the best moment of my life, so that's burnt onto the CD too. I'm going to write him a poem too, which I'm in the middle of doing, because he's always encouraging me to write more poetry because he thinks I have a special talent for it.

'For Danny on Valentine's Day'
Oh Danny my baby, oh Danny my boo
You came into my life and now it's less blue
You're big and you're handsome
And your ass is so cute
Being your girl is like jumping from a plane with no chute
First time I saw you at the youth club disco
You were dressed as William Wallace and dancing to Sisqó
I was Anne Frank's annex – you a total fox
You spent most of your night
Trying to get into my cardboard box
Danny, you served straight into my heart like Martina Hingis
You make my soul soar like Aer Lingus
And this Valentine's I hope you give me cunnilingus.

That's all I've written so far Dear Diary! I hope he likes it. He hasn't texted back though which is so unlike him. Maybe he's doing what I should be doing and studying for my Leaving Cert. Lucy just texted me asking me did I text Danny yet asking him for the cunnilingus set from the Body Shop, and I just texted her back and said, 'Yes, earlier, but he hasn't texted back yet,' and she just said, 'Don't worry, he will.' Oh my God, she is literally the sweetest friend ever for worrying about me like this!

Goodnight Dear Diary,
Love,
Ciara X

Boyz in the Would

Dear Diary,

Well, I'm basically after spending the last two hours of my life crying. Not crying about the stress of the Leaving Cert, which makes a change, or wondering what's going to happen to me and Danny if he goes to Australia after the Leaving Cert. I'm crying because I watched a load of people win awards for movies they starred in. Yes Dear Diary, I watched the Oscars. The speeches get me every time. Am I crying because they were crying? Maybe. Am I crying because my biggest wish in the world would be to win an Oscar and have it presented to me by Daniel Day-Lewis? I just don't know, but it's a seriously emotional time for me.

The African American actors of the Academy had a great night! Firstly Halle Berry won for *Monster's Ball* and Adrien Brody from *The Pianist* presented her with the award and practically shifted the face off her in front of the whole audience. Her dress was beautiful, but her speech was really annoying. I haven't seen *Monster's Ball* but all the lads in school say it's class because there's this scene where she is topless and rides Billy Bob Thornton in a sitting room! A sitting room?! Hardly the place you want to have sex when it's the same place you watch *Fair City*. The lads figure she deserves an Oscar for that alone. I tried to tell them in school that that is NOT the way you win an Oscar.

You win an Oscar if you play a famous person, or if you have AIDS, or if you're a strong female character who believes in some cause, or if you're portraying a depressed poet. You certainly don't win an Oscar for riding Billy Bob Thornton! Men are so immature. Denzel Washington won an Oscar for *Training Day* which I haven't seen either but all the lads at school said it was, like, the coolest movie ever. You should have see Russell Crowe's face when he didn't win for *A Beautiful Mind* – hilarious. What is with Americans starting off speeches with 'God is good, God is great'? They are not a priest in your local parish about to give Saturday night Mass! Denzel Washington's speech was cool all the same. There is no one in this world cooler than him. He is sexy as hell too, his teeth are honestly the most glorious set of teeth that I have ever laid eyes on. They should win an Oscar themselves they are so outstanding.

You know, in all my years watching the repeats of the Oscars on RTÉ, I've never seen as many black people win Academy Awards. Seriously, check this out: Halle Berry, Denzel Washington and some old dude called Sidney Poitier won a lifetime achievement award. It's like the Academy waited to give them these awards all together. Mum was explaining to me that Sidney Poitier starred in this groundbreaking movie called *Guess Who's Coming to Dinner* and it's about this girl who brings a black man home to her parents. It doesn't sound very groundbreaking to me. It might have been a bit different if she rocked home with Adolf Hitler or something, but what's the big deal? Are her parents not happy that she's actually bringing someone home at all? Hot Gay Brendan says he feels sorry for his cousin, she's really old now, hitting 30, and she doesn't have a boyfriend. He says weddings are a total nightmare for her. I'm sure HER parents would be happy if she brought anyone of any colour home. It got me thinking though, if I was to bring a black man home for dinner, who would I choose? The list would literally be too long because there are too many amazing black men out there, but I'll give it a try. Here is a list so far of what black gentlemen I would invite over for dinner to meet my parents:

1. *Will Smith: he will always be cool because of* The Fresh Prince of Bel-Air.
2. *Paul Ince: because we share the same birthday and he was one of the first people I ever fancied.*
3. *Pele: because he is the most famous footballer on the planet and my dad would love it.*
4. *Michael Jackson (when he was black): he is a musical genius.*
5. *Paul McGrath: because he is the biggest legend of all time ever.*
6. *Nelly: Because I love 'Ride Wit Me'.*
7. *Denzel Washington: even his name is awesome and he has two Oscars now.*
8. *Lenny Henry: I saw him a few times on* The Late Late Show *and he's funny.*
9. *Phil Lynott: because of Thin Lizzy and my parents love his music.*
10. *Muhammad Ali: because he is literally one of the best sportspeople in the world and my dad loves him.*
11. *Dion Dublin: I just want to ask him why a footballer with a surname like Dublin never played for Ireland.*
12. *Martin Lawrence: because I'd just make him say 'Mike Lowrey' a million times like he does in the movie* Bad Boys.
13. *Morgan Freeman: because he is the best actor of all time and that final scene in* The Shawshank Redemption *is the best ever.*
14. *Martin Luther King: he was an inspiring man and hopefully someone I am actually related to somewhere along the line.*

That's all I've got for now. I think that's a comprehensive enough list.

Things are back to normal with me and Danny again after that whole hilarious cunnilingus joke that happened at Valentine's. Turns out cunnilingus means oral sex, which Lucy, Rebecca and Hot Gay Brendan ALL knew. They let me ask Danny for a cunnilingus set from the Body Shop for Valentine's. They all thought it was hilarious but I felt like a complete idiot.

Even worse, Danny got caught looking up cunnilingus on the school computers and was sent to the headmaster's office, so then he got thick with me because he thought I did it on purpose and we ended up having, like, this fight on Valentine's, which then made me get thick with Lucy, Rebecca and Hot Gay Brendan, but they wouldn't even let me get my words across as they were all laughing so much.

Like, the whole cunnilingus thing. Why are humans hell-bent on interfering with body parts that have to do with bodily functions? I'll never understand it. Why can't things just be left to the mouth and that's it. It's put me off losing my virginity for another while anyway, which is probably best as I need to focus on my Leaving Cert anyway.

Goodnight Dear Diary,
Love,
Ciara X

RIP BIG — Again

Dear Diary,

I'm just going over and over my mocks results. Things are not good. Not good at all. I didn't get anywhere near the points that I need to do Arts in NUIG, unless the points go down by at least 50, which will never happen in my case because it wasn't as if I was born lucky. The D1 in Ordinary Level Maths hasn't helped either. If I was being honest, I'm surprised that I passed Maths at all. If I was going to be even more honest, I can't believe I've been allowed attend a Maths class in the six years that I've been at school.

Do you remember when kids had to wear that hat with the letter 'D' for dunce on it? They should have given me that hat the minute that I walked in the school gates. I know I'm being really hard on myself Dear Diary, but I really want to go to college and experience all those things that I've seen happen on the TV and in movies. I'm sick of treading the boards in secondary school for six years, struggling with being a girl teenager with all these hormones and feelings and sexual urges, and then finally being judged on my intelligence in seven subjects that I may never use again for the rest of my life.

Take French for example. Will I ever honestly have a French pen pal for life that I write to? Will I ever honestly buy a French magazine and translate the articles? Will I ever send a postcard written in French from a French caravan park that is also a campsite with showers? I don't plan on ever marrying a French man. Although they are very handsome and dress well, they can be arrogant and eccentric. Just look at Eric Cantona! But they are good footballers.

Take Geography as another example, if I need to get somewhere in the future, I'll buy myself a map, I'll avoid countries where tectonic plates collide and if climate change is really a thing, and the sea levels are going to rise, then I'll buy myself a boat. I got a C3 in Higher Geography. I'd say I lost points on my sketch map of Carrick-on-Suir. I never understand why they say to draw the sketch map half-scale, the coastlines I draw in always look dodgy as hell, and I hate the fact that I have to draw anyway. There's nothing more boring than drawing glaciers and drumlins and adding titles to them. I feel like I'm being really hard on Geography but it's because I'm lashing out now. I'm angry at the educational system of this country. I'm angry at the government for letting the educational system get to this point! If I were to meet the Education Minister Michael Wood right now, I would give him a severe talking to.

I would give out to him about the pressure teenagers are under, our heavy schoolbags, how the Leaving Cert is on at the same time as the World Cup, and how it is all just a huge pile of stupidness. I think it's fair to say Dear Diary that I am frustrated, and not, like, sexually frustrated like I usually am, but frustrated about life, frustrated at the struggle of teenage boys and girls across the world, when will it get easier for us? Why is life so unfair?

I think I need a miracle, like a real-life miracle. I'm not talking about the Virgin Mary appearing on a hill type of miracle, but a miracle where I grow loads more brain cells in the next four months and suddenly develop a photographic memory, and go work for NASA, all in the space of four months. I even asked Granny to light more candles and say even more prayers for me. She says that she has the legs walked off herself going up and down the church praying for me, and that I'd be more in mind to put my head into the books and start studying and never mind the Lucys and the Rebeccas and the Hot Gay whoevers. She's right you know. I'm even beginning to think that daydreaming constantly about Danny isn't doing me any favours either. I'm also distracted about what I'm going to wear on St Patrick's Day.

Speaking of Granny, she's in weird form. She's heading off tomorrow with some women from the village to go and visit some famous healer that's coming to a hotel in the midlands. Seemingly, the healer was on *The Late Late Show* once with Gay Byrne and is really popular. Granny wants to get rid of her arthritis. I didn't want to point out to her that she's been to Lourdes, Medjugorje and up and down on that bus to the Knock shrine EVERY year looking for the same thing, a cure for her arthritis, and it hasn't happened yet, so I don't know will this healer magically make it disappear. I don't know what excuse she's going to use when she's throwing hot whiskeys back into her and getting me to make her more to help 'ease' the arthritis. I hope she does get healed though. I know I give out about my granny, but I really love her too.

Was just texting Lucy, Rebecca and Hot Gay Brendan there. Lucy wants us to go over to hers and mourn and have, like, a moment for the anniversary of this rapper guy called Biggie Smalls who was shot, like, dead in 1997. I think he's called the Notorious BIG too, I'm really confused by all these rappers and the names they give each other. There was nothing 'Biggie Smalls' about that rapper either, he was obese with a capital O. The people who shot him had an easy target. He was shot in LA. I've never been to America, but it does sound glamorous.

Since the pregnancy scare, Lucy seems to have shifted her musical interests from dance music and transferred it onto rap. I was in her bedroom the other day and she has replaced her posters with ones of Eminem, Nelly and Puff Daddy, and she's taken to wearing a bandana like that guy Tupac Shakur. The way

I look at it is, may she be into anyone and anything that stops her from getting pregnant and focuses her on her Leaving Cert. She wouldn't divulge her mock results and changed the subject by saying that we should try and get in contact with the spirit of the Notorious BIG by playing his songs and asking him to send us a sign that he was listening to us. Thankfully, Hot Gay Brendan told her to fuck off.

Then Rebecca went and floored us all by telling us she got 550 points in the mocks but that she's really upset because it isn't enough for Medicine and she's stressed because she put so much pressure on herself because she really wants to save people's lives in the future. Then she started crying and the Biggie Smalls song 'Hypnotize', which was playing on Lucy's CD player, began to skip and we all freaked out because Lucy decided to declare that Biggie Smalls was in fact in the room with us, and the whole situation was just so ridiculous that we all started laughing, even Rebecca. I think for a few minutes we all forgot about stressed we were about the Leaving Cert and how worried we all are about the future.

Goodnight Dear Diary,
Love,
Ciara X

Prayers of the Unfaithful

Dear Diary,

I have spent most of Easter stuffing my face with Easter eggs. I had three of my own – a Flake one, a Kit Kat one, and a really posh After Eight one which must have cost an absolute fortune, but Granny won some money on the bingo and wanted to splash out. It's the most extravagant Easter egg I've ever eaten, but even after that, I started on my brother's eggs. Which he keeps in the fridge to give them 'that extra kick', seemingly. People are so weird.

I have turned into Fatty McFatterson, which is great because it means that after the Easter holidays not only will I be fat, but I'll be thick as shit too. I can't seem to concentrate on getting information on theorems or equations or diagrams into my goddamn head. I went on the computer earlier to print stuff off, and I ended up just playing solitaire for an hour.

Granny was a great distraction over Easter too. She rocked into the house distraught at the fact that the Queen Mother was dead. The Queen of England's mother died. Which raises the question how come she was never Queen? The monarchy in the UK is a strange thing. Granny says they are all inbred and that a corgi isn't even a real dog. Granny is a funny one, she does nothing but give out about the English, nearly vomits when she hears 'God Save the Queen', but she is just fascinated with the royal family. She made me hold her hand all throughout Princess Diana's funeral on the TV and kept wiping away tears from her eyes, and she seemed to be delighted at the fact that I was crying too, which I totally was because I, like, LOVED Princess Diana.

Oh God, I wonder is she going to make me sit through the funeral of the Queen Mother with her too. I don't know much about her bar the fact she was 101 years of age! Imagine living to be 101! Imagine all the things you would have seen and all the historical events you would have witnessed? The only things I can remember aren't even that great. I can barely remember Italia 90. There was Dustin's first appearance on *The Den*, and the time two men nearly shifted the faces off each other on *Fair City* in 1996. I remember that specifically because Granny's mouth dropped so far open in shock that her false teeth nearly came out, and we all thought it was hilarious. It was the first time that anything like that was shown on Irish TV.

Hot Gay Brendan reckons that we would all find it really weird if we were to see him shifting someone. We told him in no uncertain terms to get over himself. I don't know the science behind it, but men's tongues are bigger than female tongues, so I can imagine there would be a lot of gagging. Anyway, I've seen Rebecca shift Johnny Limp, and they looked like two animals featuring in a David Attenborough wildlife documentary wrestling with each other before fornication. So, honestly, if I were to see Hot Gay Brendan shifting another guy, it couldn't be half as gross as watching Rebecca and Johnny Limp maul each other.

Anyway, none of that compares to the time that Granny watched this woman called Annie Murphy on *The Late Late Show*. Seemingly she had had a baby with Bishop Casey which everyone was like 'Oh my God' about. Granny spent the duration of the interview shouting 'Lying Yank' at the TV and at one stage got so bad that my father had to tell her to calm down. I remember she said that interview ruined bingo for her for the whole weekend. Although I'm not quiet sure what Annie Murphy did to her personally. If I was being honest, I'd imagine Granny and her old lady friends were probably jealous. Maybe that's why older women are fascinated by priests and bishops and clergymen. Maybe because nabbing a priest would be the ultimate goal for all those so-called Holy Joes. Think about it, they are some of the most important people in the parish, they have a constant supply of wine, they have their own house, they have a direct line to the pope and God is their boss – and that's a powerful boss in fairness. They're always attending events all over the parish and I'm pretty sure, although not certain, that they can drink and drive.

Maybe I'm just after uncovering the number one fantasy of Irish women. Priests don't do it for me I'm afraid. I'm not a fan of the preaching or the rig-outs, and the gossip, I'd imagine there would be a LOT of gossip about you.

Anyway, back to the historical events that I have witnessed. I think I vaguely remember people crowding around the TV and getting excited over some wall that was demolished, I'm not sure, but I think it was the Berlin Wall and had something to do with Germany. Then of course there was the death of Princess Diana, the death of Mother Teresa and lately the breakup of Dane Bowers from Another Level and the glamour model Jordan. 9/11 of course is in there too. The time Mary Robinson was on *The Den* – that was cool. I'm sure there's something about Nelson Mandela being freed too, mad cow disease, Harry Potter, Tiger Woods winning everything in golf, Bill Clinton being peached, loads of people from Nigeria moving to Ireland, loads of people from Poland moving to Ireland, Sonia O'Sullivan winning everything. Actually Dear Diary, I'd be here all day if I was to go through absolutely everything that has ever happened.

God, if I lived to 101, I'd be exhausted. You'd get to see the good stuff, but you'd also have to see all the bad stuff too. Like, Katie Price was SO upset over her breakup with Dane Bowers from Another Level, she's even started some beef with Victoria

Beckham because Dane worked with her on that song 'Out of Your Mind'. I guess she really loved him. Speaking of love, Danny has started putting 'luv you' at the end of text messages followed by smiley winky faces. I'm like, well does he or not? Is he saying 'I love you Ciara', or is it more, 'I luv you maybe, haha, wink wink'? I've just sent back ditto like Demi Moore and Patrick Swayze in the movie *Ghost*, and then I put loads of kisses at the end, so he knows how much I love him back.

It's frustrating not seeing him that much, but he's doing an Easter revision course in Galway, so he's seriously concentrating on that. He said some of the lads from the course are going out tonight in Galway to have a few drinks, but he's not going to bother, which is cool, because I'm not going to lie, I'd have been totally jealous for the night. We all know what Galway city girls are like too, and they would totally try to get their claws into my Danny. I just know it, and he's such a nice guy that he would talk to them just to be nice, and they might see it as a sign and go in for the kill and then Danny would accidently end up kissing someone and then it would be awkward. Maybe I'm thinking about this too much ...

Oh my God! Danny just texted. He's going out with the lads tonight. My life is OVER.

Goodnight Dear Diary,
Love,
Ciara X

'Why do you have to go and make things so complicated?'

Dear Diary,

Spring has finally sprung, and along with all the flowers blooming and sheep having lambs and birds having sex with each other, I'm having a bit of a spring awakening myself. I always feel a strange melancholic feeling in my brain around this time of year. It's like I actually have to start making an effort, there's a grand stretch in the evenings as my father says, the sun is kinda out, leaves are growing on the trees, blah, blah, blah.

I have to come out of hibernation, when I don't really want to, I want to stay with the other bears in the cave and NEVER emerge to have to deal with the human population ever OR study for my Leaving Cert. But I guess I wasn't born that lucky.

I feel like comparing myself to a daffodil right now. It's their time of year to be at their most glorious, more than ALL the other flowers. And maybe Dear Diary, just maybe it's my time to bloom and be glorious over all the other flowers in my life. And for once I'm not talking about my boobs (SIGH).

I'm sitting here listening to Avril Lavigne's 'Complicated', which genuinely is, like, the soundtrack of my teenage years. Everything seems completely complicated. Life is complicated. School is complicated, my relationships are complicated. My parents won't get off my back telling me to study, the teachers won't get off my case telling me to study, Rebecca is constantly worrying am I studying more than her, I'm worrying about the fact that Lucy doesn't show any signs of studying, and Danny must be studying REALLY hard as I haven't heard from him in two days. And I know he has credit on his phone because he bought some on Monday, and it's only Tuesday now, there's no way he spent 10 euro on pay-as-you-go phone credit in less than 24 hours. Unless he's texting someone else. But all I know is, he's not texting me.

Maybe it's a good thing. Maybe if we break up, I can give 100% of my full concentration to the Leaving Cert. Maybe I'm not really into him any more. Maybe he's not into me any more.

I know what I'm going to do to settle this, I'm going to write up a list of pros and cons as to why me and Danny should still be together.

This is the closest I've ever felt to being like Eminem in my WHOLE life, because it's like I'm metaphorically 'spring cleanin' out my closet'. Okay, I'm going to start with the cons just to get them out of the way. Here goes:

- *Sometimes he gets snot bubbles in his nose and doesn't notice; at the start I thought it was cute, but now, not so much. Now I'm consumed by the fact of whether or not he'll have a snot bubble when I see him next. Once he had a snot bubble in the cinema and it literally ruined* Ocean's Eleven *for me.*
- *Playing video games with him isn't all that fun, as he can be really competitive and will never help me get through the last level of Crash Bandicoot.*
- *He calls his mother 'Mammy'. I also don't think she likes me. I think he's too close to her and that it's weird for a teenage boy to be that close to their mother, and once I'm nearly sure he kissed her on the lips which is gross. I'm supposed to be shifting him, not his mother.*
- *He talks about some day getting a tattoo of the Tasmanian devil from the cartoon on his bicep because that would be, in*

his words, 'badass'. He's couldn't even pick out Tasmania on a map.

- He puts too much mayonnaise and ketchup on everything. Even toasted cheese sandwiches! I blame his mother for that one.

- He never watched Glenroe growing up and doesn't know what Arthur's mail bag is, I mean COME ON.

- Sometimes when he says he wants to talk about his feelings, it doesn't mean talking about his feelings about us, and every time I get excited but he ends up talking about his feelings about how Liverpool are doing in the league and how much he's looking forward to the World Cup. And then when he's in, like, really bad form and says he REALLY needs someone to talk to, he'll just tell me that he's feeling sad about all eight of the Man United players and three club officials that died in the Munich air disaster in 1958. It's actually kind of morbid.

- He's kind of into love songs, but not cool love songs like Tracy Chapman's 'Fast Car' or John Lennon's 'Woman'. He likes weird ones like Martine McCutcheon's 'Perfect Moment' and Kate Winslet's 'What If'. He knows all the words! I used to think it was endearing, but now I think it's weird. Like, is this normal?

- Sometimes his Dubarry shoes annoy me. I don't know exactly what it is about them in particular, but they annoy me. Maybe it's just the way he walks.

- His hilarious stories about the lads farting in the club-house after GAA training aren't even that hilarious. I've also heard the 'better not drop the soap' joke in the shower like a million times now.

- I don't know whether he is joking or not, but he refuses to let me say the name Voldemort and insists on making me say 'He who shall not be named' as he's superstitious about a fictional series of books involving a boy wizard.

- *He was once with a bunch of lads that went up to the actor who plays Father Jack in* Father Ted *and said 'Drink! Feck! Arse!' to his face, and claims that it was the funniest moment of his life.*
- *He keeps talking about going over to his brother in Australia after the Leaving Cert.*
- *He literally has not, and I mean HAS NOT, made any attempt to have sex with me and help me lose my virginity. SO selfish.*

Okay, that's the entire list of bad ones I can think of right now. I think it's time to think of the good ones.

- *He's, like, a really good kisser, and I mean like a REALLY good kisser. As Lucy always says, 'When he kisses you, he needs to make your fanny feel funny.' And I guess he does Dear Diary. I guess he does.*
- *He's really smart, like, really smart. He knows the periodic table off by heart and is even doing Physics for the Leaving Cert! I mean, who does Physics if they don't have to?*
- *He's really hot when he pulls up in his mother's car to collect me, and then I get into the car and I can smell a mixture of his Lynx and his aftershave all in one and it makes my fanny feel funny all over again.*
- *We both like Supermac's which is really important in ANY relationship in my view.*
- *I like the way that he texts me good night and signs it off with a stupid smiley winky face and like a million kisses.*
- *I like how he supports my decision to write strongly worded letters to Irish newspapers when I feel angry about something, and then consoles me when they are not printed yet again, and he always says, 'Next time, you'll have it printed next time.'*

- *He doesn't seem to mind my obsession with celebrity couples and how upset I feel when they break up, but also joins in my celebrations when they get back together.*
- *I enjoy our stupid in-jokes, like when he pretends to be John Lennon and I pretend to be Yoko Ono, and he does a stupid Liverpool accent and I do an impression of Yoko Ono, and then he says he completely understands when I get upset all over again about the fact that John Lennon is dead.*
- *I like how when he comes over to my house on a Saturday, he'll sit there patiently drinking tea with my granny watching Winning Streak, and how he always agrees with Granny when she says that Derek Mooney is a poor man's Mike Murphy.*
- *I like his laugh. His laugh makes me laugh.*
- *I like how when I'm bitching about Lucy, Rebecca and Hot Gay Brendan, he never ever says anything bad about them, because it's okay for me to give out about them, but not him, as they are MY friends at the end of the day.*
- *He genuinely does a really good impression of Jason McAteer.*
- *He doesn't judge me when I say that I think that Dean Cain is a better Superman than Christopher Reeve, even though I feel really mean saying that because Christopher Reeve is in a wheelchair and it's, like, really sad.*
- *He doesn't make a big deal about the fact that I am a virgin and probably will be for the rest of my life or definitely until after the Leaving Cert anyway.*

That's it Dear Diary, reading over those last few reasons, maybe I don't want me and Danny to break up. Oh God, I hope HE doesn't want to break up. What if he wants to break up? Oh my God, I'll actually send myself over to the Netherlands, where I saw on the *Six One News* that they have just legalised euthanasia, or I'll end up doing a Winona Ryder on it and go on a shoplifting spree and get arrested because let's be honest, she never really recovered after splitting with Johnny Depp, which is really sad. Again, life: why do you have to go and make things so complicated?

Goodnight Dear Diary,
Love,
Ciara X

Would you Rather: Saddam or Osama?

Dear Diary,

How are you? It's just me, Ciara. The same old same old. I've been thinking a lot about you lately. You know all my secrets and about all the embarrassing things that have ever happened me. Which is LOADS in fairness. You know about my entire heartbreak over boys, my constant struggle for my boobs to finally grow, my thoughts and feelings on being very good at being a virgin and about all my feelings to do with God and how I'm dubious about that whole Virgin Mary story. AND you know how worried I am about the Leaving Cert and the future. BUT, I got to thinking, I've never stopped and asked you how YOU are Dear Diary.

Sometimes I think you might need to go to a see a therapist like that Tony Soprano guy from *The Sopranos* after all the stuff that I have told you in the past. But then I remember that you are just pages with writing on it and not a real person and I feel like a dope, but in fairness, these pages are laden down with the melancholy of my teens, so much more than Anne Frank at this stage. She is always someone that I have looked up to and identified with, but at this stage, my diary is, like, better than hers. I'm not being whatever, but she literally just wrote in a diary for two years, she was bored in that annex and had nothing else to do. I've been writing in my diary now for years and you don't see me being hailed as a voice of a generation.

Life is so unfair, it's like if I wasn't a teenager really struggling with death and war then my diaries are worthless. At this stage, Ireland would want to have another famine in 2002 with people starving on the streets and jumping on boats to go to America for my diaries to mean anything, OR I'll have to have to come out and say that I had an inappropriate relationship with a priest when I was an altar girl for my diary to make a name for itself.

So Dear Diary I popped into the local church after school the last day. There was no one in there, and if I'm being honest, it was kind of scary being in an empty church on my own. I went up to light a candle and, like, say a prayer for my Leaving Cert and the Irish team going to the World Cup, and I thought in my head that would give God enough time to send me a message or, like, appear in front of me if he wanted to, but there was no sign of him. So I lit another candle, but didn't have any more money on me, so then I felt guilty as sin, and started freaking out that God is probably going to punish me by making me fail my Leaving Cert and that something awful will happen the Irish football team when they go over to Saipan, so I couldn't think clearly.

As I was sitting in the empty church though, a story my granny told me began to freak me out, so I had to leave. I don't know why she told me this story because I was only a child, and she should have been shipped off to child abuse services for telling me in the first place, but she said when coffins are left in the church overnight after a removal, that some priests have reported lights going on and off in the church, and that one time a priest went over to check what was going on and saw the coffin on the wheeled cart going up and down the aisle of the church of its own accord! So I got out of there quicker than lads pull out of Lucy.

Then I got home and my parents were wrecking my head giving out about this new plastic bag levy that the government have imposed since March. Fifteen cent is going to break the bank seemingly. Mum was just pissed off as she forgot to take her canvas shopping bags with her doing the weekly shopping and she ended up having to fork out over a euro for plastic bags to carry all the shopping, and she says that the government are robbing people blind left, right and centre, and if she could get her hands on Bertie Ahern, she wouldn't be responsible for what she would say to him. She then started banging on about the environment and how plastic bags like that take over 500 years to disintegrate, and how many animals are going to suffer because of it. Sometimes she kinda reminds me of Saddam Hussein when she goes off on a rant about the government or a guest that has annoyed her on *The Late Late Show*, and quite frankly Dear Diary, it's like being ruled by the Taliban.

Speaking of Saddam Hussein, I was looking at the news earlier, and the news reporter was talking about how Tony Blair is saying that Saddam Hussein is a threat, and I was thinking in my own head, ummm, what about Osama bin Laden?! Still on the loose, rocking around, hiding out, having a great time for himself. Saddam Hussein is like a kitten in comparison to him. If I had to choose between marrying either Osama bin Laden or Saddam Hussein, I think I'd definitely pick Saddam Hussein. Firstly, Osama bin Laden's beard is just too much, and who knows what he is hiding underneath that turban, like, does he even wash his hair?! Also, he's one of the most wanted men in the world, and for some girls, that might be hot, but not for this girl. Is it weird that I think there's something kinda cute about Saddam Hussein? I like the way he rocks that moustache and that little hat if I'm being honest, AND he lives in a palace, which would be cool, and WAY better than hanging out in caves in Afghanistan. I think it's fair to say that Saddam is WAY more popular than Osama bin Laden at the moment too. There's something exotic about those two men, like, compared to Tony Blair and Bertie Ahern.

If I had to choose between either marrying Bertie Ahern or Tony Blair, I would probably choose Bertie Ahern, and it simply comes down to the ears. Tony Blair's ears are ridiculous; you could take him flying with those ears. Bertie has nice ears in fairness to him. Add to that the fact that you could get to hang out with Nicky Byrne from Westlife and probably get free tickets to all their concerts, and I'm team Bertie all the way.

Just got off the phone to Rebecca, she's seriously stressed and has said that she has taken to listening to Six's 'Whole Lotta Lovin'' on repeat on her CD player when she's in her room trying to concentrate on studying. It's a seriously good song in fairness that it hasn't been off the radio now in, like, two months! I've been trying to de-stress by listening to more R & B stuff that Lucy recommended, so I've been listening to Fat Joe and Ashanti's 'What's Luv', which is an awesome track. What's funny is that Fat Joe is actually fat, so it's funny that he's actually called that. A lot of these rappers could do with going to Weight Watchers down the local parish hall on a Friday if you know what I mean, even Missy Elliot who I LOVE, but she has some serious junk in her trunk. The only one who doesn't is Eminem, BUT he should consider a few sessions on the sun beds or definitely take himself off for a week in Lanzarote to put a bit of colour into those pale cheeks.

Danny has been texting me loads this week which is cool too. I've decided that we shouldn't break up, it's just too much hassle before the Leaving Cert and the World Cup, and so I've put it to the back of my mind for now. He's really excited because Paul McCartney from the Beatles is getting married in June in Monaghan in a castle to some model called Heather Mills, I think she might only have one leg or something, but anyway, he says he doesn't care that the Leaving Cert is on, and the World Cup, but that we HAVE to go to Monaghan to try and catch a glimpse of Paul McCartney. I'm like, 'Okay', but there's not a chance I'm going to Monaghan. It's at the other end of the country; it might even take days to get there! I'm not that big a fan even! Although I would be curious to see how Heather Mills manages a wedding dress with just one leg.

Anyway, I'm going to retire for the night from war-torn Connemara! Hahahahahaha!

Goodnight Dear Diary,
Love,
Ciara X

RIP TLC

Dear Diary,

I am literally so upset, I am in shock, I can't believe what I've read, I can't believe it. I haven't been able to concentrate on anything at all. I can't believe that I'm about to write this, but through the tears dripping down my face and my broken heart Dear Diary, I can reveal to you the harrowing news that Lisa 'Left Eye' Lopes from TLC is dead. She is dead. Like Princess Diana dead. Like Mother Teresa dead, like Anne Frank dead, like Joan of Arc dead. She has croaked it, she is a dead as a dodo, she is joining rappers Biggy Smalls and Tupac in the sky, she has given up the ghost, and she is outta here.

She died in a car crash last night in Honduras, wherever that even is. I'm stunned. TLC are, like, the coolest band from my generation. I know they haven't really had any singles out lately, but TLC will always and for ever be *CrazySexyCool* for God's sake. My heart is going out to Chilli and T-Boz, it would be like if something happened to Rebecca and Lucy and they died. I would literally be SO heartbroken. Out of me, Rebecca and Lucy, Rebecca would be T-Boz, I would be Chilli and Lucy would be Lisa 'Left Eye' Lopes, because in fairness, she has the biggest attitude out of all of us. TLC are like Destiny's Child and the Spice Girls put together, only EVEN cooler. These are the girls that wore condoms on their clothes to promote safe sex; these are the girls that wrote 'Waterfalls', the song that teenagers all over the world have cried to! These are the girls who created girl power before the Spice Girls even knew what it was.

Lisa 'Left Eye' Lopes is the girl who lived up to her nickname by wearing a pair of glasses with the left lens covered with a condom AND she started wearing a black stripe under her left eye AND she even got her left eyebrow pierced, which is, like, beyond cool and dedicated. I know she once accidentally burnt down the house of her ex-boyfriend because she set his runners on fire in a bath, but that was a total accident and people make mistakes, like, ALL the time. It's weird, because the last song she did with Mel C from the Spice Girls seems eerily like real life today after hearing the news, because things will literally 'Never Be the Same Again'.

I was telling Mum and Dad about being really upset over her death and they said they remembered the day that Elvis died, MY GOD they are literally ancient. Elvis must be dead like 100 years at this stage, and also, WHO CARES? They also remembered the day Freddie Mercury from Queen died, but I'm sorry, it's not the same thing because Elvis died on a toilet from eating too many burgers and Freddie Mercury had the AIDS, so for Lisa 'Left Eye' Lopes to die in a car crash is way, way more dramatic in my opinion. Ugh, they just don't get it. They just don't understand the influence she has had on my young teenage mind. They don't understand what her music and the music of TLC has contributed to modern-day society. Why don't adults understand it? Were they ever even young?!

All I know is that it's got me thinking about death AGAIN Dear Diary. What if I were to die in a car crash tomorrow like Lisa 'Left Eye' Lopes? What regrets would I have? I'll tell you what the main regret would be, and I think you'll know what that is before I even write it. It's the fear of never getting the ride. Pure and simple.

In one way, there would be benefits to me leaving this world and going to heaven a virgin, I mean it's worked out well for the

Virgin Mary, she's like a celebrity virgin, but I'm a legit virgin and, well, it remains to be seen whether she is or not. It also means I would go straight past St Peter at the pearly gates, who would probably high five me on the way in and lead me to the VIP area where all the other angels hang out. But in another way, I would have to live for all of eternity not knowing what it is actually like to NOT have a hymen. I doubt that people have sex in heaven; it doesn't seem like a heavenly thing to do, does it? Unless of course G to the O to the D is having a great time for himself, riding all around him like it's the Rose of Tralee festival every day up there. But I doubt it. It's a scary thought all the same. I wonder do they have sex down in hell, or is it too hot? I do have a thing for a bad boy so maybe that is where I actually belong Dear Diary. SIGH.

I know that this is, like, a really deep, philosophical topic to be thinking about right now when I should really be focusing on studying for my Leaving Cert and other teenage things like watching *The Osbournes*, which is supposed to be this cool new show on MTV where there are cameras inside Ozzy Osbourne's house and you get to see what him and his family get up to all the time, but I just can't seem to focus. Lisa 'Left Eye' Lopes is dead you know.

On a side note, if anyone has a direct line to hell, it's Ozzy Osbourne. My dad told me that he once ripped off the head of a dove and spat it out with blood still dripping from his lips and everything. He is legitimately the Prince of Darkness. Bet he's not a virgin though. So unfair.

And I'm also angry, because Danny came around after he heard that I was upset about Lisa, and we went for a spin in his car, where we listened to the *CrazySexyCool* album, and, like, put 'Creep' on replay. But then things got weird because I swear to God Dear Diary, didn't he only go and get, like, an erection when we were sitting there talking about Lisa 'Left Eye' Lopes dying. It's not that he was turned on by her dying, because that would be weird, but I think it was the fact that I kinda blurted out to him that I was afraid to die a virgin, and basically suggested that we have sex soon and stop this messing around because I couldn't risk not having sex as I could be dead tomorrow. I think the emotions of the whole day just came to a boil to make me so bold as to say it outright. Danny's never even touched my boob from the inside, I mean what was I thinking. I just blurted it out, then couldn't stop talking.

But then he went and got an erection, and I kinda freaked out because honestly I thought my hand was resting on the gear stick, and then it turns out it wasn't the gear stick, but a human erection, and things just got weird.

I mean there was no need for that. In fairness to him, he told me he had no control over it and that it just happens, especially when the topic of sex comes up. Well happen sometime else, not when I'm mourning the death of a singing/rapping icon. God, men are SO inconsiderate. Anyway, he just dropped me home and things were weird getting out of the car, and he was quiet and so was I, and I wanted to tell him that it was okay that he had had an erection, and if it was any other day that the day that Lisa 'Left Eye' Lopes had passed away, then it would have been okay, but, UGH, it's just a mess. And I'm embarrassed. And I want to die, but like, not die a virgin at the same time.

I can't even write any more cause I'm cringing so much. God, I hate myself and I hate bloody erections too!

Goodnight Dear Diary,
Love,
Ciara X

'Léigh anois go cúramach'

Dear Diary,

It's May! When did it suddenly become May? I'm not ready for it to be May! It's like the whole school year has gone in the blink of an eye, and now suddenly, before I know it it's going to be Wednesday June 5th and I'm going to have to face the hardest task of my life. I've just done some calculations and I nearly got a little bit sick in my mouth. 33 days to go. 33 days to go. That's 792 hours, I think, I've never been any good at Maths, but that doesn't seem like a very long time. 792 hours. I've contemplated spending the next 792 hours awake and studying so as to make up for the lack of other hours that I haven't spent studying the whole school year. Rebecca says I'll die if I do that, and to be honest Dear Diary, death might not be a bad thing at this stage.

I don't think I'm ready to do my Leaving Cert. I'm thinking of telling my parents that I might repeat, which might seem ridiculous because I haven't even sat my Leaving Cert yet, but honestly I think it's one of the best ideas I've had in all my teenage years. Or else I could fake an illness, a really bad one like AIDS or something, OR maybe I'll get pregnant, YES, and then say I can't sit my exams because I'm suffering really bad morning sickness and OH, I'll say that the father is one of the married teachers at the school, and I'm finding it all really traumatic and stuff. I can do this. I can pull this off right?! Who am I kidding!

I mean, I'm not ready. My nails have been bitten down to the very last, I mostly just sit in my room staring at my books and instead of studying them, thinking about all the subjects that

I haven't studied yet, and then I go to myself 'OH MY GOD, THIS ISN'T HAPPENING, PLEASE HELP ME JESUS.'

I've also been having this really weird recurring dream too for the past few nights. I'm sitting in an exam hall about to do my first exam, and the man's voice from the Irish aural starts playing, and the hall is filled with 'LÉIGH ANOIS GO CÚRAMACH AR DO SCRÚDPHÁIPÉAR NA TREORACHA AGUS NA CEISTEANNA A GHABHANN LE CUID A.' I'm surrounded by all the people in my year, and I'm panicking, but then I look up and see that Seamus Heaney is the examiner and he smiles down at me, and I feel calm, for literally five seconds before his face morphs into Ophelia from *Hamlet*, and she's crying and pointing at me, and then I realise that I am naked and everyone is laughing and pointing at me, then suddenly I'm gone from the exam room and I'm stranded on top of a drumlin in the middle of nowhere, and I can't get off, and I keep screaming about glaciation, but there is no one around to hear me. But suddenly a boat appears, and it's called the *Titanic*, and Lucy, Rebecca and Hot Gay Brendan are on board, but the only way they'll let me on the boat is if I recite Pythagoras' theorem, and I can't remember it, and they all start laughing like EVIL hyenas and tell me that I can't get on the boat, and that I'm going to fail my Leaving Cert. The next thing I know, Richard Branson appears from behind and shouts, 'YOU KNOW NOTHING ABOUT THE INDUSTRIAL RELATIONS ACT 1990!' and then pushes me off the drumlin, and I'm falling and falling, and all I see around me on the way down are ox bow lakes, and cirques and U-shaped valleys, and just before I hit the ground I wake up, covered in sweat, with my heart beating and with such a sense of fear and anger, ESPECIALLY at Richard Branson because he is, like, my favourite entrepreneur, and I said if I was to EVER leave this godforsaken country that I would almost ALWAYS fly

Virgin Airlines, well now he can go screw himself, the prick.

I also think a massive part of this is that I'm not ready to fly the nest, I'm scared about the future and having to move to a city. Like, I live in a village that literally has one road and a mountain, maybe I'm not cut out for all the cosmopolitan life in the big city. What if I have to end up sharing a house with strangers and they're total weirdos, what if I don't have an electric blanket in my new room, what happens if I, like, get scared in the middle of the night because I can hear police sirens going by because someone else has been murdered in the city. What if I end up getting murdered because I'm followed home at night after staying late in college to study, like I'm totally going to do, because there is an awful lot of studying involved if you do Arts in NUI Galway seemingly.

Me, Rebecca, Lucy and Hot Gay Brendan all pinky sweared with each other that we would move in together in a house if we all got the points for NUI Galway. We've even thought about how we are going to decorate our new place too. Well, we've mostly just talked about the different posters that we are going to place all around the house in different rooms, and about how we are going to get a glittery toilet seat for the bathroom. I opted for the classic black and white Audrey Hepburn poster where she's smoking that long cigarette in *Breakfast at Tiffany's*, Hot Gay Brendan because of his new found OBSESSION with Peter Andre circa his 'Mysterious Girl' days has decided on him, Rebecca has picked some shit from *Star Wars* that none of us understand, and Lucy has chosen either an old Godskitchen poster or Creamfields. She can't decide what's cooler. Or she might opt for her black and white Tupac Shakur one for diversity's sake.

She said that we need to decorate our place perfectly so that when people come back to ours for parties that we need to look like we are cultured and cool and down for whatever. Which I totally am by the way.

She said that in her brother's place (that's her brother who dry humped me with his erection by the way) they have a Che Guevara one, and another that says 'Beer, getting people laid since 1892', which is historically incorrect, because there's no way that beer was available back then. And seemingly in their kitchen they have a black and white poster of two girls kissing in bed. I don't know why but when I heard this I got a bit jealous, like, I haven't seen Lucy's brother in AGES, and we don't even mention him because Lucy was so thick with me when I scored him and didn't talk to me for AGES, but in fairness, I think it's because he is one of the first people to ever dry hump me, so obviously we have a connection of some sort, and those sort of intimate connections don't go away that easily Dear Diary, especially when your own boyfriend hasn't even tried to dry hump you EVER.

I always get a bit nostalgic when I see a dog dry humping the leg of a chair or the carpet or something, because it always reminds in a cute way of Lucy's brother.

Anyway, Lucy also said that we should throw some posters of dead celebrities into the mix, like Marilyn Monroe. I personally think I covered that with my black and white poster of Audrey Hepburn, but they are always a winner seemingly. Here is Lucy's list SO FAR. She has put WAY too much thought into this:

- *Poster of James Dean looking cool and smoking a cigarette.*
- *Kurt Cobain Nirvana one, which is, like, sad because he is dead now too.*
- *A* Simpsons *poster involving Homer but NOT Bart because we are too old for Bart now.*
- *A movie poster like* Fight Club *or* Scarface *(preferably* Scarface *because Al Pacino is, like, an acting legend).*

- *The famous poster of the men all sitting on the skyscraper having lunch, it's a nod to our Irish-American connections seemingly.*
- *The one with the woman in the bandana who has her sleeve rolled up saying 'We can do it!' because we are feisty females seemingly, and we SO can.*
- *Vincent van Gogh's* The Starry Night *because we look like we know art and are cultured.*
- *A poster of different beers from around the world, again so that we look cultured.*
- *Che Guevara, who is already mentioned, but Lucy reckons it will make us look politically aware or some shit.*
- *A funny Alien one that says 'Take me to your dealer', even though none of us smoke weed, not even Lucy, but she says she might take it back up if she gets to college.*
- *A poster of the Irish football team that played at the World Cup, because we're not going to win but we need to look like we support our country. (I personally think a topless one of our leader Roy Keane would do, but Hot Gay Brendan says it doesn't exist because he has looked.)*
- *A* Pulp Fiction *poster with John Travolta and Samuel L. Jackson.*
- *A poster of Bob Marley looking slightly to the left (again with the weed).*
- *A poster of the New York skyline.*
- *A poster of Einstein with his tongue out (which Rebecca is insisting on, not Lucy, as she has no idea who he is).*

And finally, Lucy says we need this next one in order to look smart, edgy and also like people that are really likely to 'put out after a night out':

- *'The Periodic Table of Sex', which is supposed to be the periodic table of elements I think, except it's, like, 58 positions that people can actually have sex in, and there's all these little cartoon characters in all sorts of different positions doing ridiculous things to each other.*

I don't know am I comfortable with that last one Dear Diary, I didn't even know that that there were that many ways to actually have sex to be fair. But there's the list. If anything it has given me the motivation to study now, as I REALLY want to live in a cool house with my best friends covered in cool posters!

Going to bed happier now,

Goodnight Dear Diary,
Love,
Ciara X

More Stress, Less Success

Dear Diary,

I can barely muster the energy to write this. I'm exhausted and my pen is just about managing to write these words across the page. It is now only 18 days until the Leaving Cert. The big LC. That is literally 432 hours. The day of reckoning is creeping up on my poor weary teenage soul. I feel in one way like all of those Irish emigrants who hopped on board the famine ships and headed for a new life in America. The journeys that these poor people on the famine ships took has been very like my journey towards my Leaving Cert over the past few months. A journey that has had ups and downs, the element of uncertainty about whether or not we'd actually make it, sailing through the turbulent seas of teenage life, then finally arriving tired, starving and half dead to what would be Ellis Island. Then there's actually making it off Ellis Island, some did and some didn't. I need to get off Ellis Island Dear Diary. I need to make it through quarantine and start a new adventure and life in New York City. Except in my case, it will probably be Galway City if I get enough points for Arts in NUI Galway.

I'm sitting here with the words of Eavan Boland and Seamus Heaney swirling through my head, I'm at the stage where I'm beginning to forget who wrote what. 'A Constable Calls', 'The Skunk', 'The Tollund Man', 'Child of Our Time', 'The Black Lace Fan My Mother Gave Me'. I've tried to break it down for myself and remember that Heaney writes about a skunk, a constable and a dead man found in a bog, and then I try to memorise that Boland wrote about a child, a black lace fan, and the Famine, which I'm obviously a big fan of, but I have to remember that it's also about like a woman being infertile and stuff.

There's actually too much stuff to remember. I don't know if I'm going to chance just learning off two poets but then I freak out and think what if Seamus Heaney doesn't come up on English Paper 2, but he has to right? He just has to. He seems like such a nice man, there is NO way that he wouldn't come up, that would actually be REALLY mean to all the teenagers in the country who have learned off his poetry by heart, and I don't think that he is a mean person because his poetry is SO lovely, even if he did write a sexy love poem involving a stinky skunk about his wife.

Biology revision is also causing me to hyperventilate. I have had to practise spelling monosaccharide and polysaccharide so much that I'm so freaked about spelling them that I don't even know what they mean. So I'm trying to teach myself these terms in relation to stress. So basically, I'm stressed about the Leaving Cert which means I'm either going to have an anabolic reaction or catabolic reaction, and neither of those sound good to me Dear Diary. One thing I have noticed about Biology is that there are loads of 'isms'. Too many. It's too late for me to do anything about it now, but I feel a strongly worded letter to the *Irish Times* coming on. Like seriously, tropism, phototropism, geotropism, hydrotropism, and all they really mean is a plant's reaction to stupid shit, which, unless I decide to become a gardener, isn't going to exactly help me in life is it?

The only term that's making ANY sense to me of course is 'sexual reproduction' which in Biology terms is defined as 'the union of two sex gametes'. I wouldn't mind being involved in the union of two sex gametes if you know what I mean Dear Diary. Lucy says that I should just do it before my Leaving Cert, that it would relax me and help me focus, but I think it would have the opposite effect. I think I'd spend most of the time beforehand having a panic attack wondering if my area looks okay down there, and would I do it right, like guide it into the right hole, because I'm fairly sure there's more than one down there, and what if Danny noticed my wonky boob, because I'm fairly sure one is bigger than the other at the minute, but I'm putting it down to the stress of revision and LIFE. And what about after, I'd probably fret over whether or not I actually did it right. So bearing all of that in mind, while at the same time trying to study and remember all these different terms, I'd probably have a heart attack and die.

One minor distraction is the fact that we have our graduation Mass coming up soon. It's where the entire student body from our year goes, and the teachers and the parents will gather and basically tell us how great we all are and pat us on the back for actually getting to sixth year, and not dropping out after third year like most of the lads in my year. We'll sing emotional songs and pretend that we all really like each other even though you've been forcibly stuck in a class with knobheads that have annoyed you on a daily basis since first year, but there was nothing that anyone could do because these people were born in the eighties, and sadly, they were born around the same time as you. Teachers will pretend that they LOVE us all of a sudden, and try and act like they are our actual friends, even though we have scarred each other for life, and we have probably driven them to drink at one stage or another.

I'm sure they are only dying to get rid of us, and let the next cycle of potential victims take our place come September. And in they'll come, bright eyed and bushy tailed, fresh from the shelter of their primary school, equipped with new pens and pencils, and poly pockets up to their eyeballs. And folders, they'll all have cool folders and purchase a compass for the first time in their young lives and not EVER even use it in the six years that they go to school, unless they end up stabbing someone with it for the craic. They'll buy copious amounts of Tippex, and either end up sniffing it or painting their nails with it for years to come. The teachers will feel a renewed hope of potentially moulding the minds of these youthful eejits, but they'll fail with those ones too. It's just the circle of life.

Then the other half of my brain wonders do certain teachers get attached to us at all. I mean, I think I've been a really good student in fairness. They see us coming in the school gates, aged 12/13, underdeveloped, skinny, pale, awkward, scared, and see us leaving as fully breasted, competent adults at 18. They have been through all the bodily changes with us in one way. They've witnessed the spots and acne and hickeys which must be GROSS to have to look at constantly for six years, they've seen the growth spurts, both in height and in boobular and bulge-like areas if you know what I mean. They've observed the bad hairstyles, the piercings, the puppy fat, the tears, the nose bleeds, the smell of smoke, Impulse body spray and cheap pharmacy perfume.

God, maybe I'm actually beginning to realise that teachers can be human too, human beings with feelings and emotions and LIVES outside of school. Maybe, just maybe, someday in the future, when I'm walking down the street in my future life, holding a briefcase and walking in a pair of those shoes that Carrie Bradshaw is always banging on about in Sex and the City, I'll see one of my old teachers across the way, and they'll glance my way and their face will brighten and they will smile when they realise that it's me, their favourite student of all time, and we will embrace in an adult-type way, not in a weird way, and I'll softly whisper in their old hairy ear, 'Thank you,' and they will walk away with tears in their eyes thinking to themselves, 'There goes our biggest success story, I knew her. I taught her.' That's of course if I can actually bring myself to ever talk to any of them ever again, so we'll see.

Anyway, none of us might even show up to the graduation Mass because none of us can settle on a song to sing as our 'end of sixth year' song. We did a ballot box where it was passed around and people had to write down their preference for what song they might like. Some people are such idiots, but here is a brief list of what people were thinking:

- *The Beatles: 'Get By With a Little Help from My Friends', which I don't think is even a Beatles song and it's hilarious because only some of us are, like, really friends, but it reminds me of* The Wonder Years *with Kevin and Winnie, so it's cool.*
- *Sisqó's 'Thong Song', which most of the lads in our year voted for seemingly.*
- *Baz Luhrmann's 'Everybody's Free (To Wear Sunscreen)', which is cool and all but it's just mainly a man talking and that's not technically a song.*
- *Dido's 'Thank You', thanks for what like?!*
- *Vitamin C's 'Graduation (Friends Forever)', which is pretty apt in fairness, but not, like, classy enough in my opinion.*
- *Green Day's 'Good Riddance (Time Of Your Life)', but like, was it? Was it?*

I'm sure we'll pick one of them eventually, anyway, I'm SO tired now, so I'm signing off for now.

Goodnight Dear Diary,
Love,
Ciara X

The Early Purges

Dear Diary,

Sorry that I haven't written in a while, I've just been really busy nearly LOSING MY WILL TO LIVE and trying to cram in as much studying as was humanly possible. It's here. I am in the midst of things. All the nails bitten down to within an inch of their life, all the stress, all the anxiety, all the pain and suffering, it's here. I'm in the middle of my Leaving Cert. This is actual hell on earth. I now can sympathise with every other nation of people that I've seen on the *Six One News*. You know those people Dear Diary, the ones that stare with big sad eyes into the news cameras pleading to be taken away from their godforsaken lives in, like, Russia or China or somewhere shit like that. I now know how those people feel. If a news camera were to be put in my face right now, I'd do the same, I'd look into the camera, and be all like, 'Take me the hell away from here and this goddamn educational system and this sorry existence of a life.'

There must not be a candle left in the parish as I'd say well over a million were lit over the weekend for me according to my granny, who only the last day reminded me that although she would be asking the big man in the sky for help and guidance for me, she would be praying EXTRA hard for the Boys in Green over in Saipan. Looks like she didn't pray hard enough though, as you won't actually believe what happened. I can't believe that I am actually going to write these words, and I wouldn't be surprised if the pages of this diary were to somehow suddenly burst into flames when I write what I'm about to write, but here goes.

Roy Keane has left Saipan. He's gone. He's not the captain of the Irish football team any more and he is gone. I'm not sure what happened really, as I think I was just in so much shock, but it's something to do with Roy not being happy with the training facilities that the Irish football team had to put up with and then seemingly he had a big massive fight with Mick McCarthy and he hopped on a plane and left and probably went back to Cork or some shit. Isn't that so weird! Can you actually believe it. The country is literally torn. It's like the Troubles all over again. One side of the country is supporting him, the other half is saying 'Screw him, we don't need him.'

Ummm, actually, I think we do. The news is going crazy reporting on it, people are on the radio giving out and giving their opinions, but I'm just worried about Roy to be fair. Those training facilities must have been really really bad for him to walk out like that, and Mick McCarthy must be a real pain in the hole to listen to at times, and in fairness Roy Keane is used to dealing with, like, the best training facilities at Man United and Old Trafford, and Alex Ferguson is, like, a proper manager too. This wouldn't have happened if Jack Charlton was still in charge, just saying.

The other half of me is really pissed off that Roy Keane didn't take into consideration the effect that this would have on Leaving Cert students across the country either. We had to face into THE most important exams of our life and Roy Keane goes and leaves us and causes all this upheaval. It's been massively distracting and even hurtful that he wouldn't think of us poor students slogging our brains out for OUR country when he can so easily turn his back on his. My dad thinks he's damn right, but thinks that he shouldn't have left the team, my mother on the other hand didn't hold back and says that he is a spoilt Cork bastard and reckons that Keane leaving will take the wind out of the sails of all those in Cork that think they are God. She says it might be a nice change to hear them shut up about how great they are because Roy Keane just happens to be from that county. She also thinks that Cork people think Roy Keane is the second coming of Michael Collins and they all need to get back in their box. I'm beginning to get a sense that she might have an issue with Cork people.

Anyway, I've just realised that I've done all this talking about Roy Keane and I haven't even begun to tell you about how I'm doing in my Leaving Cert. I woke up on Wednesday and I nearly got sick into the toilet with nerves, I then swallowed nearly a whole bottle of Bach's Rescue Remedy and thought I was drunk for a second. I had gone to bed listening to a minidisc of Seamus Heaney's poetry, as I thought that if I had his poetry in my head going to bed that they would just magically drop from my mind and create these amazing essays on my exam paper.

I'm not going to lie, it was really nerve-racking to walk into the regular classroom that was now an official examination site. Lucy and Hot Gay Brendan were in a different room, and me and Rebecca were sitting English Paper 1 and Paper 2 in the school library. We all had this, like, group hug before we went in, and told each other that it would all be all right. English Paper 1 was okay. The theme was family and there was some bullshit comprehension on a woman talking about the sale of grand-mother's house, and these visual pictures of families hanging out together in New York and you had to write about what they meant to you? I mean, seriously? There was also an extract from *The Grapes of Wrath* which is seemingly, like, this iconic book for a certain generation, and I honestly thought it was a bit sneaky to throw that in there as it is NOT on our Leaving Cert curriculum. But then I was really happy because Question B was: 'You have been asked to give a short talk on radio or television about a fundamental human right that you would like to see supported more strongly. Write out the text of the talk you would give.'

It was one of those moments in my life that I was totally prepared for. I have long been an advocate for the rights of gay rugby players, ever since I discovered that Hot Brendan was in fact Hot Gay Brendan, and I have spent a large amount of my teenage life writing to the *Irish Times* about the plight of gay rugby players, and although none of my letters have EVER been published it was like all that practice was leading up to this very moment. I wrote one hell of a speech in favour of equal rights for gay rugby players. I was impressed with myself, I'm not going to lie. So I think I aced that, I really do.

Do you know what pissed me off though? There was absolutely no mention of 9/11 on English Paper 1 at all, which was annoying as I'd spent a good bit of my study time practising how to spell 'Al-Qaeda'. I mean what was the point in all that happening last September if it didn't even come up on the exams this year?!

English Paper 2 nearly caused me to quit this life and march out of that examination hall for ever. I was never so ready for an exam in my life. I'm down with Hamlet and his procrastination, I'm down with his messed up family and the fact that his best friend is actually in love with him, so when the question popped up about how to write about how complex Hamlet was as a character, I jumped at it. I did think about answering the other question about the importance of Gertrude and Ophelia, but honestly, my only take on that would have been the fact that Gertrude should not have gone off with Hamlet's uncle and Ophelia was a bit of a pain in the hole what with crying all the time, and I knew that I wouldn't get as much foolscap pages out of that, so I went with the question on Hamlet himself. I think

I aced that too. I quoted, like, loads of his soliloquies and every-thing, and all was going grand until I got to the poetry section.

I had to reread the section on poetry questions again and again. I saw Elizabeth Bishop, Eavan Boland, Michael Longley, William Shakespeare, but no Seamus Heaney. I repeat. NO Seamus Heaney. I reread it again just to make sure, I turned the page up and down and back-side-over, nothing. I nearly fainted. Those bastards, those absolute exam-setting cowboys, those educationally inept pricks, those stupid sacks of sheep shit, those dog-faced spawns of a boil-ridden anus, those complete dickwads had decided not to have Seamus Heaney on the poetry section this year. HOW DARE THEY.

I could fail my Leaving Cert because of this. I wonder does Seamus Heaney know, I'd imagine he would be pretty pissed off too! I feel like writing him a letter to tell him, but I don't have the time as I have a million other things to study for right now, but six years of studying his poetry, loving his poetry, loving him, and learning off lines about a skunk for God's sake and then he doesn't even turn up on English Paper 2. I have had a lot of things happen me in this life Dear Diary, but honestly, this is the one thing that has hurt the most. I actually don't think that I will ever get over this. I ended up doing a half-assed essay on the poetry of Eavan Boland and totally winged it. Like, I just didn't care at that stage.

My hand was absolutely killing me with all the writing that I had done all day, but my heart was heavy and my head was full of no one else but Seamus. AND also the fact that Ireland were playing Germany in the World Cup with no Roy. How could the day get any worse, right? But it was actually okay in the end! It wasn't for a while though, Germany were leading for AGES, but then right at the end, Robbie Keane went and scored a goal and we were level! It ended up in a draw, thank God, but we survived. Thank the sweet Lord above for Robbie Keane. I'm not sure whether I think he's hot yet, but I'm glad he scored, I'm just really glad he scored. He even got man of the match, that's how good he was. So that's a draw with Cameroon, and a draw with Germany, so now we just have to beat Saudi Arabia, which should be easy because seriously, it's Saudi Arabia, so maybe, just maybe, we can do this and go a little further.

Anyway, I have to go and study, you might not hear from me for a while Dear Diary, because of this Leaving Cert sucking the life out of me, but I will be in touch.

Goodnight Dear Diary,
Love,
Ciara X

Treat them Mean, Keep them Keane

Dear Diary,

Well, I'm nearly there, this absolute hell that has been my life is slowly coming to an end. The trials and tribulations of doing the Leaving Cert are coming to a close, and maybe, just maybe, I will soon feel like myself again afterwards. You know, like, when a character in a movie or book goes through something really traumatic that totally changes their view of the world and them as a person? That's how I feel Dear Diary. I am Andy Dufresne from *The Shawshank Redemption*. I have done my time in the Shawshank prison that is secondary school and now, after crawling through a whole load of shit too, I'm nearly out the other side.

Once I get Biology and Business over with, it will be like that final scene in *The Shawshank Redemption* where I'm on the beach like Andy, sanding down a boat on a beautiful island, and I'll look up, and instead of Red (who was, like, Morgan Freeman), I'll see Lucy, Rebecca and Hot Gay Brendan walking on the beach towards me, and we'll just smile and realise that we are finally free.

I've probably, like, really changed over the past few weeks as I've taken on these exams with every fibre of my being and my brain. I guess this is par for the course for teenagers; this is the pinnacle of our teenage career, I guess.

Everything gets better after this, I just know it. The world will seem so new and shiny, and college is going to open my mind, and everyone will just be having sex all the time and I might even go travelling, like, go Interrailing to pay my respects to

Auschwitz and breathe in the same air as Anne Frank did before she died, or maybe even go to Australia and check out where *Home and Away* is filmed and get my photo taken down by the beach they all run to when no one wants to adopt them.

I never really understood the saying 'the world is your oyster'. Because to me oysters are gross and people eat them to have sex with each other. But I guess the world IS my oyster Dear Diary.

Before I even get into how the rest of exams went, there's more. Ireland has qualified for the next round of the World Cup! We beat Saudi Arabia 3–0. Can you believe that! Although Germany did beat them 8–0. Morto for them! Robbie Keane scored and so did Damien Duff. I am now totally in love with Robbie Keane, and Damien Duff is SO cute, he even got man of the match. So that means that Germany and Ireland have gone through but Cameroon and Saudi Arabia are gone. Poor Cameroon, I feel sorry for them because of them being an African nation, but off with you, Saudi Arabia! You can feck off now back to all your oil and playing baddies in James Bond movies.

Can you believe that we got this far without Roy Keane! There's a new Keane in town and his name is Robbie! I wonder is Robbie Keane single? He's 22 years of age and from Dublin, which I won't hold against him in fairness. He's only four years older than me. Oh my God, I'm going to spend the rest of my summer just daydreaming about shifting him. I do feel like I'm cheating on Roy Keane, but where is Roy Dear Diary, where is he?! Walking his dog back home by the looks of it.

Anyway, I'm nearly there as I said. English Paper 1, English Paper 2, Irish Paper 1, Irish Paper 2. Wrote an essay based around the word 'brod' which I guessed was 'pride'. Thank God I was right, because I wrote an essay that was a speech for an Academy Award that I had won and basically most of the speech was based on my Irish pride at winning and that the Oscar was presented to me by Daniel Day-Lewis. Honestly, I think it was the best Oscar speech ever written in Irish, and I will use it if I ever win an Academy Award when I'm older.

Maths was a different story. Maths Paper 1 and Paper 2 were just the worst. There's a really funny feeling sitting down to do a state exam for a subject that has been the bane of your life for six years. Mathematics, the only subject to have eluded me all these teenage years. I guess you could call it 'the one that got away' Dear Diary.

But, here's the thing, this is the one subject that could make me fail my Leaving Cert. If you don't pass Maths, you're screwed, and also, it's the only subject that I'm doing Ordinary Level in, so it may also bring my points down if I don't do well in it, and then I'll either have to repeat my Leaving Cert, even though I'd rather die, OR not get enough points for Arts in NUI Galway, and then what do I do?! I don't have a Plan B! Imagine how unfair it would be! Why do people even need maths in the first place? I don't plan on EVER using ANYTHING to do with the mathematical curriculum EVER again. Theorems, and statistics, and modes and medians and trigonometry can literally go and take a run and jump.

I think it's fair to say that I am no Bill Gates Dear Diary, I'm more arty farty, so there's more of a chance of me having a career rowing a gondola in Venice than sitting in an accountants office looking up numbers OR becoming a janitor with an attitude problem in a school where I just so happen to miraculously be able to solve extremely complicated graduate-level maths problems, and Ben Affleck is my best friend and Robin Williams becomes my therapist. I just don't see my life going in that direction I don't think.

Lucy, Rebecca and Hot Gay Brendan have been doing okay. We promised each other that we wouldn't go through how any of us did in the exams because, well, I think we just didn't want to hurt Lucy, because as much as we all, like, really love her, she ain't the brightest spark in the pack. But what she lacks in book smarts she sure as hell makes up for in street smarts.

She said that after the Leaving Cert she is going to make it her mission for me to finally lose my virginity. She said that she will not let another summer go by without some young fella actually getting his mickey near me. I told her that was a really mean thing to say because obviously I'm still SO in love with Danny (who is also doing okay in the Leaving Cert by the way) and that if anyone was getting his mickey near me, it was him.

She just rolled her eyes and said that I was no more in love with him than Elton John was with his first wife, which Hot Gay Brendan totally agreed with. I pretended that I got, like, really thick with both of them. Of course I love Danny, he's like, 'The One', and we're going to be together for ever, because we got together at the mature age of 18, so why wouldn't it last?!

But, deep down I think she's right. I was thinking maybe I could just lose my virginity to Danny, get it over and done with but then, like, break up with him, because surely there will be loads of guys who want to get into this box when I get to college, right?!

Anyway, I can't be thinking of lads getting into my box when I still have two subjects to get through before I am free as a bird. Business and Biology. I should be okay. I can be very entrepreneurial and I like Richard Branson and I know what picketing is. AND because of Lucy, I know the complete diagram of the male sex organs inside out and the female one too, because one night when we were drunk she made me and Rebecca learn them both off by heart. She wasn't trying to be educational in a school/Leaving Cert sense, she was trying to tell us what to expect when getting down to some heavy petting with lads, so that we wouldn't actually be surprised when fingers began to wander. She genuinely would make an awesome Sex Ed teacher, Lucy. Even though me and Rebecca couldn't stop giggling when she said the word 'shaft' over and over again. I'm actually still not quite sure what part that is again, but hopefully I'll find out some day. It sounds sexy though.

Anyway, I better go. Need to study.

Goodnight Dear Diary,
Love,
Ciara X

BORED.com

Dear Diary,

I've finally copped on to something. There is something that adults have been trying to keep quiet for years, but I have figured them out. Sneaky, sneaky adults. I have discovered that I have become institutionalised by adults, thus not preparing me for the outside world at all. I've been institutionalised for the majority of my years. Think about it. As soon as you are four years of age or younger, you head off to playschool, which is just basically hanging out with your other cousins in the village anyway. Then you go through eight years of primary school from baby infants right up to sixth class, then you get just two and a half months to adjust and suddenly you're thrown into the adolescence cycle and you are controlled like the military for another six years, and then BOOM, you're out, thrown out on your arse after the Leaving Cert and just expected to fend for yourself.

I discovered this because I am bored. BORED.com. I guess the Leaving Cert is the only thing that I have really been focusing on for literally the past few years of my life and now, well, I've nothing going on. I've nothing to do. I don't need to read any books or study any graphs or learn any verbs or recite poetry, and I'm lost if the truth be known. I don't know who I am any more. Do you know the part in *The Shawshank Redemption* where the old man Mr Brooks who runs the library is let out of prison after years and years of doing time, and then he goes to the outside world, and he isn't able to handle it, because he doesn't know what to do with himself? Well that's kinda how I feel.

It's a bit of a cop-out in fairness Dear Diary, the way adults desert us when they're done with us. No wonder so many teenagers turn to drink and drugs like those war veterans that come back from Vietnam. My mum says that I am getting an unhealthy obsession with the Vietnamese war, but it's probably down to the fact that I've watched *Forrest Gump*, like, five times since my Leaving Cert finished because I AM BORED OFF MY BRAIN.

There has been nothing else to watch since Ireland was knocked out of the World Cup, I mean what was the point in even watching it after that. It was CLASS though. Spain and Ireland played, and we were all out watching it in the pub because our Leaving Cert was finished and Spain were leading most of the match 1–0, and we were all like, 'Aren't we shit,' and how crap it is to be Irish, etc., etc., until a late penalty kick scored by the GOD that is Robbie Keane made it 1–1 in extra time, and then it went to penalties, but then Spain went and won 3–2 in the penalty shoot-out, but it was SO nerve-racking, and everyone was saying that we didn't need Roy Keane because look how far we had come without him, which I thought was a little bit mean, because I, like, love him, but still, we did so well.

Brazil beat Germany in the final thank God. Ronaldo is such a legend, hopefully with all that money that he has to be making, he'll fix that gap in his two front teeth; my mum says that it takes from him. Granny reckons the Germans lost out of karma for what their country did to the Jews, but I told her that she couldn't say things like that. She told me that at 76 years of age, she could say whatever the hell she wanted to, so I let her off.

She's bad in fairness. We were watching Wimbledon together the last day, which she loves, which again is weird because she hates the English, and she told me that if she ever won the Lotto she would bring me over there and that we would drink that fancy drink Pimms and eat strawberries but that we'd have to keep an eye out for Princess Margaret, who Granny says is the closest thing to a horse that she's ever seen. She's convinced that people who go to Wimbledon are those 'horsey' type people; they all actually look kinda horsey too.

The Irish team's homecoming was incredible too. We were watching it on the news, nearly 100,000 people went to Phoenix Park which is this park near President McAleese's house in Dublin, I think a lot of people murder each other in that park because it always seems to be in the news, but the homecoming was cool all the same. Westlife even gave a performance too, and Robbie Keane was out on the stage looking delighted for himself, and so was the Taoiseach Bertie Ahern, and it looked like there was a mad party about to happen in Dublin for it. Which also annoys me, how come Dublin gets all the fun stuff? What about all the fans from all over the country who got on their knees (during the Leaving Cert may I add) and supported the Boys in Green? Dublin is NOT the be-all and end-all. As my father says they are nothing but a crowd of Jackeens. I'd say they were all fairly quiet down in Cork watching the homecoming though. I wonder did Roy Keane watch it. I wonder did he feel a bit bad now that it's all over. I really hope that he's okay. That must have been, like, the worst breakup ever for him in his life.

Speaking of breakups, well, I know how Roy Keane feels. Me and Danny broke up. I'm okay Dear Diary. It was me that kinda said it was over I think in the end. I hope I didn't break his heart like mine has been broken a million times before in the past. It's just that we didn't really see each other coming up to the Leaving Cert, he goes to a boarding school and, if I was being honest, I think that he is definitely going to apply for a visa to go to Australia, and I read in *CosmoGirl* magazine that long-distance relationships are, like, really hard.

I'll always fondly remember the night we met. I was dressed up as Anne Frank and he was dressed up as William Wallace at the Halloween disco last October, and shifting him was so awkward because he kept on getting stuck in my box ... which was made out of cardboard and represented the annex in Anne Frank's house. SIGH. God, that's a long time, that's eight months. That's, like, my longest relationship ever. You could say it was even like a marriage Dear Dairy.

I rang Lucy, Hot Gay Brendan and Rebecca to tell them. Lucy said she wasn't surprised and that Danny had the sexual appeal of an amoeba. Hot Gay Brendan agreed and Rebecca as always said that she thought that Danny was a really nice guy but that I had done the right thing, and that if she could go back in time, she would do things differently with Johnny Limp and that they would still be together. Seriously, Johnny Limp? She's still banging on about that loser, and also that doesn't even make sense, I don't want to get back with Danny, but at the same time I don't, like, want him to start seeing other girls, because that would be weird, and technically he's still kinda mine because we spent SO much time together, and rules are rules, so if any of the girls from school go near him, I am well within my rights to go mad. Lucy says I have nothing to worry about, that no one will want to go near him, but that if they do, Lucy will deal with them personally herself. She's like Kevin Costner in *The Bodyguard* but, like, doesn't fall in love with me or anything.

I guess if I've waited this long, I might as well keep on waiting for someone perfect. Surely the perfect boy exists out there.

I've written up a small list of credentials for the next guy that comes along:

- *Better be a good kisser and must not kiss like a washing machine.*

- *Must not be frigid, because if the both of us are, then we'll never get anywhere.*
- *Needs to write love letters like soldiers in the Vietnamese war used to write to their lovers back home (again, I am a little obsessed with the Vietnamese war, I know).*
- *Better not have any aspirations to go on a working visa to Australia.*
- *Must not have an overbearing mother, I'm nearly sure I saw Danny kissing his mother on the lips once and it was gross.*
- *Must always have enough credit to text me in the morning and at night before I go to bed.*
- *Someone who is independent but also kinda clingy, but not in a possessive way, just in a way that other girls know we're together, so back off.*
- *Hold hands with me even in front of the lads and not care if the lads see and call him 'gay'.*
- *Has to be nice to my granny because she is the hardest to please because she thinks most men are an abomination just because Granddad and his mates liked to drink.*
- *Has to be smart and doing something cool like Sports Science or IT or Law in college, with a language.*

That's all I could be bothered writing for now. Is it bad that one of my first thoughts on me and Danny breaking up is that I'm now ANOTHER step away from losing my virginity? Like, now I'll have to get to know someone new, trust them, fall in love with them, make them respect me, start Immacing ALL over again, pluck up the courage ONCE AGAIN to give away my flower and then maybe get the leg over, but who knows how long that's going to take. My life is passing me by Dear Diary. Passing me by.

Lucy has started seeing a Polish guy that has just started working in town, his name is Lucas, and he seems really nice.

The first night I met him, we all drank vodka and had a Eurovision Song Contest with him and his Polish friends Dominik and Jakub, which is Jacob, but spelt with a U and a K. They kept on giving Poland top marks, which pissed me off, but Lucy said to relax, that it was just a bit of craic. I didn't want to shift either of them, not because they were Polish or anything, but I couldn't understand what they were saying and they kept on playing Scooter's 'The Logical Song' over and over again, so I ended up getting annoyed and going home. There are only so many times you can hear that song in fairness.

Anyway, I'm going to head to bed here Dear Diary because I AM SO BORED, and I kinda miss Danny, that's probably weird, maybe I'll send him a text just to say 'night, or maybe I shouldn't, oh I don't know. What if he's texting another girl, so then maybe I should text him, and see how long it takes him to reply to me, then if he doesn't reply, like, straight away, then maybe he IS texting someone else.

Goodnight Dear Diary,
Love,
Ciara X

Fisherman's Blues

Dear Diary,

There's one thing that's really bothered me over this whole Leaving Cert thing, one thing that I've definitely sacrificed, and that's my creativity. It's hard to be creative when you have to learn mountains of things OFF by heart, only to regurgitate it onto a foolscap page where some examiner, who doesn't even know you, judges you and marks you on what THEY think is best. So I've been in a bit of a funk since the Leaving Cert ended.

I told my mother that I thought I was suffering from PTSD after watching a Doctor Phil episode on RTÉ One. Mum told me to get out of the house and go for a walk, and that I no more had post-traumatic stress disorder than the man in the moon.

I'm being serious. I've read articles about American men who came back from fighting in the Vietnam War, and they were never the same again. I mean, look at Lieutenant Dan in *Forrest Gump*, he came back from the war with no legs after Forrest saved him, and he suffered post-traumatic stress big time. I've just gone through the most horrific couple of months in my life and now I'll have to wait until August to see if it was all worthwhile.

But then I got to thinking, do you know what I haven't done in a really long time Dear Diary? Something that I loved to do when I went off into daydream land, when I was alone in my bedroom with only my two hands and brain as company, when teenage lust began coursing through my veins and my teenage loins started yearning for something more, and my hand would automatically drop and find that perfect ... PEN! And I would start writing one of my famous Romantic Short Stories.

Lucy says I'm like a young teenage Mills & Boon writer. She said there needs to be more sex, but that I have potential, although I need to be like a dirtier version of Maeve Binchy.

Lucy is like Estelle, Joey's agent in *Friends*, reading over my stories with one hand and smoking a fag with the other. She says that I have to write one that she can get off to. Get off what, I don't know, but I do know that I've missed writing these, and now I can spend the rest of my summer scribbling away to my heart's content (unless I get a summer job) before the Leaving Cert results come in.

I've dug deep with this one Dear Diary. It really helped get my creative juices flowing, and I'm pretty proud of it. It's called ...

'*The Hot Fisherman*'
by Ciara King

> *She walked quickly through the village, her long hair bouncing in the wind. 'Lucky I brought over my turbo powered hair dryer from America', she thought to herself, 'because you certainly wouldn't be able to buy one in this lame village'.*
>
> *She had been in Ballinagra for a few days now. Her parents had insisted she spend a summer in Ireland to connect with her Irish roots, so she was staying with an aunt and uncle in a cottage by the sea. She loathed being there. She wanted to be back in California with her friends, hanging out in the mall and doing things that American teenagers do, but instead she was bored out of her mind in the smallest Irish village of ALL time.*
>
> *Her heart yearned to be back with Brad at the football rally in school, wearing his jacket and getting to first base with him behind the school gym. She had decided to give him her flower this summer, and her heart raced as she thought of the high school's most popular quarter back on the football team, with his cheeky American grin and perfect tan.*

Of course, that was before her parents had shipped her off to Ballygonebackwards for a few months. God, she hated them right now. She hated them for sending her here, she hated that she didn't have access to a computer or that she couldn't watch her favourite TV show, MTV Cribs, as her aunt and uncle only had two channels called RTÉ One and Network 2. And she hated how her heart skipped a beat every time she thought of that last night with Brad. Even though she was a million miles across the Atlantic, she could still feel his wet, hot kisses on her neck.

She continued walking past the cottage down to the beach, she didn't feel like eating bacon and cabbage or whatever the Irish deemed food these days. She took off her shoes and felt the sand beneath her feet, and sat staring out to sea wishing that she was on the other side of the Atlantic. Suddenly a traditional Irish boat came into view. She thought it was called a 'currach', because she had heard her uncle talking about one earlier and had thought to herself, how quaint. It was a currach alright, but that's not what glued her to the spot on the beach. It was what was on the currach that grabbed her attention. It was a teenage boy, probably the same age as her. He was wearing a vest and waders that stretched up to his groin area, which she couldn't help but glance at.

He was tanned and muscular and pulling in nets at a speed that would put Moses Kiptanui to shame. A lone fish had got caught up in the nets, and although the fish slithered and fought to escape the hands of this Irish Adonis, he managed to gently place the fish back into its natural habitat. 'Oh no,' she gasped, 'he loves animals.' She was a sucker for anyone who was kind to animals. She felt her legs begin to melt beneath her in the sand. Was this love at first sight? She began to get really nervous then. As the boat approached the shore, he hopped out of the water and dragged the currach in, his muscles bulging, his vest wet and tight against his torso, and all she could see were perfectly formed abs.

She knew right there and then that she had to have him. Her whole teenage body ached for him, and she wanted to do things to him that she had only seen in the movies. Like listen to love songs on a Discman, sit on a car bonnet with him staring at the stars, walk home with him hand in hand, then sneak out of the house later to meet him by the lake to kiss by the moonlight ... or have sex.

She sat stunned as he walked by her on the beach, his waders squelching as he passed. He nodded in her direction and muttered hello. He had a thick Irish brogue and she was instantly struck by his steely grey eyes boring into hers. He smelled of salt and sand and sex – she nearly fainted. She felt a small bead of sweat rolling down her back under her Calvin Klein push-up bra, which she had bought in Macy's before her trip to Ireland.

All she wanted him to do was stop, drop down onto the sand and kiss her till she could barely breathe OR walk.

She managed to pull herself together and stumble all the way back to the cottage. She had to find out who this mysterious fisherman was! Luckily she didn't have to wait that long, because as she approached the cottage her aunt told her to hurry up and get ready for Mass. What was with the Irish and Mass? As she slid into the pew in the small church, there he was. Her sexy, hot fisherman. He was wearing a checked shirt and casually glanced her way. Their eyes locked just as the priest came onto the altar.

At communion time, she happened to walk past him on her way down the aisle. His aftershave filled her nostrils, and with the thoughts that filled her head she knew she was one step away from confession. As he reached up to receive his communion from the priest, his elbow accidentally brushed off her chest. She wasn't sure if she was imagining it, but she thought her nipples had gone hard.

Breathing heavily, she went out to the church porch and splashed herself in holy water. She had to get out of there. Just as *she did, she saw her uncle approaching with the hot fisherman. 'Elizabeth,' he said, 'it's time for you to meet my nephew'.*

She had to lean against the church door for support. 'It can never be,' she thought. Although she knew that she would yearn for him for the rest of her days, he was and always would be ... her Irish cousin.

The End

I'm not going to lie, I feel kinda hot after writing that. Maybe this summer I'll have a summer romance myself and lose MY flower. Lucy said to stop calling it 'my flower', that any normal girl after transition year, and ESPECIALLY one that has just done her Leaving Cert, can finally call it 'getting the ride'. But I think that sounds crass, so I'm going to stick with the regular old 'lose my virginity'. I knew this would happen, I just knew it, as soon as the Leaving Cert is over, I'm right back talking and thinking about sex ALL over again.

It's a vicious circle, and one that my poor hymen is definitely bored with at this stage. I wouldn't be surprised if my hymen has gone bloody Interrailing for the summer, it's probably given up hope of getting the ceremony it deserves after all this time serving me.

Anyway, goodnight Dear Diary.
Love,
Ciara X

Death Becomes Her

Dear Diary,

Life is so funny, one minute I'm drinking vodka that tastes like petrol with Lucy and her new Polish friends, and the next thing I'm being woken up to the news that my granny has died. She's dead. They found her this morning, in her seat by the range, a heart attack they think. A heart attack? Women don't get heart attacks, men do. How is that even possible, it would mean her heart was weak, but she was the strongest old person I know? I've never seen an old person walk as fast to Mass on a Sunday morning as my granny.

Now that I think of it, I should have seen this coming. Oh my God, this is Roy Keane's fault, because Granny kept on saying that he broke her heart after leaving Saipan, and now my granny is dead, and I can't help but feel the need to blame Roy Keane. Or it could have been that penalty shoot-out between Ireland and Spain, she said afterwards that she needed to sit down, it made her weak. Or was it when she found out that Daniel O'Donnell got engaged to a woman who used to be married, and they're due to get married this summer, is that what did it?! How did this even happen?

I feel weird, everything is weird. My granny is gone and I want to write something beautiful like Seamus Heaney did with that poem 'Sunlight' about his aunt making bread in the kitchen, but I can't, firstly because I'm hungover and secondly because I think I'm in shock, I'm remembering all these random things about my granny like her grey cardigan that she got in Dunnes and never took off her, or the fact that she wore her good cardigan from Marks & Spencer's every Christmas day because it cost pounds, or how she always gave out about the English yet was obsessed with the royal family and made me sit through both Princess Diana's funeral and the Queen Mother's, and how it's funny that she has died the same year as the Queen Mother as she would get such a kick out of that.

I'm remembering the time that she got the three stars on a *Winning Streak* scratch card and we all got on a bus and went up to the RTÉ studios to support her on TV, and how she blushed and turned into a giggling school girl when she met Mike Murphy, or how she used to sit in the house on a Friday night watching *The Late Late Show* and calling Gay Byrne a 'condescending shitehawk' after a few glasses of sherry, or how she used to tut-tut her way through *Father Ted* and called it an abomination to the Catholic Church, yet laughed her ass off so much at the episode where Victor Meldrew appeared in the Aillwee caves that her false teeth fell out onto her lap.

I'm remembering that time I came home with my first pair of glasses and she told me that I looked like Deirdre Barlow from *Coronation Street*, or the time when she said, 'Well if it isn't Judy Garland' to Hot Gay Brendan's face, or the time she told me to be wary of Lucy, that she would lead me up a path of sin, or the time she told Rebecca she'd want to get up and do some laps of the local GAA pitch to lose the puppy fat because it took away from her pretty face.

I'm remembering everything so clearly and all these memories are whizzing through my mind. I remember the only time she was really mad at me. I dropped the collection basket in Mass, and all the coins and envelopes fell all over the place. Granny was mortified. It was my own fault, I was checking out one of the lads that I fancied in my year at the time, and I wasn't concentrating, and I'm so sorry Granny for laughing when you dropped the collection basket in Mass, I really am, you didn't talk to me for at least a whole week, but started again when I gave a lovely reading from the book of Genesis on the altar and you told me that I had a beautiful reading voice and slipped a fiver into my hand.

Granny, you did nothing but give out about Granddad all my life, and gave out about him being in the pub morning, noon and night, but I saw you so many times sitting by the range holding your framed picture of him with tears in your eyes whispering gently, 'I miss you, you aul bastard.' Or how your eyes would mist up when you heard John Denver's 'Annie's Song' on the radio because that was the song that Granddad used to sing to you when he was trying to get back in your good books after going missing after a session.

You were sometimes mean to my mum. Mum always said that you spoilt Dad red rotten since he was a child. You commented on her cooking constantly, and raised your eyebrows if Mum went out with the girls for a few on a Friday night. I saw Mum hold back so many times, and argue with Dad instead, and he would always say 'I'm not getting involved love,' and that would cause even more arguments.

I need to find the rosary beads you gave me, the white ones you gave me when I made my First Holy Communion. The day you put a French plait in my hair and told me that I was the most beautiful girl in the parish. Where are they? I need to find them.

I don't know death or how to deal with dead things. I mean I've imagined my own funeral SO many times, and I've changed what songs I want played at my funeral a million times too, I've only ever seen my brother's loss of his pet snail 'Billy the Whizz' who managed to escape from an empty Carte D'Or box, or see our cat Becky – named after David Beckham – be buried, and that was really sad, but this is different. It's not the same as when

Shane died in *Home and Away*, or when Mufasa died in *The Lion King*. This is different, this feels very real yet so weird.

I can't help imagining you rocking up to the big gates of heaven and giving your tuppence worth to St Peter who probably will be so bamboozled by you that he will just let you into heaven straight away. Knowing you, you'll march straight into what ever is the nearest pub in heaven and drag Granddad out on his ear like you used to when he went on a session up the village. Do you think there are pubs in heaven Dear Diary?

I can't help thinking of you telling me that the BEST day of your life was when Pope John Paul visited Ireland in 1979, or the sparkle in your eye when you came back from Lourdes and told me it was the most magical place on earth, and why wouldn't it be, sure, if it's good enough for the Virgin Mary then it's good enough for you. Or the many trips I took with you to Knock as a child where I would have to sit for hours on a bus, hours in a church and then queue for hours to bring back even more holy water. I remember you saying that your big dream would be to go to Rome and see the pope in the Vatican, but after all you've heard about those pervy Italian men, you might leave it for a bit because they would probably try and get in your knickers and you wouldn't be having any of that, and you'd tell those Italian men where to go.

You always told me to stick up for myself no matter what, and to go after what I believed in no matter what the cause. Like the time you told me you went and protested about that blasphemous movie in Galway in the eighties called *Hail Mary*, and you were very proud as you were spotted on the news protesting, and you said that you felt like a real officer of God that day.

Granny I'm really sorry that I thought you smelt funny sometimes and I'm sorry that we used to slag you and the other bingo ladies for heading off on the bus on a Friday night and I'm confessing to you now that we made up a song about ye to the words of the Venga Boys' 'We Like to Party' but instead changed the words to 'the bingo bus is coming'. I've another confession: it was me that would eat your jellies when you weren't looking and once I said that I was going to Mass on a Saturday night, but then I didn't because me, Lucy and Rebecca skipped it and went and hung out with the lads in the park instead.

And there was one time you told me to do the Lotto for you, and I said that I had lost the ticket and bought *Heat* magazine instead, and most of all I'm sorry for telling Lucy, Rebecca and Hot Gay Brendan that I thought you had a serious horn for Father Murphy, I didn't mean it. And I'm sorry, I saw your Mills and Boon books and we used to steal them and go down and read them in Lucy's and I honestly couldn't understand why you were reading those books that were just full of 'throbbing members'.

Granny, thank you for lighting a million candles for me around my Leaving Cert and every other occasion in my life so far. Thank you for being so obsessed with *Titanic* that you made Dad drive us over an hour into the cinema in Galway to see it. Granny, you literally can't be dead.

How will I never see you fall asleep while knitting by the range and have to pick up your stray balls of wool when they roll away from you? Who will tell me about how good I have it as a young girl, as you had nothing but stones growing up and had to go to school in your feet through the fields because you were so poor you had no shoes? And who is going to tell me about distant cousins that we seemingly have in Boston and New York whose mothers and fathers left here, like, in the Famine?

Granny, I can't believe you are dead. This doesn't make sense. Oh God, all I can hear is the neighbours coming in and out of the house and it smells of egg sandwiches SO bad. Oh man, I'll probably have to do a prayer of the faithful, which is seriously annoying, and my brother will probably get one of the easy jobs of bringing up the gifts or some shit like that.

I'm sorry if I let you down as a granddaughter, you died and your loser granddaughter is a virgin. I wonder did you know that before you died, God, maybe that's what gave you the heart attack.

Granny, I can't believe that we will be going to your funeral.

Goodnight Dear Diary,
Love,
Ciara X

Abracadavera

Dear Diary,

It's been a really crap summer so far. I haven't come close to the shift, my granny died and my Leaving Cert results are out soon. I'm seriously down and blue, and I guess I just really miss my granny.

Her death is, like, the first major one after Princess Diana that I have had to deal with on a serious level. I remember after Princess Diana died I became obsessed with playing Elton John's 'Candle in the Wind' over and over again, to the point where my father threatened to throw out my ghettoblaster, and he said it wasn't normal for a girl my age to be locked up in her bedroom crying about a member of the royal family. In my defence, I was 14 at the time and was going through what I like to call my Anne Frank stage of teenage melancholy.

This time I find myself in the sitting room listening to old cassette tapes of Mary Black and Daniel O'Donnell and Nanci Griffith. I've listened to 'From a Distance' like 12 times today already. Granny used to sing it, or 'try' to sing it, bless her blue rinsed hair. She used to talk about the time when Nanci Griffith appeared on *The Late Late Show*, and how it was the BEST *Late Late Show* that she ever did see, and how she made my mother let me stay up to watch it especially with her, and how it got her in awful trouble with my mother, but it was worth it because seemingly afterwards I didn't stop singing 'From a Distance' for about eight weeks. Even now my mother shudders when she hears it.

Mass isn't even the same any more. I'm going to Mass nearly every day, even when there isn't Mass, because I just want to feel close to her. Its weird though because I'm not constantly turning around feeling her eyes bore into the back of my head if I give off even a slight hint of a giggle. You know when people say that they can feel someone's eyes on them, well that was my granny. She'd fix you with a gaze so deadly as if to say, 'If you even attempt to laugh in God's holy house, and bring shame to me in front of all the other holy Joes present, I will disown you as a granddaughter.'

Her funeral was nice and sad and flew by in the blink of an eye really. It turns out that everyone is really nice to you when your granny dies. I'm not going to lie Dear Diary, I lapped up every bit of the attention and may have even amped up my sadness in front of certain people hoping they might give me money or some shit because they felt even more sorry for me. I tried the 'I don't know who's going to put money in my college fund now' line and it worked on a handful of people before my father told me to stop. Isn't it annoying though that it takes someone dying for people to be nice to you?!

This one woman, who is a complete gowl by the way because she once reported back to my parents that I was seen cycling on the wrong side of the road when I was younger and I could have gotten myself killed if she hadn't had the common decency as a neighbour to tell my parents, blah, blah, blah. Her little neighbourhood report lead Mum and Dad to take my bike off me for a week. Well, she was there, with a bang of Avon cosmetics off her, and she was all like, 'Oh, your grandmother was such a great woman, and she would have been SO proud of you dear,' which is complete bollix in fairness, and honestly, Granny was always talking about her anyway, saying that her husband had an awful soft spot for young ones. I just shook her hand, but made a mental note in my head to flirt with her husband the next time I saw him. Big gowly head on her.

The only bit of craic was at the wake when a local man from a nearby village who's known for sleeping in bushes and for not really having any fixed address rocked in to show his respect, having known my grandfather and fished with him – back in 1845, by the gimp of him. He produced a bottle of poitín and after about an hour broke into The Dubliners' 'Seven Drunken Nights', and it was not the time or the place.

Lucy took full advantage of the wake and people smoking in the house. I rock into my kitchen, like my HOME kitchen at one stage and see Lucy smoking using one of my mother's good vases as an ashtray, and Rebecca and Hot Gay Brendan are drinking hot whiskeys. I mean it was nice of them to come and all, but like, this wasn't a party, we weren't exactly celebrating anything. And it was just weird, like, it's my parent's house and they were smoking and drinking in it like it was a youth club disco, and my granny was lying dead as a dodo not a few feet away. But all rules go out the window at a funeral. Adults will literally let you do what you want. It's the one time you'll get away with anything because people are so sad and dying for pints that they just don't care.

Lucy told me that she wouldn't go in to see my granny's coffin because she literally cannot touch or bear to be around dead people. She was made kiss her dead aunt once, and says that she will never ever forget that feeling of cold dead forehead on her lips. She said from that day on she made a pact with herself that the only hard things she would touch going forward are ... AND I had to stop her right there before she said anything else. It would only be Lucy that would bring up dick at a wake, and it is certainly NOT the place for Lucy to be talking about her favourite hard things.

That was fine by me, if Lucy came within two inches of my granny she would literally rise from the dead and tell her to piss off. There was no love lost between those two. What was it that

Granny used to call her again? Oh ya: 'dirty jezebel'. That was it. Rebecca stood by Granny's coffin and said a prayer which was sweet because she is sweet in fairness. Hot Gay Brendan hovered over Granny's coffin for ages looking perplexed, and then I nearly fell over because I saw him reach into the coffin and do something with Granny's hair! I thought my father was going to have a heart attack, but in Hot Gay Brendan's defence he said that he fixed it and made it look more like my granny, and he did, to give him credit.

I had to help my mum make decisions in terms of prayers of the faithful and readings and stuff. It was, like, the most adult thing I've ever had to do. I think I did all right at it. Granny loved a good prayer of the faithful. She loved the ones that focused on victims of injustice and poverty. I suppose she spent most of her life giving money to those little black babies in Africa, that it only seemed right to include one.

We chose a reading from the Book of Wisdom because in fairness she was a very wise woman, and had all these old sayings like 'What's in the cat is in the kitten,' and 'There's no use boiling your cabbage twice,' and 'Even black hens lay white eggs,' I never really grasped what she was saying but she'd continue on muttering them anyway.

The second reading was my special shout out to her. After my mum said that I couldn't use one of the poems that was read out at Princess Diana's funeral, I decided that the second reading should come from the book of the prophet Daniel. Granny was Daniel O'Donnell's biggest fan after all. My only comfort in this whole awful ordeal is the fact that Granny won't be around to see him get married later this year. It would have broken her heart. The track that played at Communion was Daniel O'Donnell's 'Here I Am Lord' from his *Faith & Inspiration* album. She played it religiously, so she would have been happy with that. Afterwards at the graveside all the old fogeys that Granny went to bingo with stood around and sang 'Nearer, my God, to Thee', and I would have totally slagged them under normal circumstances, but I was crying too much.

I met up with Lucy, Rebecca and Hot Gay Brendan after my family had gone to the pub and everyone had totally destroyed all the soup and sandwiches the local hotel put on for the mourners. Some of my family were making their way home, others were settling in for a session, and I just needed a break. I wanted to go drinking or just do something mad, so I found myself with the rest of the gang down drinking with the Polish lads that Lucy and Rebecca are scoring this summer and who Hot Gay Brendan wishes he was scoring. Rebecca only started scoring him the last night, so it's all new, but knowing her she probably fell in love with him instantly. It was grand, I was glad of their company. I didn't even mind the fact that Lukas basically had his hand up Lucy's top the whole time we were there, but then everything changed. In walks Lucy's brother. I've never seen a lad remove his hand from up a top in lightning speed as Lukas did right then. It turns out Lukas did work on Lucy's brother's car, and they're buddies.

Bear in mind Dear Diary that the last time I saw Lucy's brother was when we had dry humped at a party about a year ago, and then again at a rave when he was off his head, so that doesn't count. Lucy found out about it and didn't talk to me for, like, two weeks. But there he was. Fresh back from Interrailing across Europe, looking like a total ride in the Polish lads' kitchen.

Maybe it was because my granny had just been buried, or maybe because I've matured a bit, but I didn't go red or pretend to even care he was there. I was just like one of those French girls in the movies who smoke a cigarette and shrug their shoulders. If I was being totally honest though, I was more petrified that

Lucy would catch me looking at him, so I just stayed chatting to Hot Gay Brendan and didn't really look at him.

The next thing I know he's sitting beside me and he's saying, 'I'm sorry to hear about your granny, Ciara,' and he's looking at me, like right into my eyes, and I can feel my skin begin to prickle, and suddenly I can smell him. And he smells divine, he smells of Daz washing up powder and Gillette shaving cream that my dad uses, and he smells of after-sun, and Red Bull, and petrol, and weirdly enough, Monster Munch, and it was right then Dear Diary, through the haze of Polish vodka that tasted like turpentine and pure raw grief about my granny, right there in that exact moment, that I knew I wanted to lose my virginity with him. Lucy's brother. He's The One.

Goodnight Dear Diary,
Love,
Ciara X

Your Books will Grow (And Other Life Lessons)

Dear Diary,

It's hard to be a teenager. All these thoughts, emotions and feelings – it's, like, exhausting sometimes. I know this might sound weird, but there are times that I don't even want to be in my own head.

In saying that, I have learned a lot these past few years and I want to tell those coming up the teenage ranks behind me that it's not all bad. Here's some of the teenage wisdom that I have learned along the way:

Bright-blue eye shadow is a no-no. No one can pull that off – it doesn't matter if you got it free in *Mizz Magazine*.

Don't get anything pierced that you can't hide.

Saying you have period cramps will get you out of almost anything at school, but don't overdo it!

Go easy on the Immac and try not to burn the box off yourself.

If you're bad at Maths in first year, then you're pretty screwed for the following five years. That's just the way it is, so deal with it.

Also, it's hard to believe, but teachers are human beings with real lives, who have feelings like normal people and, believe it or not, some people actually marry them.

If you fancy someone in first year, it's almost a certainty that you won't fancy them in sixth year, but you will definitely have shifted at least one of them at a Youth Club disco.

The best advice I can give you to try and make someone notice you is to ignore them ... OR stalk them so you keep bumping into them accidentally on purpose.

Get over the fact that you couldn't finish the last level of Crash Bandicoot. Metal Gear Solid is WAY cooler anyway.

Be nice to other girls – the quiet ones, the smart ones, the loud ones – we need each other, so BE NICE.

Be nice to the nerdy boys, the quiet boys, the weird boys, the larger than life boys, even the boys who listen to Metallica – they're not dangerous, just confused.

Jealousy is a waste of time.

If someone behind you starts flicking your bra strap in class, tell them to stop flicking your bra strap.

Be careful when sending notes in class about lads you fancy. The teacher will find them and they will know who you fancy FOREVER. Do not give them that power – it's us against them, remember.

You know what, guys? Hamlet is actually an alright dude. He's had a lot to deal with, what with having a dead father and his mother marrying his uncle, so go easy on him.

Also, Michael Collins was a ride.

When it comes to handling a hickey, always have a good scarf from Penneys or toothpaste in your bag. Toothpaste is a lifesaver.

You will think that other students are hotter or funnier or skinnier than you, but remember: contact lenses exist, retainers and braces are not for ever, and you will not be a virgin for the rest of your life.

Your boobs will grow! Just when you've given up all hope, they will grow. I promise you!

Friends will come and go, but remember the loyal ones. You might question their life decisions, but you should never have to question whether they have your back or not.

Don't dumb yourself down for anyone.

Listen to your parents, they might even surprise you.

Imagine, you could be the next Sonia O'Sullivan or Roy Keane. How cool is that?

Rugby players can be gay, and a lesbian ex-nun can come runner-up in *Big Brother*.

Stand up for what you believe in, but please do us all a favour and don't be annoying while you do it.

Don't be a music snob. Nobody likes a music snob.

Not even David Beckham can pull-off wearing a sarong.

Love your grandparents.

Your parents are like the FBI: they will find out and you will be grounded.

You don't need others to like you, YOU need to like you.

Don't wait around for anyone to text back. If they're worth it, they will.

Never, ever, ever write mean comments on the internet.

Be kind. Always be kind.

Laugh at yourself, you absolute eejit.

You are loved.

There is always someone there who will listen.

And remember (most importantly), BIGGER BOOBS!

Good Night Dear Diary,
Love,
Ciara X

'Period Pains' by Ciara King

My uterus is cramping
My ovaries have packed up and left
My cervix is crying loudly
Period pain has left me bereft

My emotions are all over the place
My hormones are going mad
To have been born a male right now
Would make me very glad

Having Aunty Flo visit is highly distracting
Especially when you can feel your fallopian tubes contracting
Having Munster play at home is no easy lark
But mainly because my cervix is not Thomond Park

The Panadol isn't working
The hot-water bottle won't ease the pain
What is a woman's loss, it seems
Is typically a man's gain

For men don't know how it feels
For your boobs to get sore
Or how really bad cramps
Leave you curled on the floor

Or how embarrassing it can be
To cry at random things on TV
But there's a light at the end of this menstrual tunnel,
    to a degree
My period pains will get me out of PE